Smothered

A Whipped and Sipped Mystery

G. P. Gottlieb

With love + murder !
Galit

D.X. Varos

Dedicated to my father Alex Joseph Pinsky (1928 – 2020)
to whom I was always a bit of a mystery.

Cast of Characters

Alene Baron, 38, owner of the Whipped and Sipped Café, mother of Sierra, Quinn, and Noah

Blanca, 47, Alene's cleaning lady, Cal's caregiver

Brianne Flynn, 52, Alene's neighbor, owner of bar next door to café

Cal Baron, 65, Alene's father

Edith Vanza, 60, Whipped and Sipped staff, former owner's sister

Frank Shaw, 42, homicide detective, Alene's boyfriend

Harrison Huff, 32, Stanley Huff's son

Heather Evans, 30, Sylvie's daughter, dating Miles Taylor

Jack Stone, 34, Whipped and Sipped staff, Alene's neighbor, stepbrother of Kacey Vanza

Jocelyn DeVale, 24, Whipped and Sipped staff

Julian Evans, 34, Sylvie's son, married to Phyllie for 6 years, father of Evan and Richie

Kacey Vanza, 24, Whipped and Sipped staff, Alene's neighbor, dating Kofi

Kofi Lloyd, 26, Kacey's boyfriend, bartender at Tipped, part-time trainer at Better be Fit,

LaTonya James, 23, Whipped and Sipped staff

Lee Bautista, 41, Frank's partner

Lawrence Habern, 70, Lillian's beau, was Stanley's lawyer

Lillian Blum, 64, Ruthie's mother, Sylvie's best friend, dating Lawrence Habern

Lydia Baron, 34, Alene's sister, estate lawyer, married to Theo King, 36

Michael Jay, 32 Alene, Brianne, and Gary's personal trainer, used to work for Stanley Huff

Mitzi Dunn, 67, Alene's ex-mother-in-law

Miles Taylor, 35, Heather's boyfriend, works at Better be Fit

Neal Dunn, 43, Alene's ex-husband, father of Sierra, Quinn, and Noah

Noah, 8, Alene's youngest child

Olly Burns, 24, Whipped and Sipped staff

Phyllie Evans, 34, wife of Julian Evans, mother of Ethan and Richie

Quinn, 10, Alene's middle daughter

Rhea Huff, 32, wife of Stanley's son, Harrison Huff

Ruthie Blum Rosin, 38, Alene's best friend/pastry chef mother of Shaily, 12, Eden, 10, Avi, 8

Sierra, 12, Alene's older daughter

Stanley Huff, 59, owner of Better be Fit

Sylvie Huff, 62, mother of Julian and Heather, married to Stanley

Toula Savas, 43, customer with gap between front teeth, married to Royce

Vivian Baron, Alene's deceased mother Zuleyka Martinez, 23, Whipped and Sipped staff, Alene's babysitter

Chapter 1

Alene fretted as she walked to work, first about Frank, second about her children, and third about her father. Frank hadn't made it over to the apartment the night before. Was his work as a homicide detective always going to come before their relationship? Nobody ever said life would be easy for a single mother of three, but it had been a long time since anyone had held her.

She needed to do something to stop the foul language Sierra picked up from Alene's ex-husband; she was a rotten mother for putting off the attention-disorder testing that Quinn's fourth grade teacher had recommended at the end of the school year; and she hadn't yet been able to get Noah to stop biting his nails. It wasn't even six in the morning, and she was already gnashing her teeth.

Mostly she worried about her father's deteriorating health. He'd probably have an easier time swallowing if he didn't keep insisting on drinking ice water. Should she pester him about resting more and insist on room temperature water like the doctor had advised?

At least she had Blanca, who'd morphed from cleaning the apartment into caregiving for her dad. Blanca would come at eight that morning, take care of the children, and stay until Cal fell asleep after lunch. Alene would probably get home before he woke up. She worried that he'd fall if left alone, since myasthenia gravis, finally diagnosed the previous year, caused muscle weakness. What if he dropped a glass or something, and she came home to find him bleeding on the kitchen floor? He hadn't yet been rushed to the hospital, but it could happen, and Blanca couldn't be there around the clock.

Alene turned into the alley, and saw Edith, a longtime employee, pacing at the back entrance to the Whipped and Sipped Café. Edith Vanza resembled a cranky neighborhood librarian who made late returns feel like punishable offenses. Even from afar, she looked put out because she had to wait for Alene to unlock the door. Alene didn't trust her with the alarm code after an incident involving firetrucks and a false alarm citation.

Alene passed the shoe store on the corner and then Tipped, the bar just before the café. Her friend Brianne had managed the bar on her own ever since her husband died, eight years before. Alene would never forget seeing him lying on the bike path, other riders flying past, none of them stopping to help. If only she had Brianne's confidence and positive attitude.

Alene noted garbage bags strewn on the ground in front of the fitness facility just past the café. Maybe she could rally Brianne and other fellow business owners into demanding that Stanley Huff, owner of the fitness place next door, keep the alley clean.

She didn't have anything against fitness facilities or personal trainers. Michael, her own fitness trainer, whose first job out of college was to work in one of Stanley's earlier Better Be Fit locations, was wonderful. He knew everything about the human body, but he also read books, followed the news, and was intelligent enough to carry on a thoughtful conversation about the world while urging Alene to hold her plank for a few more seconds.

It bothered her that in addition to fitness training, Stanley Huff sold vitamins and a host of medical-sounding

2

but probably dangerous weight-reducing supplements. He also peeked at himself in her café's window whenever he passed by, admiring his thick silver hair and bulging muscles even though he was well into his sixties and nobody cared. Just the day before, he'd strutted into the café, smelling like he'd bathed in a musky aftershave, his face over-tanned and one of his eyes swollen. He'd flirted with one of Alene's customers, an attractive woman with long, golden-brown hair and a gap between her front teeth, and he'd argued with Edith Vanza about the healthful properties of the smoothies Edith made versus the ones he sold.

Alene had overheard him tell the customer with the long hair that his business was tremendous, and that he was planning to open another Better Be Fit a few miles west. Great, she thought, then more Chicagoans could spend money that they'd literally flush down the toilet the next day. Edith said she'd heard that Stanley had some dedicated followers. Hard to imagine he was that good at fitness training, although in those tight shirts he favored, his muscles had muscles.

In the alley, Alene greeted Edith, unlocked the café's back door, and turned off the alarm. Edith went right in, but Alene stopped to pick up one of the bags that Stanley or one of his trainers had tossed much too close to the café's back door. It looked like it was filled with papers, wrappers, and receipts. Everything was computerized at Whipped and Sipped – why did anyone still want or need paper receipts? She should contact the neighborhood alderman and ask his office about littering policies. It would be fitting if Better Be Fit had to pay a huge fine.

Businesses focused on healing should not be tossing trash on the ground, Alene thought. Maybe later in the morning, she'd bring over a smoothie and hand Stanley the garbage bag she'd picked up. If he said something patronizing, like the day she'd come into the condo building winded after a run and he'd remarked that someone her age should be in better shape, she'd give him the look she'd been practicing in her mirror. Then she'd scrub her hands and face to get rid of the cigarette smell combined with the musky scent he wore.

As Alene walked in, Edith complained about how cold it was in the kitchen. "It's going to be over ninety degrees today and the ovens will be on in a few minutes," Alene said, tossing Stanley's trash bag under the desk in her little office, wondering what she could possibly learn from it. She put her purse in a desk drawer and tied on an apron. Edith followed her into her office. "Maybe you could just wear your sweater until you warm up, Edith." Alene dreaded the thought of becoming a cranky old lady.

They had two hours before the café opened. They washed up, and Edith began chopping fruit and vegetables while Alene turned on the ovens, chose one of her self-made playlists of calming music, and pulled trays of prepared dough from the refrigerators. While the ovens heated up, Alene set out ingredients: oils, flours, vanilla beans, fruits. Preparing to bake usually soothed her, but her mind was all over the place. Maybe she needed to take up one of the meditative or self-defense practices her employees were always talking about, like meditation or yoga.

Jocelyn, for example, practiced Krav Maga, and Olly taught Jiu-Jitsu classes. Both in their twenties, they'd been close friends since high school, kept up a running conversation in the café, and wanted Alene to try out their respective disciplines, each promising increased strength and mental clarity. Alene went running on mornings when she didn't open the café and worked out with her trainer every other Monday, but that didn't help her concentrate during the rest of the week. She didn't want to take on something without her children, but what if she could find a class that they could all take together?

Edith returned to the kitchen and a smile flickered as she pushed a cart of supplies out to the café. The smile was a good sign. Lately, Edith had seemed grateful to have recovered from that blow to her head at the beginning of the summer. Before being attacked, she'd have already lobbed

4

several more complaints and Alene would have already started losing patience.

Now Alene began measuring ingredients for the pastry chef's Almond-Berry breakfast cake, since Ruthie always took Saturdays off. Alene's kids were usually with her ex-husband on Saturdays. Today, he'd probably take them to work at his car dealership and let them run around. He'd no doubt bought them fatty, salty food the night before and would do the same at lunch, unless he took them to his mother's apartment. His mother would make them feel loved and they'd come home smiling. Would Neal ever figure out how to do that, or would the children always come home bickering and fighting with each other? Alene tried to stop thinking about home and focus instead on getting the café ready to open.

An hour later, more employees signed in, washed up, and put on their aprons. Two of them got busy with batters and dough. Jocelyn DeVale greeted Alene with a broad smile and a warm hug and started filling trays for the dessert case. Alene wished her own ponytail was lustrous, like Jocelyn's, and that she wasn't just another sallow-skinned, late-thirty-something mom with bags under her eyes.

Olly Burns, Jocelyn's best friend since high school, struck a boxing pose and whispered something that made Jocelyn laugh. Alene could count on Olly to make a joke out of everything, which sometimes annoyed her, but he was a hard-working, good guy. Like all of Alene's employees, he washed his hands constantly, and she always noticed how scarred they were from his other gig, carpentry. After Jocelyn left the navy and came home, Olly had helped her get the café job and had partitioned his bedroom so she could have a place to live.

Kacey Vanza, daughter of the café's previous owner and Alene's across-the-hall neighbor, came in looking depleted. Maybe because of her new boyfriend, thought Alene. Kacey got to work cleaning, cutting and prepping vegetables to roast. She'd turned into someone Alene could count on. Olly Burns, with a little help from a new employee, prepared and began frying huge pans of mushrooms and onions. Everything smelled so smoky good, Alene started thinking about adding a plain bowl of roasted and sautéed veggies to the menu. She pulled out her cellphone and texted herself a reminder.

The kitchen's smells, and sounds weren't as soothing as usual, because Alene was still disappointed that Frank had cancelled their date the previous night. She'd finally felt ready for their relationship to take the next step and had already spent an hour cleaning up, washing her hair, and getting dressed when he called to cancel. It hadn't been his fault that yet another Chicago homicide required his attention. Alene had been one of the people who wondered what the police did all day, since there was so much crime, until she saw how much time Frank put into his job.

Kacey Vanza took a break from chopping vegetables to give Alene a hug. What a pleasure to see her beautiful smile, her sea green eyes sparkling behind her glasses, her skin clear and bright. Alene had babysat for her when she was a curious, cuddly little girl, but as a teenager, Kacey had gotten into drugs, lost her way, and dropped out of high school. While she was still using, her skin had seemed gray and her eyes had looked glassy and red-tinged, like a night animal's. She'd spent time in one rehab after another, but now she was back, living across the hall from Alene and sharing the apartment with her stepmother, Joan, and Joan's thirty-four year old son, Jack Stone, a relatively new employee, who was now cleaning the front windows.

"It's never as much fun in the kitchen without Ruthie," Kacey said now, her dark-blonde hair pulled back in a ponytail, her voice low and serious.

"Because we all have to work harder," said Alene, guilty because she'd started thinking about Frank again. The truth was that she always felt kinder and less bitter when Ruthie was around. She'd thought her marriage to Neal would last forever and had never imagined raising the children by herself. She knew that she spent too much time mired in self-pity. Ruthie, still her closest friend after twenty years,

6

had to continuously remind her about what was good in the world.

Alene unlocked the front door at eight, and customers began streaming in. She noticed, as usual, how different the weekend crowds were; people had more time to sit and enjoy their drinks on a Saturday morning without jumping up to go to work. She loved this part of the day, greeting regulars and welcoming newcomers, but it was hard to look at all the couples smiling at each other, eating from each other's plates, and holding hands.

The customer Stanley had been bragging to about opening another training facility came in wearing a snug Better Be Fit T-shirt over leggings, her long hair in a single side braid. She'd been stopping by nearly every morning all summer, and usually ordered a vegan omelet smothered in onions. Alene didn't know her name, or the name of the thick-necked man who sometimes came in with her, but she usually took one of the large tables, even when she was alone. Now, Alene noticed her standing at the counter for a long time while two employees chatted near the espresso machine as if they didn't see her.

It was the third time Alene had to point out waiting customers to Jocelyn and LaTonya, a barista who was slowly working her way through a graduate degree in urban studies. LaTonya's intricately braided hair gave her a few additional inches so that she was as tall and striking as Jocelyn. They were both usually excellent baristas, but occasionally got too immersed in conversation. All month, Alene had been conferring with Ruthie about how to get employees to be more attentive to customers.

They'd been overwhelmed with pride when the café won both "Healthiest Breakfast," and "Best Hot Drinks," in the Lakeview neighborhood newsletter competition. Whipped and Sipped was known for its art exhibitions, story hour and knitting group, and always co-sponsored Pride Parade and Lakeview Arts Fest. Everyone loved Whipped and Sipped, but it could all collapse if Alene wasn't vigilant.

After the breakfast rush slowed, she headed back to her office, intending to check her email and confirm that the schedule was set for the next day, Sunday, when she'd be off. Sitting at her desk, she read Frank's text and felt herself blush, even though she was alone. Hopefully, her daughters would never search through her texts. The second line was about rescheduling their date for that night. Alene would probably have to decline if her children came home from their day with Neal feeling clingy and needing attention. She texted Frank that she'd have to get back to him.

Then she closed her office door and put on a pair of rubber gloves.

She opened the trash bag she'd found in the alley and read through a few of the bunched-up receipts. Alene felt a little uncomfortable about going through Stanley Huff's trash, but it wasn't as if she stole something. The rest of the bag was filled with crumpled wrappers for those ludicrous protein bars Stanley sold at Better Be Fit. People didn't need as much protein as they imagined. And, just as she'd suspected, Stanley didn't recycle.

Chapter 2

Thirty minutes later, Alene was back behind the counter, watching Phyllie Evans open the café door for her husband, Julian, who pushed a stroller in which their two open-mouthed, red-faced little boys slept. Phyllie and Julian lived in the neighborhood and came in often. Now, they waved at Alene and lifted their sons out of the stroller. Then they left it standing in everyone's way, as usual.

The two boys rushed to the dessert case and pressed their faces against the glass. The four-year-old, who had a sweet face and frizzy brown hair like both his parents, called out, "Where's Ruthie?" in a gravelly voice. The younger one managed something that sounded like "Roofie." He had sparse hair, and his crooked mouth and flat nose made him look like a boxer who'd seen better days.

"I'm sorry, boys," said Alene. "Ruthie's not here on Saturdays."

From the moment Alene and Ruthie met in the Northwestern dorm where they'd been assigned as roommates, Alene knew they were going to be best friends. Everyone loved Ruthie. Especially children, including, much later, Alene's three. Twelve-year-old Sierra often called Ruthie for advice or to complain about Alene, and ten-year-old Quinn had told Alene that Ruthie was more patient than her at teaching all the art projects Quinn and Ruthie's daughter liked to do together. Eight-year-old Noah loved playing with Ruthie's son, and constantly asked if he could stay overnight at the Rosins', because it was more fun than at home.

Alene wasn't hurt that all three kids loved being at the Rosins. A big part of the allure was Ruthie's husband, Benjie. He was a handsome bear of a guy who fixed, built, invented, and had endless patience for all of it. He was the kind of loving dad they longed for instead of the kind they had, who dragged them to his workplace on a Saturday and left them to their own devices.

Alene loved being with the Rosins too, especially when Ruthie's mother was around. In one of those small-world stories that Alene loved encountering, it turned out that Ruthie's mother had grown up with Phyllie's mother-in-law. And Phyllie's mother-in-law, Julian's mother, turned out to be Sylvie Huff, the wife of Alene's self-absorbed, bodybuilding, fitness center-owning, supplement-selling neighbor, Stanley Huff.

Phyllie said, "Don't worry guys, we'll come back and see Ruthie tomorrow." She ushered them back to their table.

Edith stood at attention behind the counter as Phyllie ordered a cappuccino for herself and a green smoothie for the boys. "My husband has reflux and has been belching all morning," Phyllie said. "What would you recommend for that?" Both Edith and Phyllie spoke in loud, inescapable voices. Jocelyn leaned over to tell Zuleyka, another barista, what Phyllie had just announced to the entire café, and they both giggled. Zuleyka, who was Panamanian, spoke English well enough to serve behind the counter, but didn't always understand every word.

Julian approached the counter. "My mother was rushed to the hospital last night, while I was at a Jiu-Jitsu tournament," he said, swallowing a burp. His voice wasn't as loud as his wife's, but it was nasal and could cut through other restaurant chatter. "It's not unusual to feel stressed when your mother's blood pressure shoots through the roof." Phyllie and Julian both worked at the middle school Alene's twelve-year-old daughter attended; Julian as a science teacher and Phyllie as a librarian who often recommended books to Alene.

"I drink a glass of water with apple cider vinegar every morning," said Edith, "and that helps me enormously. I'm sorry to hear about your mother, because I know what it feels like to be sick, I mean, I ..."

"Hi Julian," Olly interrupted, bouncing up from behind the counter where he'd just replenished a tray. He whispered loudly to Alene, "Maybe it's the vinegar that gives her the prune-face." Zuleyka and Jocelyn giggled again, stopping only when Alene tilted her head at them, her eyes opened wide in an expression of "What's wrong with you?"

"Would you like a pot of chamomile tea, Julian?" Alene, who also drank water with vinegar every morning, scowled at Olly and smiled at Julian. "The banana muffins and ginger molasses cookies are still warm."

Edith said, "Or, you can have smoothies made with flax meal, hemp, chia seeds, goji, maca powder, romaine lettuce, and fruit. I think drinking smoothies makes me feel much better despite the serious head injury I suffered recently." Edith needed to mention the attack at least once a day.

Julian, distracted from his worries, asked, "What is maca powder, exactly?"

"Ah," said Edith, who rarely missed a chance to give a boring description of ingredients. "Maca powder comes from the root of an herbaceous biennial plant, meaning they do not have a woody stem above the ground, and they take two years to finish their biological life. Sweet William and hollyhocks are biennials, for example. Anyway, Lepidium meyenii is part of the crucifer family of plants, like mustards and cabbages. It comes from the Andes Mountains in Peru."

Phyllie and Julian stood motionless, and even their sons seemed hypnotized by Edith's droning. Zuleyka and Jocelyn were serving other customers but kept looking over at Julian and his family. Alene said, "How about that pot of tea, Julian, and something for the boys?" The order was taking forever.

Phyllie ordered breakfast for the family and turned to Alene, her sullen expression and brown hair nearly identical to her husband's. "He'll be with his mother all day. Here we are on another Saturday morning and again she has some unexplained malady requiring the attention of her one child who has a family to inconvenience." She turned her back to Julian and sat down at the big table next to the counter, muttering, "She probably has hiccups."

Alene said, "I'm sorry to hear about your mother, Julian." She and Ruthie had taken voice lessons with Julian's mother when they were first pregnant. Back at Northwestern, they hadn't been accepted into the chorus they'd wanted to join, and worried that their future babies would cry if they tried to sing lullabies. Sylvie, when she wasn't bragging about herself, had taught them how to breathe correctly. The lessons must have worked because none of the kids had ever covered their ears, and Alene thought she'd gotten pretty good at singing to them. "How's she doing?"

"It's more than hiccups," said Julian as he paid for breakfast. Julian had brown, sloping eyes, just like Phyllie's. The two of them were similar looking, but Julian had a straight nose, his features weren't quite large enough to fit his face, and he usually seemed defeated in some way. Alene's daughter, Sierra, had hated him as a teacher. She said he let the class disrupters get away with everything and never sent them to the principal's office.

"If there wasn't something seriously wrong with my mother," said Julian, now carrying his and Phyllie's hot drinks to the table, "they wouldn't keep her overnight at the hospital."

Alene's mother had spent a lot of time at the hospital during her final months, after the cancer had metastasized and the doctors said there was nothing more they could do. Alene remembered how difficult it had been to be surrounded by beeping machines in airless rooms. "I hope your mom gets to go home today," she said. Julian and Phyllie had chosen the table closest to the counter.

Ethan, the older child, was now sitting up straight, and asked in a croaky voice, "What's wrong with Grandma Sylvie? Can I make her a picture?"

"Picture," growled Richie, the two-year-old, with a twist of his upper lip, as though he were issuing an order to one of his henchmen.

"Awesome idea, boys," Julian bent down to kiss the tops of their heads.

"Your mother always gets sick just in time for the weekend," said Phyllie. Alene cringed when people spoke about their mothers in a negative way.

Julian said, "Stanley's son and his wife came over and upset her, which isn't that hard a thing to do. My mom thinks those two are judgmental, but then she ranted about Rhea's broad shoulders and Harrison's hair plugs for ten minutes."

Alene interrupted, "Hold on, I never paid much attention, but didn't Stanley have two kids?"

"Two sons," said Julian, his eyes darting to where Jocelyn and Zuleyka stood near Alene giggling about something. Alene gave them both a stern look. "Harrison is the older one," Julian continued. "He's thirty-two, two years younger than me. He does something in real-estate. And the younger one is about twenty-four. My mother married their dad when Heather and I were ten and twelve, but we never lived with them or anything, so we were never close. I hate when my mother complains about them, especially when she focuses on silly things, like hair plugs and shoulders."

Jocelyn turned from setting a cup of something on the counter and said, as if she were a part of the conversation, "Rhea has broad shoulders because she was a swimmer, Julian. She's an interior decorator, perfectly nice, but she does whatever Harrison wants, and Harrison is a bully, as you probably know. He's never thought about how his words and actions effect other people. And he's the kind of real-

13

estate broker who will say whatever he needs to say to close a deal. He probably said something appalling and hurtful, something that could have really upset Sylvie. So, Harrison's got hair plugs?"

How did Jocelyn know Harrison Huff and his wife? Alene put a hand on Jocelyn's arm and said, "Next customer, Jocelyn." She also nudged Zuleyka to get moving. She didn't want to offend the people standing in line behind Julian.

Edith, a few sentences behind the conversation, said, "Your mother might have had a stroke, and if you don't treat a stroke immediately ..." She stopped talking when Alene looked at her with what Edith fortunately understood to be the same "what's wrong with you" face Alene had just used with Jocelyn and Zuleyka. How many times in one day was Alene going to take issue with Edith? In the training on responding to difficult customers, one of the main points was to stick to the menu.

Moments later, when they were ready, Alene brought the plates to Phyllie and Julian's table. Phyllie said, "Thanks, Alene. We've got twenty minutes together because Julian's mother is sick again, as I mentioned, in some mysterious way that's going to require lots of attention. He's planning to leave here as soon as he finishes eating."

Alene wished some of Ruthie's sweetness would rub off on her and she could respond in an empathetic way. She said, "Hope you all enjoy your breakfast then." Alene didn't really know Phyllie that well, although she'd recommended some wonderful books over the years.

"My mother-in-law is beyond difficult," Phyllie continued. "She invents a new drama every weekend to get Julian to come over." Alene's eldest daughter had complained that he talked through his nose, told too many stories, and graded too hard, but Sierra had only liked two of her teachers that entire year.

Phyllie pulled wipes from her purse and cleaned the boys' faces. "I just wish Julian would cut the cord," she added. Alene often saw Julian at her condo building on weekends; a big-boned, hunched-shouldered guy pushing

14

his stroller in and out of the elevator, on his way to or from visiting Sylvie. Sometimes he also came on weeknights. Alene hoped at least one of her own children would be as attentive.

While the little boys ran in circles around Julian, Phyllie told Alene about the time a few years before when Stanley put his hand up her skirt. It had felt like an assault. "That's the kind of family I married into," Phyllie said. "I wish I'd kicked Stanley in the balls instead of just running out of the room."

Alene wasn't sure how to respond. "I'm so sorry," she said again, wondering how Sylvie could have stayed married to Stanley after he made a move on her daughter-in-law. Someone should have warned Phyllie that you marry the family along with the man. Alene's marriage had failed, but she was still close to her ex-mother-in-law. "What happened after you reported him?"

Phyllie shook her head. "I probably should have," she said, "but I didn't think anything would come of it." It must have been before the #MeToo movement. Alene apologized a third time, thanked Phyllie and Julian for coming in, and hurried to help behind the counter thinking that she should have another talk with her girls about what to do if a man ever tried to touch them inappropriately.

The pretty woman with the golden-brown hair with whom Stanley had been flirting the other day had managed to nab the largest table again. She had a Better Be Fit bag next to her purse and Alene was about to ask her to move tables, or at least to put the bag away, but her partner with the thick neck brought two cups of coffee and sat down. Jocelyn delivered their food, and Alene was glad she hadn't said anything about the table or the bag.

Now, Ruthie's mother, Lillian, entered the café with Lawrence, her new boyfriend. He was a gentleman about Alene's dad's age, early seventies with a receding hairline, who stooped over a bit and had very thin lips. Alene, consciously pulling back her shoulders, crossed the café with her arms open and greeted them both, "How nice to see

15

you!" Alene adored Ruthie's mother. She was calm, didn't get easily frazzled, and always looked put-together. She'd also survived and flourished in the twenty years following the death of Ruthie's father, but her hair was completely white. "You know that your daughter doesn't work on Saturdays, right?"

"I know," said Lillian, "but we wanted to bring some healthy pastries to my good friend, Sylvie Huff. She's in the hospital."

Alene said, "We heard about it from Julian, who is here now with his family." She pointed at them.

Lawrence said, "I've been looking forward to visiting the famous Whipped and Sipped Café." Alene liked his warm greeting.

"So, we want half-a-dozen of whatever you think are the best things Ruthie baked yesterday," Lillian said.

"It's all best," said Alene, admiring how Lawrence kept his hand behind Lillian's back as though to protect her from falling over. Maybe it was a generational thing. She noticed Lillian's pale-pink fingernails, and as expected, impeccably applied make-up. Lillian once said that she hadn't left her house without make-up since the day at age fourteen when she'd worn lipstick to school, and a boy had smiled at her. Alene loved that story about Lillian, who'd taught both Ruthie and Alene that their efforts at self-improvement should be both internal and external. Ruthie was better at remembering the advice than Alene.

"I've already drunk enough coffee today, but I'd love a cup of green tea, please," said Lillian.

"For me as well, please," said Lawrence, glancing around the café. He gestured with his thumb, "This is a terrific neighborhood." He listed the shops and restaurants he knew and liked, and then said, "One of my former clients owns the gym next door."

"Lawrence did some legal work for Stanley Huff," said Lillian, gazing fondly at him, "a long time ago. Ruthie might have mentioned the connection."

16

"We've been tangled up in a lawsuit against him for over five years," said Lawrence.

"That must be frustrating," said Alene. She wasn't surprised, considering Stanley's generally rude behavior, but for all she knew, Lawrence was the one who'd wronged Stanley and not the other way around. "Ruthie never mentioned it." That was because Ruthie avoided gossiping.

Alene listened to Lillian while out of the corner of her eye she watched Kacey's new boyfriend lock up his bicycle. He was a street artist who collected garbage and transformed it into sculptures. Alene saw him stop to admire the sculpture he'd made that was now attached to the café's outside wall. The Rainbow Sculpture was Kofi Lloyd's signature piece, well-known as a fixture in Lakeview. Alene wondered if she should investigate how to organize a neighborhood art walk.

Kacey had told her she'd never fallen so hard for anyone before. Kofi was tall and thin with adorable dimples. While building his career as a sculptor, he worked as a bartender next door at Tipped. He'd already helped to bring out Kacey's artistic side. In the six weeks they'd been dating, he'd gotten her to try her hand at sketching and photography and had spent a lot of time teaching her how to use his high-tech, expensive camera. He'd even gotten Kacey to sign up for a community art class starting in September.

Maybe he'd be willing to create a map of Lakeview's public art. It could be both on paper and online. Alene and Ruthie could help him approach the local Chamber of Commerce. Most neighborhood businesses would want more customers, and like Whipped and Sipped, would probably be willing to pay for an advertisement. Someone must have gone back to alert Kacey, who ran out of the kitchen and into Kofi's arms.

Lillian smiled with her perfect, white teeth as she continued speaking. She'd once told Alene that she'd felt like an ugly duckling when her mother couldn't afford to have her teeth straightened. She'd worked at the corner drugstore after school and saved every penny to pay for her own braces. It was supposed to be an inspirational story, but Ruthie's twelve-year-old daughter had been horrified and demanded assurance from Ruthie and Benjie that they'd pay for her braces.

Customers came in and lined up at the counter. Alene went back to help, passing Julian's younger child, who sucked his drink with the satisfied expression of someone smoking a cigarette. Behind the counter, Alene loaded a box with pastries and presented it to Lillian. Lawrence reached in his back pocket for his wallet and Alene stopped him. "I'd never charge the mother of my best friend and pastry chef," she said.

As they thanked her and left the café, Alene admired how Lillian camouflaged her hooded eyes with smoky shadow and mascara. She'd once shown Ruthie and Alene, but neither of them had ever managed to pull off the look. Lillian had learned her make-up skills from Sylvie, who'd once been, according to Lillian, a spirited redhead with a gorgeous voice. It was hard to imagine, because whenever Alene saw her, Sylvie's hair was brassy, her voice was adenoidal, and she looked uncomfortably bloated.

Another customer entered the café carrying a Better Be Fit bag. Stanley had probably talked the guy into buying some unnecessary crap. Phyllie started trying to get the boys back in the stroller. "Do what you want, Julian," she said loud enough for the entire café to hear, "but we're going home for naps. It'll be nice if we can have some family time today."

Julian mumbled something about how his mother was also family. Jack came back out of the kitchen then with his bucket and mop. And through the open kitchen door, Alene heard Kacey scream.

Chapter 3

Alene rushed through the back door in time to see a young man with a red face and blond hair hurtling up the alley. It was one of Stanley's trainers, wearing a Better Be Fit T-shirt over shorts. He was running towards Kacey, who stood facing Better Be Fit's open back door, holding several large plastic garbage bags. He reached her and clapped a hand on her shoulder. "What are you doing?" he yelled.

Alene checked her watch. Didn't they open before eleven on Saturdays? Maybe Kacey had seen another rat. Alene had been vigilant about ordering traps and making sure the café's garbage bags went into the closed dumpsters, as did most of the neighbors. But Stanley tossed trash bags to the ground and smoked cigarettes near the café's doors. She'd watch him squint as he inhaled, and the exhaled smoke seemed to linger for hours. She hated getting in an elevator in her building after one of the smokers, like Stanley, had been there. At the café, employees and customers would sniff and look around suspiciously whenever he walked in. It bothered Alene that someone who sold the promise of better health, could also carelessly litter the ground and the air.

Kacey's bags fell, her knees buckled, and she slid down to the filthy gravel, the back of her head making a final loud thud. Jocelyn, who'd come to stand behind Alene at the café's back door, shot across the alley and squatted down beside Kacey. Alene felt her stomach lurch at the sight of Kacey's thick caramel-colored hair splayed against the oily-black ground. Hopefully, she hadn't cracked her head open. Imagining the bugs and bacteria swarming in the alley, Alene rushed over to bend down on Kacey's other side.

"Who the hell are you?" Alene asked. The guy, who looked like a roasted tomato, seemed to be in his late twenties. He stood nervously clicking the set of keys he'd pulled from his pocket and combing his other hand through his straw-blond hair. Before Alene could yell at him for scaring Kacey, Jocelyn, gently cradling Kacey's head, glowered. "What the hell is wrong with you, Miles?" Another person Jocelyn already knew.

"I thought she was trying to break in," he said in a defensive tone. He continued to jostle his keys and looked warily at Kacey as he got his breath back. Keys, as if there were no such thing as electronic security systems. He told Alene that he was a trainer at Better Be Fit and asked who she was.

She told him and pointed to the café before turning to point at the gym's back door. "Better Be Fit's door is open, so you don't need your keys." Alene whipped off her shirt hoping that her camisole could pass as a summer top, and placed it under Kacey's head. She looked warily around in case a rat did show up.

"I didn't mean to make her faint," Miles mumbled, turning away to step inside. He had pretty-boy good looks, but his teeth looked too white against his bright red skin. From where she crouched next to Kacey, Alene watched Miles push open the door. Now she could see a whole head of silvery gray hair on the floor just inside of Better Be Fit. Miles turned abruptly around and ran back outside, covering his mouth as though he were about to hurl.

"I'll go in," said Jocelyn. She stood and strode through the open door. Then she gasped, "No, how can this ..." Alene rushed inside and saw Stanley Huff on the floor, pale and motionless. She couldn't tell if he was still breathing, but his signature smell of musky aftershave and cigarette smoke lingered in the air. She glanced briefly around his office and ran back outside to help Kacey.

Alene's first thought was that he must have had a heart attack and slid down to the floor from wherever he'd been standing. Medics would probably try the defibrillator on him. "Miles, call 911," she said. "Then when Jocelyn comes out, go try to make Stanley comfortable, maybe cover him with something, but don't move him."

Miles nodded and wiped his sweaty brow with the back of his hand. He fumbled with his cellphone and managed to make the call. Alene rubbed Kacey's forehead and murmured her name in the same sing-song voice she used to put Kacey to sleep when she was a little girl and Alene was babysitting.

Miles put his phone back in his pocket and managed a few steps towards where Stanley was lying just as Jocelyn stepped out into the alley. Alene shouldn't have left her in there alone for so long. She looked wan. "Are you okay?" Alene asked.

Jocelyn gave a short nod, her face blank except for a vein throbbing in her forehead. "I couldn't find his pulse," she said, kneeling on Kacey's other side and scooping her up to carry her back into the café.

Alene grabbed the soiled shirt she'd put under Kacey's head, and said, "Look for his pulse, Miles. He might still be alive even if Jocelyn couldn't find it. She's not a medic."

"Yes, of course, I will," said Miles, in a scratchy voice, still glued to the ground. "But I'm not a medic either."

Alene ran ahead to hold open the café's back door. Kacey's eyes fluttered as Jocelyn carried her into the kitchen. That was a good sign. Olly stopped stirring the onions that Kacey had abandoned on the grill. He stared.

"Something happened to Stanley," said Alene, rushing past them all to clear the sofa in her office. Jocelyn's hands trembled after she set Kacey down. The kitchen staff gathered by the office door. "Did he try one of his moves on her?" someone asked softly. They'd all heard about Stanley.

"I hope she knocked him out," said Olly. They all watched Kacey, hoping she'd come out of her faint. "If he hurt Kacey, I'll march over there and break a plate over his head." Sometimes Olly sounded like Alene's dad, or like a dad from an old television sitcom.

"He didn't do anything," said Jocelyn, her brow creased as she swept Kacey's hair away from her face. "She'll be fine in a few minutes."

Alene said, "He might have had a heart attack. He's on the floor near the back door and Miles Taylor called for an ambulance."

"He was probably taking statin drugs for his heart," said Jocelyn. Maybe he'd mentioned it when they were both outside in the alley vaping or smoking.

Olly brought Alene a dampened cloth to hold against Kacey's forehead, then ran out of the kitchen to discuss Stanley with everyone behind the counter. Jack Stone hurried over and hovered above Kacey like an anxious mother until Alene shooed him away. "She's my sister, Alene. I should help take care of her," he said.

"Really, Jack?" Earlier in the summer, he'd begged Alene for a job. He hadn't ever actually worked, aside from dealing drugs. Alene had taken chances on other employees who'd worked out, and Ruthie had convinced her to do whatever was needed to make sure Jack succeeded. Kacey was Jack's stepsister, a decade younger than him, but he'd always acted like she didn't exist. Alene couldn't wait to tell Ruthie that Jack felt like he should help take care of her. It was just the kind of thing they'd hoped for.

Alene said, "That's really good of you, Jack. Maybe keep an eye on her and prepare her something to drink for when she wakes up. She'll probably be thirsty." Maybe, after six months or a year of working at the café, Jack would have a steady-enough work history to rent his own place.

Alene headed back to the counter, where a line had formed. On weekends, customers sat in the café and ate and drank and had real conversations instead of working at their laptops, as they did during the week. Alene served two women and started to remove empty muffin trays from the display shelves. She'd heard sirens approaching and now they'd stopped, so they were probably already taking care of Stanley. When they revived him, would he understand the irony of having a heart attack after all that touting of vitamin supplements? Alene felt a little ashamed of her harsh attitude. She forced herself to imagine how awful she'd feel if something like that happened to someone she loved.

She peeked in on Kacey, whose eyes flickered and then popped open as Jack waved a peppermint teabag under her nose. "Where is Stanley?" she asked in a groggy voice. Alene rushed to her side and helped her take a sip of water.

"He's dead," Olly piped up breathlessly from the kitchen door.

"Are you sure, Olly?" Alene asked.

"I just asked one of the paramedics," Olly said, "and the annoying old guy is definitely dead."

Alene wondered if it was necessary to respect the dead even if they were horrible alive. "No matter what we thought about him, he was a human being," she said.

"Right you are," said Olly, not at all contrite. "And now he's a dead human being."

She wasn't going to change Olly anytime soon. "At least you can get back to work now. You too, Jack." Olly made a face and tossed his curls at her before heading to the sink. "We all should," Alene added.

Jocelyn shoved past Jack and sat at the edge of the couch near Kacey's feet. Usually unmoved by chaos, Jocelyn had tears in her eyes. She whispered, "He wasn't that old."

"You're not going to faint too, are you?" Jack, still hovering, asked. He made a skeptical face at Jocelyn.

"Didn't you see people die when you were with the army in Iraq?"

"I was with the navy in Afghanistan," Jocelyn replied in a now steely voice. "And it doesn't matter where I was, because there wasn't a lot of death in the coding division, Jack. Just give me a few minutes if you don't mind." Her hands were shaking.

"Maybe you're low-sugar," said Olly, who'd come back to Alene's office. He thought everyone had low blood sugar. "I'll make you a smoothie," he added, pushing Jack to the side and rushing out to the counter.

She'd have to remind Olly about not being pushy, but she liked when her employees took care of each other. Alene and Ruthie had always tried to create a kind of Whipped and Sipped family. "Sorry. I'm all right," said Jocelyn, exhaling loudly. She rose from Alene's couch and smoothed her silky goldenrod-yellow top before stepping back into the kitchen.

"They're still running around back there," Jack called out.

Alene didn't really care to watch the police or paramedics and was relieved when they'd finished and left not long after. Lunch customers were lined up, and she could hear whispering about what was going on next door. Olly handed out small paper cups of fruit and vegetable smoothie, trying to drum up interest. He passed Alene and said, "Why don't you call your boyfriend since he's a cop?"

Alene gave him a look. He asked, "What about the wife? She's related to Ruthie, isn't she?"

"Ruthie doesn't answer the phone on Saturdays," said Alene, "but I can call her mom." She texted Lillian, and then Frank. Alene hadn't expected to see another dead body so soon after the last one, Kacey's father. That had only been six weeks ago and had been shocking. She'd known immediately that he was dead. She hadn't been as sure about Stanley because there hadn't been any blood, and she'd only seen him for a brief moment.

She went into her office when her phone rang a moment later. "Hi Alene, I was just thinking about you," Frank said.

"Before you say anything, we're next door at Better Be Fit and will be coming over soon to talk with you and your employees."

It was nice to hear his voice, and she always liked when he said her name. "But you're in homicide," said Alene, hoping she'd have time to check her hair before he saw her. "Stanley was just a middle-aged-guy with a weak heart."

"That's the kind of helpful CPD officers we are," said Frank. "What about you, are you okay?"

Alene sat back in her chair. "I'm all right, thanks, but it's a long story."

"I hope you'll tell me later," he said. "And, Alene, I'm sorry I couldn't come over last night." Alene had hoped they'd have been able to have their first night alone together, but he'd had to work late. "Would later today work for you? Can we do dinner or take a walk?" He sounded sweet, sincere. Maybe he'd have said something about wanting to hold her in his arms if he was alone in the car.

"I'm not sure tonight will work," said Alene, kicking herself for having to decline. It depended on how the kids felt after a day with their father. "But can we talk later?" It felt weird to consider plans for the evening while Frank was dealing with Stanley's death. Were their plans always going to be last-minute? And Lee, his partner, was with him. Did Frank mean that they'd both be on the walk?

"Rain check, then," he said in a melancholy way. Her dad used that phrase too.

"Of course," she said, rising from her desk and heading into the kitchen as they said their goodbyes. The second she slid her cellphone into her back pocket, Olly was at her elbow.

"I could help make phone calls about Stanley," he offered.

"That's sweet of you," said Alene, telling him that it was probably taken care of and he could get back to work. Olly was always generous like that.

She checked Ruthie's list and began taking out ingredients for a batch of chocolate sauce that also made an ideal frosting for several of Ruthie's cakes. Alene was proud of the recipe she had invented, and now she'd make enough to put in jars that they'd sell along with some of her specially made bean and vegetable dips. Lillian called back just then, and Alene told her that Stanley Huff had collapsed in his office.

"That's awful," said Lillian, "but he's not a healthy person, so I'm not totally surprised. Lawrence and I are with Sylvie at the hospital right now. Maybe they're both sick, but if Stanley has a virus, the last thing she needs is exposure to him. Hold on, she needs me now, so I'll call you back."

"But ..." said Alene.

Lillian had clicked off. She called back a few minutes later and said, "Hi again. They're trying to get her blood pressure under control, and Sylvie might be having a psychotic episode, although it's unclear. We came out to the hallway while the nurses are in there with her."

Alene heaved a sigh. "I'm sorry."

"Sylvie and I have been friends for a long time," said Lillian. She shared how difficult Sylvie had become and how hard it was to recognize her lately.

Alene tried to explain that Stanley was dead, but Lillian interrupted again, now whispering, "She's babbling about how she wanted to be an opera singer." Lillian started to say something about taking Alene and Ruthie to see Don Giovanni at the Lyric, but then stopped abruptly and said, "The nurses are leaving so we're going back in the room. And Sylvie is gesturing at the phone because she wants to talk to you."

Suddenly Alene was on the phone with Sylvie. She flashed back to voice lessons and remembered singing endless syllables into a mirror while Sylvie ordered her and Ruthie to stop slouching. She remembered collapsing with laughter at how silly they looked and sounded during those lessons. Although Sylvie had spent a lot of time bragging about her tragically truncated opera career, she'd also taught them how to inhale deeply into their diaphragms and exhale while imagining a deflating balloon. Sylvie would occasionally sing a phrase or two, and they'd both been amazed at her voice, even though she constantly fretted about having lost her ability to sing. Ruthie and Alene had tried to convince her that she still sounded fantastic, but she had waved them away, telling them that they didn't know the opera world.

"Lillian doesn't understand," Sylvie said now, in a gravelly voice, "what it's like to be married to someone who hates you."

"Oh," said Alene, simultaneously horrified and sympathetic. "This is Alene Baron." There was no way she could tell Sylvie that her husband was dead. "I'm sorry to hear that you're in the hospital."

She could hear Julian in the background saying, "Mom, do you know you're talking to Ruthie's college friend, Alene Baron? She's the one who owns the café." Then she could hear Julian telling Lillian the plot of a story. It wasn't interesting to Alene, but Lillian was probably nodding and smiling, too polite to say what she really thought.

"It's a highly-flammable, corrosive agent that could melt the metallic spacesuit without affecting the skin or anything made of cotton," Julian said. "The guy would be left standing there in his underwear."

"I need to talk to Lillian," Alene repeated loudly as she shut her office door. "Could you please give her the phone?"

Sylvie said, "Did you know that I got accepted into one of the most prestigious opera festivals in the country?" She slurred her words. "Then I got sick and had to come home."

Alene thought about hanging up and trying to call Lillian back later. She'd heard Sylvie's opera stories back during her voice lessons. Sylvie continued, "A girl with a voice like a frog snagged my role. Everyone said I would have made a better Carmen."

"Mom, that was a hundred years ago," said Julian in the background. "And they wouldn't have given the part to someone who couldn't sing. Now, give the phone back to Lillian."

She must have done so because Lillian said, "Hi Alene, sorry this is kind of a hassle, but they gave Sylvie something and she'll hopefully fall asleep now. Then, I hope to convince Julian to get out of here and go meet his wife and kids at the playground. Lawrence and I can stay with Sylvie for a while."

Maybe one day, Ruthie would be just like her mother, fielding phone calls if Alene ever had to be hospitalized. Alene would have to find someone else for Saturdays though, when Ruthie was home celebrating the Sabbath with her family. "Lillian," said Alene. "I've been trying to tell you. Stanley. Is. Dead."

"Oh," said Lillian. Alene thought she must have been holding her breath. "Actually, Alene, I don't think it's a good time to relay that information right now."

Alene quickly wished Lillian luck, said goodbye, and texted Ruthie, who wouldn't get the message until after the sun went down. The rest of the day dragged by with the usual ebb and flow of a Saturday afternoon. Alene was grateful when the café emptied out, the closing staff finished up, and she was ready to lock up.

Neal called as she walked home, telling her that the children were at his mother's and asking if they could stay another night. Sierra confirmed that all three wanted to stay because Grandma Mitzi was giving the girls makeup tips and letting Noah take a bubble bath in her jacuzzi. Plus, the next day, Neal was going to take them bowling. Alene didn't think her girls, with their big blue eyes and flawless skin, needed a speck of makeup, but she was delighted that Neal wanted them to stay another night. She hoped it meant that he was starting to enjoy his time with the kids. She thought about calling Frank back, but she was done in and she hadn't seen her dad since he'd gone to bed the previous night.

At home, she whipped up a quick fish chowder using ingredients she always had on hand. After Alene and her father finished dinner, they sat at the scuffed pine table sipping tea while she told Cal about Stanley. He nodded off as she spoke; his eyes seemed droopier than usual and she wasn't surprised that he wanted to go straight to bed. Shuffling back to his room, Cal said, "In The Odyssey, Homer said, 'There is a time for many words, and there is also a time for sleep.'"

Alene remembered the long hours he'd worked when he advised clients about their finances. He used to come home every day and nap for ten or fifteen minutes in his favorite chair before popping up again, totally refreshed. He hardly ever seemed refreshed these days. She kissed his forehead and said, "Sweet dreams, Dad."

It was just after eight on Saturday night and the sky was a dark azure, Alene's favorite color. She wondered if Frank was still at work. If only she hadn't been in such a low mood, they could have had an entire evening alone together. Or even just a nice conversation. Maybe she could slip him into the apartment after the kids were in bed one night during the week, and he'd leave well before they woke up. He'd probably dislike being treated like a sixteen-year-old boyfriend, but she didn't want to be the kind of mother who exposed her children to the men she dated. On the other hand, it might be good for them to see what a healthy relationship looked like.

Just before ten, she was reading in bed when Frank texted again to apologize for not coming the night before. He promised to stop at the café every single day if that was the only way he'd get to see her. After they said their goodbyes, Alene got a text from Ruthie saying that she was running a fever and coughing, too sick to come in the next day. Alene was grateful that Neal was already planning to have the kids for another night. She made a mental note to thank him later. Next, she arranged for Zuleyka, who babysat when her school and café schedule allowed, to come at eight to help her father and make sure the kids got to their various Sunday activities after Neal dropped them off. Then Alene read a Georgette Heyer mystery until sleep pulled her under.

Chapter 4

From the minute the café opened at eight, everyone was on their feet. Usually on Sunday morning, Ruthie would be supervising the kitchen and Alene would be at home, sipping coffee with her father, trading sections of the New York Times and watching boats gliding in and out of Belmont Harbor. In the winter they'd gaze out at the empty docks and watch the waves, the hardy birds, the bare trees. Now, Alene glanced around at the customers, recognizing only a few. None of her staff ever talked about how much more family-centered it was than the Saturday crowd.

Julian made an appearance for the third day in a row. He said he'd come to pick up something tasty to bring to his mother, so he was alone, without Phyllie or the stroller. Alene suggested the guacamole salad and a slice of Ruthie's freshly baked pumpkin apple cake. Then she asked about Sylvie.

Julian said his mother hadn't been terribly surprised that Stanley was dead, which seemed both odd and suspicious to Alene. Could Sylvie have given him something to make his heart stop, like feeding him deep fried hotdogs or slipping some foxglove into his soup? They'd probably been married for nearly twenty years, so why now? Alene didn't ask, because Julian was still talking about Sylvie's blood pressure five minutes later when LaTonya handed him his order.

Then Alene was swept into the rhythm of the café with its honey-vanilla smells and the undulating sounds of conversation. She greeted two fresh-faced young women wearing cumbersome backpacks and a woman dressed too warmly for a bright summer day, who looked like she'd been crying. If Ruthie were there, she'd have listened to the woman's story, but Alene didn't have the bandwidth to be that empathetic. Finally, she left the counter and headed back to the kitchen to scrape overdone zucchini-orange muffins from a muffin pan. She hoped nobody would tell Ruthie that someone had overbaked the muffins.

She walked back out to the café in time to see Kacey's tall, thin boyfriend, Kofi, locking his bicycle to the iron bike stand in front of the window again. He had a new cut on his cheek and a bandage on his neck, but his intricately braided hair was still intact, and he could still flash his dimples. Alene turned to help two little pigtailed sisters who were having trouble choosing between a cookie or a muffin. Out of the corner of her eye she saw LaTonya make an obscene gesture at Kofi before stomping away. Now what? How many times would Alene have to remind her employees to leave their squabbles at the door?

Kacey came out of the kitchen for her break and broke out in a radiant smile when she spotted Kofi. She'd already whipped together a smoothie in anticipation of his visit, so now she followed him to a table where they sat close together, sharing the smoothie and whispering.

After Kofi left fifteen minutes later, Alene led Kacey back to the kitchen, where she checked Ruthie's list. She was pleased to see that the baking team was keeping everything on schedule. "Seems like everything's okay with Kofi, huh?" She didn't want to pry but couldn't help worrying about Kacey getting hurt. And LaTonya's angry gesture, although inappropriate in the café, was none of her business.

"We're good," said Kacey, starting to grill a batch of yellow onions that Olly, now red-eyed from the task, had chopped. "But Kofi wants me to meet his family." She'd lost her smile and was back to her usual serious face.

"That sounds like a great idea," said Alene, pouring batter into a prepared loaf pan. "Why not?"

Kacey shrugged. "I don't know. I really like Kofi, but I just don't know." Alene liked Kofi too. She wished more of her employees had his work ethic. Aside from bartending four nights a week at Brianne's bar next door, and taking Jiu-Jitsu classes on the other nights, Kofi spent hours searching for materials to create his unusual sculptures. The rainbow sculpture in front of the café had led to a couple of small commissions and helped advertise the café. Kofi was more of a go-getter than Kacey. Maybe some of his confidence would rub off, and Kacey would find something to be passionate about.

Olly, who kept popping up everywhere, said, "He's a good guy and he's phenomenal at Jiu-Jitsu. I don't say that about just anyone. Go meet his family, Kacey. What's the worst thing that can happen?"

Kacey stopped stirring the onions and said, "They could think I'm not good enough for their son."

LaTonya had burst through the kitchen door in time to hear the exchange, and said, "That's ridiculous, Kacey. Kofi Lloyd doesn't deserve you."

Olly and Alene exchanged looks. "What's up with you, LaTonya?" Olly asked. "Kofi is probably going to be a famous artist, and did you know that he's a fifth level brown belt in Jiu-Jitsu?"

"I don't care about Jiu-Jitsu, Olly," LaTonya said. She pressed her lips together and waved her hand as she headed to the restroom. "It's just a bunch of boys showing off their moves."

Olly followed her and called through the closed door, "It's one of the most powerful disciplines there is, but you wouldn't know anything about discipline, would you? And what's your problem with Kofi?"

Alene straightened a tray of pastries. Was she going to have to get involved? She wanted her employees to get along with each other. She also wanted customers to know that Whipped and Sipped was a place where everyone would be comfortable and welcome.

Olly, who hated not having his questions answered, nabbed LaTonya before she could walk back behind the counter and confronted LaTonya. "I'm not interested in martial arts," LaTonya grunted. "And Kofi gets on my nerves with his artist garbage-picking crap," she said. "What bothers me most though is all these customers who keep asking me if we're related. Is it the braids or do we really all look alike to them?"

Alene sighed. "Of course not, LaTonya. I wish people weren't so clueless."

LaTonya said, "You mean white people."

"But Kofi has dimples and he's way cuter than you," said Olly. "It's definitely the braids."

Jocelyn had just returned to the kitchen after vaping in the alley and gave Olly an exasperated look. LaTonya smacked him lightly on the arm. Alene couldn't blame her after his comment. Jocelyn said, "You can't let other peoples' narrow-mindedness hurt your feelings, LaTonya. They're just being asinine."

LaTonya said, "I'm used to it. Every Black woman I know is used to it. I just get tired of it sometimes." She let Jocelyn and Olly hug her. "This doesn't mean I'm interested in taking one of your classes, Olly, so don't even start."

Olly said, "That just shows that you're prejudiced. Brazilian Jiu-Jitsu isn't just a martial art, Latonya, it's a lifestyle."

"Stop it, Olly," said Alene. "This is serious. I'm really sorry, LaTonya, but it's true that people can be limited. And not just about race. You can't believe how many customers don't get the concept of vegan food, and I have to explain again and again that Ruthie doesn't bake with any animal products."

"And there are people who don't get the concept of self-protection and have preconceived ideas about Jiu-Jitsu," said Olly, looking pointedly at LaTonya.

"Give it a rest, Olly," said LaTonya. Everyone in the kitchen weighed in about what they'd like to change about people they knew, customers, and family members. Alene thought her employees would be better off concentrating on improving themselves. LaTonya could be less touchy, Olly could take things more seriously, Kacey could gain some self-confidence. And maybe she herself could be less judgmental. Also, what kind of a person was she to completely avoid thinking about the neighbor who'd just died the day before?

The day sped by and Alene left, leaving Jocelyn in charge of closing. At home, Zuleyka, who had been one of nine children and knew how to keep Sierra, Quinn, and Noah busy, reported that there'd been a lot of quarreling after the kids got dropped off, but they'd all gotten to their tennis lessons on time, and were now immersed in their screens. For dinner, Alene made pasta, and a chicken skillet with mushrooms, scallions, and red peppers. She also served a chopped salad with a garlicky dressing. To prove that she could be as fun as Neal, they ate sitting around the coffee table, watching an old movie about children sentenced to a juvenile detention facility who are forced to work for hours in the hot sun. It was filled with silly coincidences and had a happy ending.

Monday morning at five, after a fitful night of dreams about people she knew dying of heart attacks, Alene jumped out of bed and ran to her gym. It was small but packed with training equipment and exercise machines. One entire wall was a mirror, and the other three walls were filled with posters of fine-looking bodies engaged in sports of one kind or another. Michael, the owner and Alene's trainer, said, "Where's my coffee? You know I can't function without my coffee," spoken robotically without inflection in order to better mock what he viewed as a ridiculous obsession. He was about six years younger than Alene, still able to party through the weekend and jump up without a hangover early on Monday morning. He had a quick mind and moved with the agility of a gymnast.

Alene tried to smile at him. "I'm just so tired," she said.

Michael tipped his head to scrutinize her with narrowed eyes. "Did you sleep in a coffin again last night? It seems like the sunlight is bothering you."

Alene, who usually enjoyed sparring with Michael, told him what had happened to Stanley Huff.

"So," Michael said, "You're saying being a jackass and smoking cigarettes didn't kill him after all?" Michael still sometimes mentioned how dreadful it had been to work at one of Stanley's earlier Better Be Fit locations after he finished his degree in kinesiology. Stanley had been grudging and petty, constantly complained about his costs, and gossiped about some clients to other clients.

Then he'd added the clients Michael had brought, into his own database. A year later, when Michael left to set up his own gym, Stanley had sued him for stealing clients. Michael had gone through a severe depression and had been forced to borrow money from his parents to fight the lawsuit. Stanley lost.

Now, Michael said, "Get on the elliptical and tell me all about it. Should I be concerned that two people you know have died so far this summer, or that both deaths happened to be in your immediate vicinity?"

"I can see how that could be interpreted as very unfortunate karma," said Alene, feeling a little more energetic.

As he guided Alene through her exercises, Michael held forth on how there is no such thing as karma and no reason for anything that happens. He said, "We might as well toss a coin to determine the future." Then later, as she left his gym, he added, "But if you come across a third death in the next month or so, we'll have to sever all ties. Nothing personal, you understand, but you might just be rotten luck."

She laughed, which felt good, and Michael gave her an impish parting smile. Then she felt dismal about having laughed; there was nothing funny about death.

At home, Alene showered and dressed, and was leaving notes for the kids when Blanca appeared. This month, her thick, layered hair was dyed in shades of purple and green. Even first thing in the morning, she wore a curve-hugging top, plum lipstick, and olive-hued eye shadow. But today she looked tired. She was in her late forties, about ten years older than Alene. "No, I'm fine," she insisted when Alene suggested that she go home as soon as Cal took his nap instead of waiting for the kids to get back from camp. "I don't get sick."

"Okay, but take it easy," said Alene. Blanca had started working for Cal after Alene's mother died, so she'd been taking care of him and the apartment for over seventeen years. They should invite her next time they rented kayaks along the Chicago Riverwalk. Cal could sit in the back of a double and just enjoy the ride.

That morning, Jocelyn had opened the café, turned on the ovens, and started baking. When Alene arrived, the baking team was measuring and pouring according to Ruthie's directions. Jack Stone was scrubbing a batch of trays. LaTonya, Jocelyn, and Edith were behind the counter looking at pictures of each other's cats, and the tables were half-filled with customers. A few minutes later, Frank and his partner, Lee, came in. By the time they took their seats, Alene had their drinks ready along with a plate of apple-cinnamon and sunflower chocolate chip cookies, and assorted other sweet or savory pastries.

"To what do I owe the pleasure of such an early visit?" she asked, taking a seat at their table. She immediately worried that she should have greeted them more formally. She'd interrupted Frank in the middle of saying something to Lee about neighborhood store owners and managers. Neither looked like they'd enjoyed a good night of sleep. Maybe there was something going around that caused bloodshot eyes in everyone she knew. She felt Frank watching her. Did he think she was starting to look closer to forty? He was probably way more observant than a typical man.

Frank smiled and thanked Alene for the food and drinks. "I don't mind being called to your neighborhood because everything you serve here is excellent. And I get to see you." Lee blinked and nodded. Alene felt sorry for him. He was still scarred with adolescent acne and blinked excessively. Frank sat with one leg folded over the other, quietly chewing forkfuls of almond breakfast cake.

Frank was freshly shaved, and Alene noticed a tiny spot where he must have nicked himself that morning. Six weeks wasn't enough time to really know a person, she thought, and it didn't count that she and Frank had first briefly met eight years before. But she liked the way he spoke to her, the way he listened, the warmth of his gaze. Too bad his work and her kids were making it so tough to get their relationship moving.

Maybe he'd say something sweet about hoping to revisit the plans that had been stymied Friday night. Instead, he said, "We're here about Stanley Huff."

"I meant to ask you about that," said Alene. "I thought it was something about his heart."

"His heart definitely stopped," said Frank, "but we think someone else was involved."

If there was one thing to make Alene forget about being lonely, it was an unsolved murder. "I didn't know him well. How can I help you?"

She remembered, from her fleeting glimpse, that Stanley's office had been messy. She'd seen the couch with a colorful afghan bunched to the side, litter on the floor, an overturned chair. Had it been ransacked? While Lee picked apart a lemon-pistachio muffin, Alene directed her questions to Frank. "Was he strangled? Were there signs of a struggle or bruises on his neck? Also, did you check if Stanley made or received any phone calls beforehand? I mean just in case he got some horrible news or something that could have elevated his blood pressure." Was it Phyllie

38

who'd talked about Stanley's older son and daughter-in-law recently moving back to Chicago?

Frank grinned. "Sounds like you're itching to get back in the game, Alene."

"I'm just asking," she demurred. Either he wanted her opinion, or not.

Frank, taking a sip of coffee, said, "There were signs of a struggle."

"I thought so too," said Alene, leaning forward and shaking her head. She'd read murder mysteries that involved overturned furniture, dumped soil, and spilled wine. Earlier that summer, she'd been the one to figure out who'd murdered Kacey's father. Did Frank want her input? "Was there anything under his fingernails?" she asked. "Small capillary hemorrhages on his face? Skin discoloration? Inhaled material in his lungs?" Oops, she was going at it again, dramatizing the possibilities with sweeping arm gestures. She'd recently finished a novel in which a man with a heart condition is murdered by someone who grinds his heart medication into a powder and inserts a massive amount of it into the victim's capsules.

"You're pretty fluent in murder, Alene," said Frank, now smiling while Lee pointedly looked at his watch and tapped his foot. "I mean that as a compliment. And we're talking to all the neighbors."

"What about his swollen eye?" Alene said, her attention on Frank's red-rimmed eyes. "I remember thinking someone must have popped him one."

"We saw the eye," said Frank as he exchanged a glance with his partner.

Alene added. "He was always arguing with someone or other."

"We don't need to hear what you didn't like about him," said Lee. Alene wondered how he ever got anyone to say anything of value when he spoke like that.

Frank squinted at Lee and said, "Actually, we do need to know what you didn't like about him."

Lee said. "Just give us the facts." He reminded Alene of the unsmiling detective in a television show her dad had loved as a kid and sometimes quoted.

"You already know that Kacey was the one who found him." Alene sat up straight and considered what she remembered. Frank had just called her fluent in murder. He wouldn't suspect her of leaving something out on purpose, but Lee would.

She told the story, including the part about Miles scaring Kacey into fainting. Frank thanked her and said, "Sorry to bother you about this, Alene, but it's totally routine."

She didn't respond because she was distracted by the smell of his aftershave.

Lee said, "We'll ask if any of the neighbors saw anything on Friday night."

That pulled her out of her trance. "We close at four in the afternoon," said Alene. Could one of her customers have murdered Stanley and then come in the next morning for multigrain pancakes with maple syrup and berries? "But didn't he die on Saturday morning?"

"Kacey found him on Saturday at about 11:00," Frank said, leaning towards Alene, "but we think he died on Friday night between about 9:00 and 11:00."

Alene had thought he'd come to work and keeled over that morning. She wished Frank could just take her in his arms and whisper what he needed from her. Then she could say what she needed from him. "I could tell you who worked and who closed on Friday."

Frank nodded, and she went back to her office, printed Friday's schedule, and headed back into the café, nodding to the guy with a receding hairline who always added cold milk to his double latte and then complained that it wasn't hot enough. The three women who usually huddled over their laptops were unexpectedly sitting up straight and conversing over iced drinks. Two sets of moms towing young children of various ages sat sipping coffees and nibbling muffins or other pastries. It looked like the sun was

40

scorching the pavement outside, but the temperature in the café seemed exactly right. Alene handed the schedule to Frank.

Frank grabbed her hand in both of his as she was about to head back to the counter. He said, "Catch you later?" She nodded and closed her eyes for a second, wishing she didn't act like a besotted teenager around him. Frank placed both their cups in a bin and the two detectives left the café.

Alene helped behind the counter for the next hour until Jocelyn elbowed her. Miles Taylor was holding the door open for a woman with thick, dark auburn hair and the kind of eyes that made her look half asleep.

Jocelyn whispered, "Miles has been dating Sylvie's daughter, who is a piece of work. She looks better than she used to. Can you believe she's Julian's sister?" Alene vaguely recognized her face, but nothing about Heather looked healthy.

"I don't think she's ever been in the café before," Alene whispered back. "When I first started hanging out with Ruthie, I used to see her and Julian at holidays because of Sylvie's friendship with Ruthie's mother. But Heather was just a little girl back then. I wouldn't have recognized her."

As the couple approached the counter, Jocelyn said, "Welcome to the Whipped and Sipped Café." She gestured with her arms and introduced Alene as the owner. Heather nodded at Alene.

"So nice to see you, Heather," Jocelyn added with a dusting of snark. "You remember me, don't you? I'm Jocelyn DeVale, and it's been over a decade since we last met. So, Miles, are you planning on scaring anyone to death today?"

Alene interrupted before Jocelyn could say anything else. "Condolences on your stepfather's passing." She would have liked to caution Heather that good-looking guys like Miles generally aged badly. Or they had affairs with younger women, convinced that beauty was more important than loyalty and love. "And I hope your mother is feeling better," Alene added. She studied Miles's face. If Stanley had treated him the way he'd treated Alene's trainer, they might have

41

been having it out on Friday night. Miles could have left the back door open on purpose so that someone else would find Stanley's body the next day. Maybe that's why he came to work so late that day.

Heather shrugged, "Thank you, but I'm fine. Stanley was a horrible person who ruined my childhood, and my mother is a pitiful old witch who tries to manipulate everyone with her drama. Miles and I both want green tea and we're going to share the vegan quiche, please." She'd pulled her auburn hair into a tight ponytail so there was nothing to soften the harsh angles of her face. Her sleepy eyes seemed childlike, but her hands were skeletal.

Alene wanted to point out that Heather's mother, Sylvie, probably deserved patience more than pity, but only asked, "Would you like toast with that?" She gestured to LaTonya to complete the order.

Jocelyn turned her back to the customers and mimed sticking a finger down her throat. Alene murmured, "Just focus on your work, okay?" She smiled in a way she hoped seemed understanding, then turned to ring up a box of assorted muffins and cookies, make two mocha lattes, and deliver the usual onion omelet and drinks to the gap-toothed woman and her thick-necked partner. The two of them ate wordlessly as usual, scrolling through their phones, or eavesdropping on everyone else's conversations.

Alene introduced herself as she set their food on the table, hoping to put names with their faces, but neither responded. They both stared down at their plates. Alene asked if the woman wanted hot sauce or anything else with her omelet. She declined with a shake of her head, and the man didn't respond. Alene understood that customers didn't always want to be interrupted, but how about a thank-you? They seemed so tense, she wanted to shout that it was a picture-perfect summer day, and they should just get over themselves and be grateful to be alive. Too bad there was no room to put a few tables on the sidewalk in front. The woman took tiny delicate bites of her omelet.

Alene straightened chairs as Heather and Miles headed to a corner table near the art wall. From the side, Heather looked like she could pass as a classmate of Alene's twelve-year-old daughter. Miles had a moist-looking sheen to his face as he carried their drinks. He might have been considered handsome by some, but Alene thought the red sheen made him look constipated. And he towered over tiny Heather, who seemed fragile and bird-like. Alene walked around the café making sure everyone was content, and slowly made her way to their table.

"How are you?" she asked. "Everything okay here?"

Miles grunted, rhythmically clenching his fists with noisy crunches. Heather said, "He's upset because he had to cancel his clients for at least the next two days."

"I'm screwed," Miles said, "if Better Be Fit closes for good."

"You still have a plan, Miles," said Heather.

He flashed her a quick smile, which softened Alene. "But I don't know if I can still make it work," said Miles, now biting his left thumbnail.

"You can find lots of other gyms that sell supplements," said Heather, sipping her black coffee. It was hard to tell if her eyes were open or closed from Alene's angle. "And there are plenty of other trainers like Stanley Huff."

"Yeah, maybe, but I put a lot of time and effort into this place," said Miles with a sullen expression. "If I'd just had time to wrap things up."

"Sounds like you're in the middle of something," Alene interjected. "I just wanted to say hello, and again, I'm sorry for both of your losses."

Back behind the counter, Jocelyn thanked a customer and leaned closer to whisper in Alene's ear, "Maybe Stanley tried to put the moves on Heather, and Miles flipped."

Alene nearly choked. "Really, Jocelyn, Heather is Stanley's stepdaughter."

"You don't understand people like Stanley," Jocelyn scowled. "Or like Heather Evans. They're both bullies. I knew her when she was a kid, and she was mean. Also, I

43

don't think she's ever held a job for longer than two months. What the hell does she do all day? Aside from batting those bedroom eyes of hers, that is."

"Maybe her meanness had nothing to do with you, Jocelyn," said Alene quietly. Ruthie always reminded her that everyone was battling their own demons. "She probably just hates herself."

"Well, that makes two of us," said Jocelyn.

Alene gave her a quick hug. "Luckily, all you need to do is smile and serve people what they want," she said. The café was filled again with regulars; the guy who wore shirts that showed his belly button, the woman whose arm was tattooed with a floral design that reminded Alene of wallpaper, and the usual assortment of young moms with strollers or baby slings. One mother was frantically trying to latch her crying baby onto her breast. Alene watched from behind the counter as she helped serve the lunch crowd and thought wistfully of the days when she could calm her children's tears by popping a nipple into their little mouths.

An hour later, when Alene had time to sip her latte and look around, she saw that the café had turned over except for the shapely, gap-toothed woman, still sitting by the crimson wall staring into space. She asked Jocelyn the woman's name, and Jocelyn whispered that it was Toula Savas and her husband, Royce, who stared into his empty cup. At the table to their left, two teenage girls wearing similar sundresses and carrying identical purses stood up and left without placing their cups and plates in a bin.

Julian came in and got in line. "So, you can order all by yourself, without your wife?" Jocelyn said. "I'm shocked, Julian."

Alene tapped her lightly on the arm and mouthed, "Cut it out." They were all on edge, but there was no need to be rude to customers, no matter how exasperating they were.

"I teach middle schoolers, so sarcasm doesn't really bother me," said Julian, blinking his heavy- lidded eyes as he watched Alene hand a lentil, eggplant and mint salad to a woman wearing long beaded earrings. He ordered the same thing, with a melon-berry smoothie.

Alene was relieved that Julian hadn't been insulted by Jocelyn's snippiness, and pleased to see that the salad was selling well. "How's it going?" Alene asked Julian.

"I'm exhausted," he answered, "thanks."

Alene asked if he'd like a receipt, but he must have thought she'd asked about his relationship with his wife.

"I fell in love with Phyllie the minute I saw her," said Julian as he rocked from one foot to the other. "We were in college, and the first thing I noticed was that her eyes were the color of chocolate pudding."

Alene smiled, thinking that they should serve ramekins of vegan chocolate pudding. Ruthie would probably be willing to experiment with chia seeds, although there was also the possibility of an algae-based binder.

"I know this is going to sound atrocious," Julian continued, "but Phyllie and I are both relieved about Stanley. He never acted like any kind of father. He was always making moves, touching Phyllie or making sexual innuendos. We couldn't stand him."

Alene handed Julian his smoothie. "That must have been challenging," she said. "I hope you reported it to the police." Phyllie had told her about how Stanley groped her. Maybe he'd tried again, the police hadn't been helpful and Phyllie had decided to take care of it by herself. She was stout with muscular arms. She could have gone to his office and knocked him down. He was strong, but she could have surprised him. Or what if she injected him with something untraceable like potassium chloride, which could cause a heart attack? Alene had recently watched a British mystery in which the murderer nearly got away with doing exactly that but was caught by a brilliant sleuth. Potassium chloride was the main ingredient used in so-called "humane" executions.

"At the time, we didn't think it was a big enough thing to report," Julian told her as she came out from behind the counter. "But I wish we had. And now Phyllie's mad at me

45

for offering to help with Stanley's papers." Alene wondered what papers he was talking about. He continued, "We were never close, but I always felt bad for his sons. He was especially mean to the younger one."

Alene didn't know anything about the sons but couldn't help thinking that they probably felt equally bad for Julian. Stanley might have been difficult, but Sylvie was no picnic. She told Julian about Lawrence, Lillian's boyfriend, having been one of Stanley's lawyers. "He might have records, and I can get you his phone number if you don't have it." She wished Julian a good day and headed to the table where Toula and her thick-necked husband had been sitting. They'd left their plates and flatware on the table; why did some customers not understand the purpose of the bins?

Alene went back to the kitchen to prepare a tray of leftovers. Ruthie always baked extra on Mondays and Wednesdays so there would be enough to send to the nearby women's shelter. Someone would come to get it before the café closed, but Alene planned to leave early so she could be home when the kids got back from camp.

She finished and wrapped the tray, said her goodbyes, and headed out. On the way home, Alene stopped at the grocery store to get fresh salmon, capers, horseradish, and pistachios for a dish they all liked. She wondered what was to become of the gym and vitamin store now that Stanley was dead. Maybe it would close, and a florist would take its place. That would be wonderful.

Chapter 5

The ovens had been churning out pastries, cakes, and breads for hours by the time Alene got to work on Tuesday morning. She was relieved to see Ruthie back at work, singing along with an Alicia Keys soundtrack as she measured monkfruit sugar for her pineapple-carrot muffins. Ruthie's eyes were bright and her olive skin glowed, probably from the heat of the ovens. Alene thought she herself looked like she'd fought a war every time she was recovering from anything, but Nine, her nickname for Ruthie, seemed as serene as though she'd spent the past few days at a spa instead of in bed with a fever. Alene said, "You're smiling like we just won Best Café in Chicago."

Ruthie grinned. "I'm sorry you didn't get Sunday off, Six." Their nicknames for each other sprang from a course they'd taken in college. "And I'm smiling because I'm happy to be back here. I missed all this." She gestured around the kitchen at the comforting symphony of humming blenders, working ovens, and murmuring bakers. Kacey, who was running a sharp knife along the edge of a vanilla bean to scrape out the seeds, looked up and waved.

"We missed you too," said Alene, tying on her apron and glancing at Ruthie's to-do list. "Did Kacey already tell you the whole story about finding Stanley Huff on Saturday?"

Ruthie said, "That must have been shocking." She wore one of her bib aprons over a long skirt with a black short-sleeved top. A black scarf patterned with tiny yellow daisies covered her thick, nearly black hair. Ruthie had the kind of dark complexion and almond shaped eyes that led people to wonder about her heritage. Alene thought she looked adorable no matter what she was wearing.

"It wasn't a big deal," said Kacey. She spoke in a monotone and seemed stiff and uncomfortable, stretching her neck, and stopping to crack the joints in her hands. Alene thought it had been an extremely big deal for Kacey to find Stanley's dead body. It was the kind of trigger that could very well send her back down the rabbit hole of addiction. Would Kofi Lloyd be able to keep her out of it? Could anyone?

"What else did I miss?" Ruthie asked, using a red pen to mark off items on her list; quick breads, challah, savory rounds and two kinds of cookies.

"Nothing," Kacey said, placing the scraped vanilla bean pod in a specially marked mason jar. Alene thought about giving her a task that didn't involve a sharp knife, but it would make Kacey feel babied.

"After that whole drama, it was just business as usual," said Alene, "plus Frank and his partner came in to ask questions." They hadn't questioned everyone, so they'd probably be in sometime that day or the next. Frank had requested a private space, so she'd let them use her office. "You'll be pleased to know I was already wearing tinted lip gloss and as soon as I saw Frank, I ran back to the restroom and brushed my hair."

"I think you always look beautiful," said Ruthie, now washing her hands.

"We're all fading," Alene replied. Except for Ruthie, who had just the tiniest crow's feet radiating from the corners of her caramel-colored eyes and a few silvery strands that looked like she'd paid to have them added. Alene was quite sure that everyone with her own mousy-brown color covered up their gray patches every six weeks, just like she did.

"Come on, Six. We're not even forty," said Ruthie.

Alene made a disgruntled face. "Then why do my feet hurt from all this standing?"

LaTonya had come back to the kitchen for a break. She made a gurgling sound. "Please let's not talk about feet or I'll start thinking about bunions and gnarled toes." Ruthie frowned, but everyone else chuckled.

Even though there were occasional disagreements, it was nice working together in the cinnamon-scented kitchen, chitchatting as they baked. Alene thought about how women had been bonding in kitchens for generations, but her grandmothers would never have been able to own and manage their own businesses. That's what had changed, thanks to the feminism of her parents' generation. It was a step in the right direction, but too bad the baby boomers hadn't managed to put an end to racism or solve major issues like climate change, inequality, or poverty.

As they measured ingredients for the next batches, Ruthie asked about Stanley's funeral. Alene felt awful that she'd forgotten about him for a while. She said, "I guess they'll do something or other after Sylvie gets out of the hospital, maybe a memorial."

"My family makes a big deal about funerals," said LaTonya, picking up a tray of muffins to bring out to the café, "but my guess is that they cremated Stanley and that's it." She walked out in her distinctive way, swinging her hips and tilting her head back.

Alene, tired of Sylvie and everyone associated with her, tried to change the subject by asking about Ruthie's kids, who always found a reason to be happy, unlike Alene's children, who often found something to complain about. Ruthie told Alene about how her children were trying to persuade her and Benjie to get a dog. Edith came by during the conversation and weighed in about the merits of cats, and everyone took sides in the pet debate.

The kitchen was already feeling toasty and Alene suspected that it was going to be another sizzling, impossibly humid day. Olly brought a pitcher of iced tea to share with the kitchen crew. Ruthie and Alene went out to the café and circled the room, stopping to greet customers or clear dishes.

Then it was time for the Tuesday knitting group. Alene welcomed the diehard knitters, who didn't let the summer heat stop them from carrying around bags of yarn and wooden needles. The five who came were more accomplished knitters than Alene. They were all working on afghan blankets to donate to refugee families settling in Chicago. She wished her fingers flew as fast and accurately as theirs. These five women were finishing their second blankets while Alene worked on edging her first. Three of their blankets were boldly patterned and colored while the other two were in marshmallow shades and smaller, perfect for new babies. Alene imagined her blue, green, yellow, and brown striped comforter warming somebody's young children on a cold winter day.

It looked like some of the customers were baring their souls to Ruthie, who was still walking around the café, chatting. She always got completely rapt in whatever anyone was telling her. Alene was interested in her customers' lives, but not enough to stand for ten minutes while someone bragged about a grandson's college graduation or a refinished bathroom. After the knitters left, Alene went over to join Ruthie. She'd sat down with Toula, who wore a low-cut, long-sleeved blouse and was sitting at the large table even though she was alone. Alene again noticed the gap between Toula's front teeth and thought about how her daughter, Quinn, was going to need braces to fix that exact problem.

Alene was surprised when Toula mentioned Stanley, saying she'd started working out with him in another Better Be Fit location, before the one next door had opened six months before. "He was the best personal trainer," she said, fiddling with her necklace. "I'll never find anyone like him."

"I've heard that it's tough to replace a good trainer," said Ruthie, who started to introduce Toula. Alene told her they'd already met.

The name Toula reminded Alene of the character in My Big Fat Greek Wedding, who by ditching her glasses and getting her hair done, metamorphoses into someone who can attract a husband. As if that's how real life worked. "If you're looking for a new trainer," Alene said, "mine is great, and he knows what he's doing. He's helped build up my strength and stamina, which I need to run this place."

Toula murmured, "Thanks," as her husband approached the table. Toula introduced him to Alene. Royce Savas nodded, unsmiling, and Alene wondered if he was shy or just unfriendly. Ruthie said she hoped Toula and Royce enjoyed their breakfast before turning to greet two women at an adjacent table. Alene said she hoped they'd come back soon, although as she spoke, she realized they had been coming in nearly every day. She headed towards Jack Stone, who was staring out the window and needed a brief reminder to empty the trash bin near the front door.

By two in the afternoon, everybody's hair was frizzing out from under the hats and scarves they wore while baking and serving. Maybe the customers going in and out had drained the air conditioning, which meant a higher electricity bill, more greenhouse gases, and uncomfortable customers. Or fewer customers. If only they had a revolving door, or a door that closed automatically, but everything cost money that she didn't have. Alene was just heading out of the kitchen with a tray to refresh the dessert case when Frank and Lee finally returned.

She passed the tray to Zuleyka, who was coming out from behind the counter, and poured drinks for the detectives, even though there were three customers already in the line. Lee gawked at Zuleyka, who had a petite frame, a seductive way of walking, and flashing eyes. Last thing she needed was the attentions of a spindly detective with no personality and an eye problem, but Zuleyka had probably been dealing with unwanted attention for years and knew how to handle herself. Now, she sank down behind the counter to unload the tray, which effectively took her out of Lee's sightline.

Maybe Frank was going to repeat his invitation from Sunday to go for a walk. That was about as romantic as they were going to get under the circumstances. She could head out after dinner, while the kids were watching TV with Cal.

Three women with varying shades of blond hair were sitting to the left of the two officers, giggling over pictures on one of their phones. Nearby, a young couple sat sipping drinks, holding hands and whispering. Lee peeked over at the counter every few minutes while scrolling through his phone. Frank, his forehead beaded with moisture, sat back in his chair. He could have asked her out for some other night of the week after she declined his Sunday invitation. Of course, she could have asked him. It wasn't as though they were still living in the 20th century.

Frank downed a glass of water and told her that the police department had been working on solving several difficult homicides. The entire CPD, he said, was depressed by the stream of weekend shootings and the backlog of cases. "We're getting asked to help in other districts while the city struggles to keep up." The line on his brow deepened and he smiled tiredly when Alene handed him a black coffee. He never cared what kind of roast, it just had to be black.

Jack passed by with a mop, and she could tell from the look on his face that he was about to say something inappropriate. "Just try not to shoot any Black teenagers, Frank."

Frank pressed his lips together and Lee pretended not to have heard by busying himself with his drink. Alene signaled Jack to go back to the kitchen. It had been a difficult summer in Chicago, particularly on the South and West sides, with dozens of people, mostly young Black men, killed each week. The police were under fire for all kinds of misdeeds and the city needed to come to grips with decades

52

of segregation, poorly performing schools in the worst neighborhoods, redlining, and insidious racism.

Alene tried to educate her kids about what was happening while still preventing them from hearing about every violent shooting, but her dad liked to share Tribune statistics about who and how many. Noah had asked her just the week before if he could wear a bulletproof vest to camp. And then there were the drills they'd gone through and would go through again when school started at the end of summer.

Alene hoped Frank hadn't been offended. She offered gluten-free almond-maple muffins, but they both declined. Frank sipped his coffee and exhaled heavily. Alene liked hot drinks during hot weather also. She pictured the two of them sitting on a picnic blanket at Montrose Beach with mugs of hot tea, watching the sun rise over the lake after a night together.

Frank clenched his jaw. She wished she could rub his shoulders to help him relax. Maybe he'd be the kind of man who would always look at her lovingly, the way Julian looked at Phyllie. It wouldn't matter if she hadn't slept well in three nights or that her skin was glossy with sweat. "Earth to Alene," her mother used to whisper. "Pull yourself together."

Alene shook herself. "Give me a minute to check on the kitchen," she said. She ran back to the staff restroom to reapply lip gloss, smooth down her hair, and make sure she hadn't spilled anything on her shirt. Then she made herself a café americano and carried it to Frank's table. As soon as she noticed his uneasy expression, Alene realized that she'd better lower her expectations.

"We need to talk," he said, quietly, "about Stanley Huff."

If only he wanted to discuss anything else. "Okay. Did you figure out what happened?" That seemed like a polite enough question.

"We're working on it," said Frank. Lee looked at her with his customarily disdainful expression, still blinking. He should really get his eyes checked.

Frank asked, "What do you know about the Huffs?"

"Well, Stanley's wife, Sylvie, grew up with Ruthie's mom, Lillian," said Alene, shrugging. What did it matter if she knew what they ordered when they stopped by the café, or if she occasionally met one of Sylvie's kids at Ruthie's house? "Ruthie has been my best friend since college, so I've known Sylvie's kids, Julian and Heather, for about twenty years. I can get you phone numbers if you need them."

"I've got contact info for Sylvie's kids already," said Frank. "Do you know Stanley's children?"

"I know he had two sons," said Alene, "but I've never met them, and I don't know their names." Jocelyn had said something negative about one of them, and she remembered that Julian had said he'd pitied the two sons for having Stanley as a father. Sylvie had said that they blamed her for their parents' divorce and never accepted her. "Julian told me he was about twelve when his parents divorced, but I don't know how old Stanley's kids were. And Julian said the older one recently moved back to Chicago."

Frank said, "Yes, that's Harrison Huff and his wife, Rhea. The younger one is here too." His fingers tapped an imaginary piano on the tabletop. "His name was Jonathan, and he left the navy about half a year ago to come back to Chicago. He changed his name."

It took a moment for the pieces to fall together. In slow motion, Alene stood up and looked at Jocelyn, who was whipping up a cappuccino behind the counter. She'd known that Jocelyn had transitioned, but why hadn't Alene known that Jocelyn DeVale had been Jonathan Huff?

They exchanged glances and Alene remembered when Olly brought Jocelyn in to interview for the job. It had been just weeks after she got back from Afghanistan, and she hadn't been nearly as polished as she was now. Would it be insensitive to tell her that, maybe congratulate her? Moments later, Jocelyn stood at Alene's office door, her arms at her sides, chin raised as if it was time for morning roll call.

Then, Jocelyn looked down at her shoes and spoke in a low voice. "Hello, Frank." Jocelyn had been religious about taking the hormones but, as she'd once told Alene, there were more ways to be a woman than the one that required pills, including unending attention to hair, nails, skin, clothes, speech patterns, the way she walked or sat, and everything else. Since Jocelyn started at the café, she'd gotten better at applying make-up and had learned to dress less like the magazine version of women and more like Kacey, LaTonya, and all of Alene's other young female employees. She seemed to have gotten more comfortable with who she was meant to be.

"How are you doing, Jocelyn?" Frank asked. Alene understood that she'd been entirely wrong about the reason for Lee and Frank's visit.

"Just to confirm," Alene said, looking at Jocelyn and hoping she'd gotten it right. Her voice came out wobbly. "Stanley was your father?"

"Yup," said Jocelyn, standing with one hand on her hip. Alene wondered if she was the only one in the café who hadn't known. She felt like she was in a soap opera.

Lee said, "She was born as Jonathan Huff." He was good at stating the obvious.

"Would you like to speak in private, Jocelyn?" Frank asked in a respectful tone.

"No thanks," said Jocelyn, squeezing Alene's shoulder. "I don't have secrets from Alene." Except for that enormous one about Stanley being her father.

Frank said, "I'm sorry we have to ask these questions during such a difficult time. I know from other family members that your father refused to acknowledge you." Frank invited Jocelyn to take a seat. "That must have been extremely painful after your transition." So, he'd known all along. Lee didn't say anything. She should ask Frank if Lee ever let his guard down, like did he ever gossip about sports while they were driving to and from crime scenes?

Jocelyn said, "Gender confirmation. It was more of a gender confirmation than a transition." She sat down, placing the carafe on the table, and putting her hands in her lap. "And some people are more understanding than others, but I refuse to let that dictate how I live my life." Her turquoise eyes sparkled as she blinked away tears. After a brief pause, she continued, speaking more smoothly than Alene would have thought possible. "I took this job because it was next to Stanley's gym. I wanted my father to be forced to see me."

Frank said, "That couldn't have been easy." His empathy made Alene want to put her arms around him, but she also wanted to hug Jocelyn.

"It wasn't," said Jocelyn with a determined look, "but I thought he'd see that I'm finally happy." Jocelyn patted her eyes with a tissue. Alene always kept a box in her office. "I left home when I was fourteen, but I tried to have a relationship with him."

Alene watched the exchange with a combination of dread and curiosity. "I'm so sorry," she said, wishing she could have helped in some way. Jocelyn must have felt torn all those times Alene had bitched about Stanley: his cologne, his behavior, his cigarettes. If only she'd followed Ruthie's advice about not speaking badly of anyone, ever.

"I was waiting," Jocelyn continued. "But it never happened."

"That must have felt awful," said Frank.

Lee, apparently acting as the bad cop, said, "You were seen vaping in the alley right before Stanley was found, Ms. DeVale, and then you were in his office for quite a while after he was found." Alene remembered rushing out as Jocelyn stood frozen over Stanley. It hadn't been completely clear that he was dead, but Alene had been worried about Kacey at the time.

Jocelyn stared at Frank's partner. "I was trying to see if he needed help while someone called an ambulance. Isn't that the normal thing to do?" Now she was wringing her hands.

"Absolutely normal," said Frank, softly.

Lee jumped in, "A witness told us that you were inside Stanley's office for over five minutes before you came back out to the alley." Alene knew that the witness must have been Miles Taylor.

"We're only talking here, Jocelyn, just trying to figure out a few things," said Frank. "But we might need you to come down to the station to give us a complete statement. For now, we're wondering if you could tell us what you were doing during that time in your father's office."

Jocelyn scowled. "Isn't it also absolutely normal to want to check the pulse of someone you find passed out on the floor?" She looked at Alene and back at Frank. "Never mind, just give me a minute and I'll give you my statement now. I don't want you to suddenly cuff me and push me into the back of a police car." She turned and headed to the kitchen.

"We don't push people," Lee muttered. "I have a feeling she's hiding something."

Alene felt sick to her stomach. "Stanley was her father," she said. "Jocelyn would not have hurt him." Hadn't Jocelyn just said that she'd taken the café job in order to be close to him? And she wouldn't lie to Frank. Alene couldn't imagine any of her employees capable of murder, although Jack Stone had been capable of committing plenty of other crimes. She'd even briefly considered good-humored, song-loving Olly as a suspect when Kacey's father was stabbed. But Alene would never consider Jocelyn as a suspect. Jocelyn wasn't the kind of person who would do something like that.

Frank stood and said, "I'm sorry, Alene, but we need to follow up on everything."

Alene sipped her drink. "Fine," she said crossly. "But I was there, and Stanley was already on the floor when Jocelyn went into his office. That's when she was trying to check for a pulse."

"She might have gone in earlier," said Lee.

"She's trying to quit smoking. She wouldn't give up her vaping time to run next door and murder her father." Alene shook her head and added, "Also, Jocelyn wasn't the only one who spent time in the alley. I've seen other Better Be Fit trainers strutting around out there. One of them could have gotten mad enough with Stanley to push him into the wall and knock him out."

"We're just asking questions, Alene," Frank said, placing a hand on her arm. "We're not accusing Jocelyn of anything."

"Stanley pissed off everyone," Alene said, moving out of Frank's reach. She felt herself getting worked up. "Maybe a customer spent a fortune on supplements and was mad about not gaining enough muscle or losing enough weight. Or Stanley owed money, or he screwed someone over the way he's been known to do. You should ask Michael Jay about how Stanley treated him. He's my personal trainer and owns his own gym now, but he used to work for Stanley." She hoped Michael wouldn't be upset that she'd mentioned him to the police. "That was years ago, and it was resolved in a lawsuit, but you get my point."

"We're collecting information," said Frank, rotating his neck in circles with a crunching sound. "Do you know any of Stanley's employees?"

"He had five trainers working for him," Lee added. "At this location."

They were digging for information without giving her any. "I've only met Miles Taylor," Alene said. She peered at the crimson wall and noticed a thin crack going nearly to the floor. Maybe if she paid him extra, Olly would be willing to spackle the crack and repaint the entire wall.

Frank looked down at his notepad. "All Better Be Fit trainers are part-time," he said. "And the other four had started looking for other jobs even before Stanley died."

"I'm not surprised," Alene said, thinking about Edith Vanza. "Some people have a way of generating hostility."

She led Frank and Lee back out to the café. Just as Jocelyn reappeared wearing freshly applied make-up, Edith rushed up to ask Jocelyn if everything was all right, buzzing around her like a mosquito. Jocelyn calmed her down and

58

hugged her. "I want to know who murdered my father," she said with her usual composure. "So, I'm going to help the police however I can. Don't worry about me."

Edith said, "Let me know if you want me to feed Bella Donna if you're not going to be home in time." Edith wore a self-satisfied look, as if she were the only one in the café privileged enough to know the name of Jocelyn's cat. Anything involving cats seemed to bring out Edith's soft side.

Jocelyn said her goodbyes and rushed off. The detectives had to hustle out the front door after her, as though they were her bodyguards. Alene was consoled by the thought that Jocelyn wouldn't have gone with Frank and Lee if she had been worried about incriminating herself. She'd told Alene how she had trained in the military to give just her name, rank and serial number. She'd probably get more information from them then they'd get from her.

When things slowed down a while later, Alene went back to the kitchen and pulled out the next item on Ruthie's list, a sourdough starter for pumpernickel bread dough. She wondered if Jocelyn was hiding anything else from her, and raised her voice to ask everyone in the kitchen, "Did any of you guys know that Stanley was Jocelyn's father?"

Everyone was bent over various tasks. LaTonya, filling a tray of fresh muffins and cookies to bring out to the pastry case, asked, "How would I know that?" She wiped her hands on her apron.

"I knew," said Kacey as she chopped up herbs.

Ruthie said, "It wasn't my story to tell." Alene usually admired Ruthie but couldn't understand her refusal to talk about other people. Ruthie often told the story of a woman who repeated an untruthful story and hurt the feelings of the person it was about. The woman was full of remorse and asked her rabbi how she could make things right. The rabbi instructed her to shake all the feathers from a pillow, and once the wind blew them around, to put them back. The woman knew that doing so was impossible. "Just like words," Ruthie always proclaimed. "Once you say them, they can't be retracted."

Ruthie had told the story so often that all she had to do was say, "Feathers," and Alene would stop talking. She understood how important it was for Ruthie not to repeat gossip, but she could have told Alene that Stanley was Jocelyn's father. They were both tall and had strong jaws, but they looked nothing alike. How could Alene have ever made the connection?

In the half year she'd worked at Whipped and Sipped, Jocelyn had been occasionally haughty and tense, but mostly patient, sweet-tempered, and generous. Nothing like Stanley Huff with his judgmental digs at anyone who didn't have a perfect body, or his inconsiderate behavior in the lobby and elevators of their building. Alene's cellphone rang and she took a quick look. "It's your mother," she told Ruthie.

"Why is she calling you?" Ruthie asked.

Alene shook her head and shrugged as she answered the call. "Hi Lillian, I'm here with Ruthie in the kitchen, and you're on speakerphone because she wants to know why you're calling me."

"Hi girls," said Lillian. "I'm calling because Sylvie is really agitated, and she wants to talk to Alene."

"Give her my love," said Ruthie, turning around to continue working on a batter as Olly came through the kitchen. He liked to know everything going on and often eavesdropped on their conversations.

Last thing Alene needed was Sylvie calling her in the middle of the day. Lillian said, "You're always so patient when she comes to the café, Alene, and she says you never interrupt. Do you have a few minutes to talk to her?"

Alene watched Kacey pour herb batter into a greased muffin tin, and through the kitchen door, noticed customers waiting to order at the counter. If Ruthie hadn't been standing there, she'd have begged off. "I'm happy to help, Lillian," she said, grudgingly, "but we're closing soon so I don't have that much time."

60

Lillian said, "I'll let you tell her yourself."

Suddenly Alene heard Sylvie's dramatic sigh. She pulled out the earbuds she kept in her back pocket and connected them. "Alene, honey?"

"Hello," said Alene. Sylvie Huff was one of the most egocentric people Alene had ever met. "I hope you're feeling better and I'm sorry about your loss." Alene could hear Julian and Lillian in the background, so she knew Sylvie's phone was on speaker. Alene placed her cellphone back in her pocket before washing her hands and finishing up a dough for peach breakfast cake. The fruit could be added the next morning just before it went into the oven.

"Losing my career was worse," Sylvie moaned. Hadn't her parents died, and hadn't she gone through a divorce before she'd married Stanley? Sylvie went on about how her career as a singer had been cut short, a story Alene had heard several times before. Sylvie must have recognized Jocelyn as Stanley's child, her stepchild. Why hadn't she ever said anything, all those times Jocelyn had fixed her drinks or brought plates to her table? Alene could hear Julian groaning in the background. Now she understood his awkwardness during that encounter with Jocelyn at the café.

Sylvie babbled on about auditioning for parts, men who'd wronged her, and highlights of her brief career, also stories that Alene had heard. Then, she began talking about how her first marriage, to Julian and Heather's father, fell apart. Julian interrupted to say he didn't need to hear her complain again about his father, that she'd been the one who'd wanted the divorce, and that parents were not supposed to badmouth each other to their children.

Alene finished the coffeecake batter and began measuring oat flour for another one of Ruthie's unusual vegan cake recipes. She tried hard to never criticize Neal in front of the kids, no matter what thoughtless, idiotic thing he did. Now she let Julian rant at his mother while she continued measuring ingredients. Maybe she should listen to interesting podcasts while she worked. She was getting quite a lot done.

Finally, Lillian got on the phone and said that Sylvie had drifted off to sleep. She thanked Alene, who clicked off and put her earbuds back in her pocket while wondering if Sylvie was psychotic or just devious. She could have had herself checked into the hospital after first stopping to murder Stanley. Maybe she'd wanted to punish him for having affairs. Alene washed her hands and flicked the water instead of using another paper towel.

Jack entered the kitchen and headed to the sink to scrub pans. He said, "Kacey's bartender just came in. I really can't stand that guy. I hope he falls into one of the dumpsters he's always digging in."

Kacey had just placed a batch of dough in the proofer. She flipped the bird at Jack and stuck out her tongue before rushing out to the café to fling her arms around Kofi. "Why don't you like him?" Alene asked Jack after the kitchen door closed. She'd checked Ruthie's list and started working on a recipe for chocolate chip cookies that she'd made hundreds of times. They were a huge seller in the café. "He's a good guy, and he makes Kacey happy."

"He steals stuff to make sculptures," said Jack as he filled the sink with hot, soapy water. "I don't want Kacey to get hurt. He says he's always banged up from riding his bike, but he could be running a dogfighting operation or selling drugs."

Since when had Jack ever expressed concern about anybody? Alene said, "He doesn't steal, Jack. He finds things that people threw away and recycles them. Did he do something specific that made you distrust him?" Jack chewed on a fingernail and ran his hand through his hair, two more unhygienic habits he needed to break if he wanted to keep working in the café.

Ruthie looked up from setting balls of cookie batter on a baking pan, and said, "Why not give Kofi the benefit of the doubt, Jack?"

"Because he's not nice to me," said Jack, "and I learned a few things about people before I stopped selling."

"You're doing great now, Jack, that's all behind you," said Alene as she poured wet ingredients into a bowl of pulverized oats, chickpeas, coconut flakes, baking soda, and salt. Was there really such a thing as recovering from selling drugs? Was it like programs for alcoholics? Did he go to meetings with other recovering dealers and talk about why they were drawn to making money by destroying other people's lives? What a shame if he slid back into it.

"Anyway, Kofi could probably kill someone with his bare hands," said Jack, running a sponge around each indentation in a muffin tray the way Alene had taught him. It made her feel good about her ability to teach, although now Jack was working himself up, attacking the next tray as if he meant to beat it clean. He added, "I think he had something to do with Huff's death."

Ruthie looked up and spoke in her soothing voice. "If that's the case, Jack," she said, lightly stirring the ingredients in her bowl, "Frank will figure it out."

"But I could be right," Jack muttered. He'd moved on to the large baking pans and was scraping scraps into a trash bin. Through the kitchen door into the café, Alene watched Kacey bring a lemonade to Kofi and then join him next to a group of women sipping iced coffees. Jack continued, "A lot of guys could fall for Kacey. I think Kofi is suspicious, that's all I'm saying."

"Don't you want her to be happy?" Alene asked, wondering how long Jack's protective step- brothering would last and if Kofi being African American had something to do with his suspicion. She knew that Jack had not been raised to view the world with much insight or understanding. Maybe he couldn't see that Kofi was an interesting, considerate guy with art school under his belt. Even more important, he was kind and patient, exactly what Kacey needed.

"Yeah," said Jack, "but Kofi knows his way around Chicago alleys. Maybe Stanley caught him stealing something and there was a fight."

"He's not a suspect, Jack," said Alene. Calling him a racist would not change his outlook. She and Ruthie were going to have to plan some additional employee training. "And let's not forget about his rainbow sculpture. Do you know how many customers that piece has attracted?"

"It's not that hard to build a rainbow," Jack said. "Anyone could have done it."

Alene had lost her patience by then. "But nobody else did, Jack. Now, I want to know why you didn't tell me about Jocelyn."

"Tell you what about Jocelyn?" He batted his eyelashes.

"How long have you known?" Alene was in no mood for games.

"I've known since I met her, Alene. I keep my eyes open, unlike you," Jack answered. "I'm trying to be a better person, you know, like Ruthie or something." Ruthie was bending over the oven and couldn't hear them.

Alene didn't want to discourage him, because he really was trying to be a good employee, so she offered a high five on her way to the refrigerators. She also wanted to be a better person like Ruthie, or something.

Chapter 6

At home, Alene stepped over the sneakers and backpacks the kids had tossed on the floor. Thinking she'd go crazy if they didn't learn to put their stuff in the cabinet, Alene sifted through and removed lunch leftovers, wet bathing suits, towels, leaves, twigs, and rocks. The apartment was hushed, and her dad was still in his room. The kids were probably sitting on their beds playing games or watching shows on the tablets Neal had given them for Christmas even though Alene had been clear about not wanting them spending their free time on screens.

She headed to the girls' bedroom, knocked softly, and waited just a moment before opening the door. Quinn never heard anything while she was absorbed by a book and Sierra had on her headphones. Alene planted a kiss on top of Sierra's head. Both girls had inherited her light brown hair; Quinn's was fine and straight, Sierra's thick and wavy. She'd be grateful for that beautiful hair one day, but now, in middle school, she spent an inordinate amount of time trying to tame it. "Mom," said Sierra, her voice dripping with adolescent disapproval. "I'm listening to something."

That was how things had been lately. Alene wished she'd spent more time cuddling with Sierra before this preteen phase started. "Sorry, sweetie," said Alene, "I guess I'll just have to give all my hugs and kisses to Quinn." She plopped down on the second bed and tickled Quinn's bare feet.

Quinn wiggled away and hooted, a sound that still filled Alene with delight. If only she could make sure her children had reasons to laugh every day. The girls had also inherited her overbite, but their smiles would be perfected, as hers had been, with braces. Sierra had her first orthodontist appointment scheduled for later that summer.

"Mommy, did you know I'm reading Island of the Blue Dolphins?" Quinn asked. "This girl gets left on an island, and then she has to figure out how to survive. And she has a secret name, it's Karana. I want a secret name, and Quinoa doesn't count because it's the name of a grain."

"It's the name of a grass, not a grain, stupid," Sierra said from her side of the room. "And can you go somewhere else to talk? Puh-lease."

Alene said, "I don't want to have to remind you again, Sierra. In this house, we don't use that word."

"Which word don't we use? Please? OK, fine, I won't say please," said Sierra. Alene folded her arms and stared at her until Sierra gave a half-hearted apology. "Sorry."

Quinn made a face at her sister. "And you'll never guess what I did today, Mom. The clue is beeswax, as in 'none of your beeswax.'"

Alene pretended to think about it as she stroked Quinn's soft, pixie-cut hair. Did any mother love her children as much as Alene loved Sierra, Quinn, and Noah? She asked, "Did you make a beehive?"

Quinn laughed with a musical, infectious sound that reminded Alene of Neal's laugh back when he was fun to be with. "No," said Quinn. "We made candles, Mom, and we got to bring them home. I waited for you to come, so can I light my candle now? I was going to do it in the kitchen on foil like at camp and then I would have let Noah toast marshmallows with me. But I know you don't want us to use matches while Grandpa is sleeping."

66

"I don't want you to use matches ever, Quinnie," said Alene, wondering what the next almost emergency was going to be. Just two Sundays before, Quinn had wandered away from where they'd all been having a picnic lunch at the beach. They'd spent ten desperate minutes searching until Alene recognized her laugh and found her playing with a puppy not far from where they sat.

"Everyone knows that ten is old enough to be responsible, Mommy," said Quinn, "and remember at school when we had a whole unit on fire safety? I was the one who organized a safe spot for our family to meet in an emergency."

"That was a good idea," said Alene, although she couldn't imagine being separated from her children or needing a place to meet. She pulled Quinn closer into a hug, wishing she could just freeze moments like these.

"So, I don't think you should be nervous about ME starting a fire," said Quinn, squirming out of Alene's hug and pointing at her brother, who'd entered the girls' bedroom and was hopping up next to Alene onto the bed.

Quinn yelled, "Get off my bed with your dirty shorts, Noah. You probably sat on dog poop today."

"I did not," said Noah. "That's a lie. Quinn's lying about me, Mom." Well, thought Alene, that was a nice moment. She reached forward to hug Noah, but he wriggled out of her grasp too. He was an exact replica of his father, who'd also been an adorable child according to the pictures. Noah had Neal's full lower lip, his perfect teeth, his dark brown eyes that shrank into slits when he smiled.

"No, I'm not lying," said Quinn. "Everyone walks their dogs in Lincoln Park and my counselor said that if you sit down on the grass, you have an 85 percent chance of sitting where a dog did its business. That's why our group sits on a tarp."

"Mine does too," said Noah, bouncing first on one foot and then the other. He smiled showing all his teeth, just like his father used to do.

Sierra, whose blue eyes always got darker when she was agitated, pulled out her headphones and jumped off her bed. "Will you all go somewhere else if you want to discuss dog poop, puh-lease? I'm trying to watch something. Can't I be alone for five minutes? Mom, please take them out of here."

Alene hoped Sierra would one day be sweet and patient, and that none of them would remember how difficult she'd been at age twelve. Her own younger sister, Lydia, had been terrible to their parents for a couple of years back then, but she'd never stopped confiding in Alene. Until recently. And Alene had no idea why her relationship with Lydia had become so strained. Was it because of Theo? Alene thought her brother-in-law was benign but irritating; the way he repeated things, the way he laughed like a whinnying horse, and the way he talked endlessly about his mother. Lydia never shared anything about their relationship, but Alene could see from the way they talked that it was strained.

She tried to be supportive, especially about Lydia and Theo's struggle to have a baby. They'd been trying for three years already, and Lydia didn't want to talk about it. Theo, on the other hand, couldn't stop talking about it. Now Alene stood and said, "Come on, guys. Who wants a snack?"

"I already had an apple," said Sierra. Quinn and Noah followed Alene to the kitchen, and Sierra slammed the door after they left.

Alene's father would be waking up from his nap at any moment, and he usually enjoyed a cup of warm cocoa no matter how hot the day was. He'd been losing weight lately, so Alene had brought home several tempting pastries to serve with his cocoa. Or maybe he'd prefer a smoothie. She started blending the ingredients.

"Quinn, would you please grab the café bag from the entry table?" Alene asked. "And after you wash your hands, put the pastries on a plate for Grandpa." Alene walked down the hall and knocked on her father's door. After several minutes without a response, she walked in. It was already four-thirty, but the window shades were down, and the lights were still out. If he slept any later, he'd have trouble falling asleep for the night. "Dad?" She said, softly. "It's time to wake up, Dad."

He stirred and moaned. Alene flicked on the light and looked at him. Tears were streaming down his cheeks and his mouth hung open. His breathing was ragged and uneven. "Oh, Daddy," said Alene. She'd been warned that myasthenia gravis could spike into a crisis. His muscles could weaken enough to make breathing and swallowing difficult. They'd been lucky, so far. Except for that first episode that led to his diagnosis, he'd only experienced mild slurring and weakness in his legs.

She kept pressing incorrect numbers on her cell. It took a moment before she managed to punch 911. What if her bumbling caused a delay in getting an ambulance? She ran to tell the kids that Grandpa needed to go to the hospital. All three nodded solemnly before she ran back to Cal's room. She caressed his heavily veined, damp forehead and told him that he was going to be fine, that the ambulance was on its way.

She called downstairs to inform the doorman. Then she called her sister, who answered after the fourth ring.

"Is this important or can I call you back later?" Lydia asked.

Alene closed her eyes and explained that Cal was sick, and she'd already called an ambulance.

"Are you sure he needs to go to the hospital?" Lydia asked with a long, anguished sigh.

"Yeah, I'm sure," said Alene. "This is Dad, our only living parent, who took care of us and made us pancakes and took us to the zoo on Sundays and comforted us during those horrendous years when Mom was sick."

Alene sat on the bed and held Cal's hand as he stared with hollow eyes, his mouth still open. "Fine," said Lydia, "You don't have to make a drama out of it. I'll get there as soon as I can." Alene slipped her phone in her back pocket, wondering if another invitro fertilization had failed. She wished there was something she could do to make her sister feel better.

The children came into Cal's room and huddled behind Alene. Sierra asked, "Will Grandpa be okay? Why does he have to go to the hospital?"

"He's having trouble breathing," Alene said, thinking she might have misjudged Sierra's capacity for empathy. Cal had closed his eyes and now he didn't look so desperate. "Remember how the disease makes his brain send confusing messages to his muscles? Right, Dad? But the paramedics will give him something for that and he's going to be just fine."

"Then why are you crying, Mom?" Noah asked, holding her hand. Quinn hugged her from the side. They were both better at expressing empathy, but Sierra had a few tears in her eyes.

Alene wiped her face with the back of her free hand, and said, "I was talking to Aunt Lydia and remembering when our mom got sick. I hate when someone I love gets sick, but the doctors will probably adjust Grandpa's medicine and watch him for a few days. Then he'll come home, and everything will be back to normal."

She was trying to be optimistic for the kids, and it was probably good for Cal to hear her calmly lay out the plan. That is, if he could understand what she was saying. She texted Kacey Vanza to come stay with the children, and set sheets, a pillow, and blankets on the living room couch. When Kacey was little, she used to love coming across the hall to sleep on that comfy couch. Then, Alene texted Ruthie about bringing in backup help at the café for the next few days.

The paramedics arrived and had Cal on the gurney, hooked up with oxygen and out the door within moments. Alene threw together a bag with essentials for Cal and another for herself. Then she kissed her children, warned them to mind Kacey, who'd already walked over from across the hall, and followed the paramedics down the elevator and into the ambulance.

After she'd completed the Medicare paperwork in the emergency department, Alene tiptoed into the curtained-off

70

cubicle where Cal lay sleeping. He looked a little less strained than he had at home. She sat down and spent the next hour and a half researching myasthenia gravis on her phone, but didn't learn anything new. She was relieved when they finally admitted him, moved him into his own room on the tenth floor, and hooked him up to an I.V. drip. Alene couldn't stand how helpless he looked, his forehead veined and tense even with his eyes closed.

She looked up the names of the drugs they were giving him, intravenous immunoglobulins and plasmapheresis, just like after his first episode. He'd had a hospital roommate that time, who swore and screamed all night. Cal had gotten better but said he hadn't had a good night of sleep until they sent him home. Alene set out the book he was reading about FDR, his magnifying glass, and the ceramic cup he liked to use for coffee in the morning. He would not enjoy sipping mediocre coffee from a Styrofoam cup.

Alene realized that she was starving. The cafeteria's offerings were sparse this late in the day. Only a few apples and oranges, containers of salad that had probably been wilting for hours, stale-looking cakes, sugar-filled yogurts, and plenty of chips or candy. If Cal had to stay for a few days, Alene would have to bring her own food. She bought an orange and a carton of vanilla yogurt and tossed them in her bag before heading back to the room. She wanted to be at Cal's side when he woke up, in case he was disoriented.

Back on the tenth floor, she leaned against the wall next to her father's room, reached into her bag for the yogurt, and pulled off the lid with her teeth. Then she unwrapped the spoon and started eating. The door to the room next to her father's was wide open. From inside, she heard a woman's voice say, "That's not true, Julian."

Oh great, it was Julian Evans. What were the chances that her father would be placed in a room next to Sylvie Huff?

Julian responded, "I was twelve and Heather was only eight years old when Dad moved out and you started up with

71

Stanley. You left us home by ourselves, night after night. Then, you'd come home in the morning and start yelling at us to get ready for school."

Sylvie responded in her brassy voice, "That's ridiculous, Julian. I never left you and Heather alone at night."

"You did, Mother, and you chose Stanley over your own children." Why was Julian dredging up adolescent memories about Sylvie's failings as a mother? Maybe he could only get her attention when she was hooked up to a machine in the hospital.

Sylvie said something unintelligible.

Julian said, "I won't come back tomorrow if you talk to me like that." Good for him. Alene was scooping up the last spoonful of yogurt and had taken a few steps towards her dad's room when Julian charged into the hallway. He blinked at her.

"Hi, Julian," she said. "It's Alene Baron, from the café. How's your mother doing?"

"Oh, hi Alene," he said. He looked even more bedraggled than he did when he came into the café with his wife and the two little boys. "Sorry, I didn't recognize you right away. I'm dealing with a crazy person. What are you doing here?"

She pointed to Cal's room. "My dad has an autoimmune disease that sometimes flares up. It's called myasthenia gravis."

Julian's blank look told her he was one of many who'd never heard of it. "It's rare," she said, going on autopilot. "The symptoms get worse with activity and improve with rest."

Julian said, "Sorry to hear it. My mother is having an obnoxious-controlling-crisis. She hates being alone in the hospital and always starts arguments so that I stay longer."

"Oh," said Alene, now hearing Lydia's heels tapping against the floor and spotting her charging up the hallway. Alene couldn't remember what had caused the rift between them – was it around the time Lydia married Theo, or the following year? Maybe Lydia had hated Alene's wedding

72

toast, or what she wore, or how Theo's friends kept asking her to dance. What if Lydia kept starting fights so that she didn't have to talk about what was really bothering her? "And here's my sister, Lydia, heading towards us."

Lydia looked fabulous, as always, in her finely knit, striped suit and black high-heeled pumps. Her long, frosted hair was pulled back into a low ponytail, highlighting her pointed chin, oval face, and stunning earrings. Alene thought she looked prettier and softer with her hair down, but Lydia preferred to project power. "I've got about an hour," she announced. "I have to get home; haven't seen Theo since six this morning."

"It's good that you came," said Alene, wondering if she'd ever again have a husband to rush home to. Lydia pushed past Alene and into the room. She sat in the chair next to Cal, who was still asleep, pulled out her laptop and started working. Alene hoped Lydia would finally get pregnant and have a child who'd be as challenging as she was. Of course, during Alene's difficult adolescent years, their mother had often said she wished the same for her.

Lydia kept typing, but Alene, reading the first of a paranormal mystery series set in Alabama, noticed her pausing often to look with an impatient expression at their father. At the end of the hour, Lydia stood up and announced, "It's already after nine. Looks like I came here for nothing." Her crisp tone didn't fool Alene. Lydia had always tried to overcome fear with bravado. That was it – Lydia was scared.

"It wasn't nothing, Lydia," said Alene. They'd been close as children, whispering secrets under the covers, inventing games, presenting a united front against their parents. Alene had stood up for Lydia when Jack Stone was bullying her in middle school. Lydia had read to Alene and taken care of her after she had her wisdom teeth removed. When their mother's cancer was first detected during Alene's senior year of high school, they'd leaned on each other, holding hands while their parents explained the prognosis and treatment plan.

After the school year ended, the sisters had gotten more involved in their mother's care. They'd shop for groceries together, cook meals, accompany their parents to Vivian's chemotherapy sessions, and cry on each other's shoulders. Lydia had been upset that Alene was still planning to go off to Northwestern, but Vivian had refused to let Alene take a leave of absence. Alene had promised to come home every weekend, or whenever she was needed. She'd already started working at Whipped and Sipped on Saturdays back then, and it was only a few blocks from home. Edith's brother, Gary Vanza, had owned the café back then.

They'd been so relieved when the treatments worked, and Vivian went into remission. But three years later, the cancer returned. After their mother died, Lydia hadn't wanted Cal or Alene's help in choosing a college, graduating from high school, or getting ready to move into her Penn dorm at the end of the summer. They texted sometimes and Alene called now and then, but Lydia only reached out once during her four years of college, after her first serious boyfriend broke her heart. Alene had flown to Philadelphia the next day to spend the week taking care of her sister.

After she got her degree, Lydia spent a year traveling the world. She posted a blog about her travels, but the only time she wanted Alene to come was when she ended up in a hospital in England. It had taken Alene two days to get there, and she stayed for two weeks while Lydia recuperated. Then, when Lydia was in law school at the University of Chicago, she rarely had time to talk to Alene, until the day she had a psychotic breakdown. Again, Alene dropped everything to take care of her. Maybe they'd always have a be-there-in-a-pinch relationship. It wasn't the worst thing, but sometimes Alene wished for more from Lydia than an occasional request for emergency nursing.

Now, Alene reassured her sister. "Even though it looked like he was asleep, I'm sure Dad knew you were here."

"I hope so," Lydia said. "But I've got to get home. I'll call you tomorrow."

After Lydia left, Alene tried reading more about the rookie Birmingham cop, but nobody else's story seemed important enough to divert her attention from her father. He looked calmer; his hands were no longer clenched, and the muscles in his face seemed more relaxed. She was pleased to hear from one of the nurses that his heart was no longer racing and his blood pressure was closer to normal. He must have been scared to death when the MG symptoms started. She should have gone immediately to his bedroom the minute she walked in the door. Or she should have called out to him from the girls' bedroom, and when he didn't answer, she'd have known that something was wrong.

She remembered to text Blanca to tell her about Cal, made herself as comfortable as possible on the chair that tilted back, and somehow managed to doze off. She must have slept a while, but at some point, a kind nurse promised to check on Cal at least once an hour and convinced Alene to go home.

Alene walked in the door at eleven, tip-toed past Kacey sleeping in the living room and got herself to bed. She woke up late the next morning, and quickly checked her messages. Ruthie had texted several times to report one thing or another: they'd finished unpacking her supply order, someone had bought four trays of pastries, and they'd had to completely restock the display case. Good to hear that everything was going smoothly, Alene thought as she read Ruthie's texts.

Then she panicked about the children and ran into the kitchen. Kacey had already gone back across the hall and now Blanca was sitting with a cup of coffee at the table, wearing mascara and shadow on her already expressive hazel eyes, deep-red lipstick enhancing her already full mouth.

"How are you, Miss Lazy-sleep-all-morning? Kids already eat breakfast and go to camp. Everything under control," Blanca said in her Polish accent. She wore mid-calf leggings with a flowing top, a long gold necklace and diamond studs in her ears. She'd told Alene that she always liked to be prepared to go out on a date, just in case.

That morning, she had let herself in, gotten the kids up, given them breakfast, made their lunches, and confirmed with Zuleyka about pick-up that afternoon before she walked them down in the elevator and waited for them to be picked up. She'd already packed sandwiches and was ready to walk to the hospital to visit Cal. Alene nearly wept with gratitude as she hurried to get ready. When she was ready to leave, she slipped on her shoes and told Blanca that she didn't need to spend the day at the hospital. Blanca said, "Your father needs to see me like a normal day."

Outside, the sky was hazy, it was already hot, and the green canopy of trees was lush and full. Alene felt herself starting to sweat as they walked to the hospital. She told Blanca about Jocelyn having been Stanley's son. Blanca scrunched up her face and said, "I have a girl cousin who turned into a boy like that. Some accept and some make big fuss, but my mother says it's okay. She makes her brother call cousin by his boy name."

"Wow," said Alene, embarrassed that she'd assumed people from old Eastern Bloc countries like Poland were less accepting about gender preferences than Americans. At the hospital, they rode the elevator up to Cal's floor. Alene hoped for a miraculous recovery.

Passing nurses, therapists, and other staff members wearing identification badges over hospital coats of different colors, Blanca said, "Maybe Cal enjoys hospital. He likes the pretty girls."

"Some of them are boys," said Alene, "I mean men." They heard yelling as they passed Sylvie's room. "And I forgot to tell you who's next door to my dad. Sylvie Huff, from the twelfth floor. You know, she's the one who is close friends with Ruthie's mom."

"Yes, of course I know Ruthie's mother. Very nice, very good clothes, very organized," said Blanca. "And I know Sylvie, too. Feh." Blanca scrunched her face as if she'd just tasted a lemon. She still cleaned or took care of a few other people in the afternoons, but only accepted clients who didn't expect her to pick up their discarded clothing and put away their knick-knacks.

"What do you mean, 'feh?'" Alene asked.

"Sylvie husband, he's not nice. And Sylvie, she's loud, not right in the head," Blanca said. "What she's sick with?"

Alene whispered, "Something with her blood pressure or her heart."

"Oh," Blanca said, shaking her head. "Maybe Stanley is dead so her heart breaks."

Maybe, thought Alene. They'd reached Cal's room, but the door was closed. Alene knocked softly as she asked Blanca, "How did you know them?"

"Two times I clean their house," said Blanca, making a spitting sound. "So messy, I tell her no more. Then Stanley asks I should clean his office. Then I come, and he smells like bad flowers and he's always touching. I tell him he touches me again I beat the crap out of him."

"I hope you made him pay double," Alene said, knocking again on her father's door. Stanley had never touched her, but if he tried, knowing that it was his modus operandi, she'd kick him in the balls. Too bad if he was an old guy. "No doubt he deducted the cost of cleaning from his taxes."

Blanca, behind her, said, "Nobody gonna touch me that I don't like. Single, nice man, I say okay, maybe. Not mean married man with big muscles."

"I totally agree," said Alene, now slowly opening the door to her father's room. What a relief to see him leaning back against the pillows. He opened his eyes. His hair stuck up in wisps and his smile looked more like a grimace, but he no longer had a panicked expression on his face.

Blanca swooped over and gave him a hug. "Why you at hospital again, Cal, what they give you, some nice cocoa like I make?" Cal was smitten with Blanca, always asking Alene to make sure his pajamas were clean and worrying that he was going to spill something.

Cal blinked. "I'm. Sore." His mouth wasn't gaping open like it had been the day before. The I.V. meds must have started kicking in. "They said. Crisis." He could hardly speak.

"I know, Dad," said Alene, "but you're going to be fine. They'll stabilize you and send you home soon."

"You want I read from newspaper, Cal?" Blanca asked. She mispronounced words and made stories hard to understand but Cal enjoyed being read to. And he helped Blanca with her reading, correcting some of her mistakes and explaining phrases she didn't understand.

A nurse came in and pulled up Cal's chart on the computer next to the bed. Alene and Blanca went out to the hallway. They watched Julian Evans approach from the elevator, his shoulders sloped like an old man's, his eyes half-closed like his sister's. Alene whispered to Blanca, "If Julian's just coming now, who was Sylvie yelling at when we passed her door?"

Blanca shrugged. "Why you have to worry about those people?"

"Don't ask him any questions or we'll be standing here for an hour," said Alene.

Blanca nodded. "I push him into wall for you." Alene looked at her and pictured Blanca ramming Stanley into his office wall after he tried to do more than just touch her. Maybe she'd actually tried to defend herself, and Stanley's death had been an accident. "Joking," said Blanca, waving her hand through the air in a gesture that meant everything from "Are you crazy?" to "Stop bothering me" as she headed to the solarium next to the elevators. Alene really had to stop suspecting her.

"Hi, Alene," Julian said as he approached. He held out a hand for Blanca to shake, "I'm Julian Evans."

"Blanca," she said, looking at his face without responding to his hand. Blanca thought shaking hands was unhealthy. "I clean two times your mother's apartment."

Julian looked at Alene, but she pretended to be busy watching a couple of white-coated doctors rushing up the hallway. Julian asked, "How's your dad today, Alene?"

"He's better, thanks," said Alene. "And your mom?" Blanca sidled away to stand in the hallway outside Cal's room.

"I don't know, I just got here," Julian said, "and obviously my sister is too busy to visit. She won't give Mom her number and I'm only allowed to call in an emergency even though she's the one who needs help." He mumbled under his breath, "She's going to be sorry one day."

"That's sad," said Alene, wondering if he meant it as a threat, and thinking that no matter how mad Lydia made her, she wouldn't talk about her like that, in a hospital corridor.

"I've only met her boyfriend once. I heard he worked at Better Be Fit," said Julian.

Alene said, "I just met him on Saturday." She'd probably seen him before that, heading to or from Better Be Fit, but she hadn't ever spoken to him.

"As long as he makes Heather happy," said Julian, pausing to look at his phone. "Not sure why I still care about her. She barely talks to me."

Alene said, "I hear you. Siblings can be complicated."

"Step-siblings are even more complicated," said Julian. "I already told you I think Harrison Huff caused my mother's blood pressure to go through the roof when he went to visit her. She nearly had a heart attack. But he was ten when our parents got married and I know for a fact that he never liked my mom."

Alene had been wondering when the nurse would finish so she could go back into her father's room. Now she remembered that Jocelyn didn't think much of Harrison either. "I'm sorry your family had so many relationship problems, but I don't think you can cause someone to have a heart attack by saying something mean, Julian," said Alene. "I don't want to argue with you, but that only happens in the movies. In real life it's not so easy to make someone's heart stop."

"Yeah," said Julian, "but he calls her nearly every day, so it's accumulative."

"What a frigging nightmare," said Alene. "Imagine the horror of having a stepson who cares enough to call every day to see how you're doing after you've lost your husband." Blanca stood ten feet away, leaning against the wall outside Cal's room and scrolling through her phone.

"No, that's not it," said Julian. "My mother says he keeps badgering her about Stanley's Last Will and Testament, and I have to stay here all day listening to her complain. As soon as Lillian gets here, I'm going home to spend time with my boys." Alene knew that Lillian worked in the northern suburbs, so she wouldn't get to the hospital until much later. "They'll probably be in bed already," he added, shaking his head.

Was he a devoted son or was he just putting on an act? Alene felt bad about being so suspicious but couldn't help herself. The nurse came out of Cal's room then, pulling off her vinyl gloves and humming a tuneless melody. "Maybe you'll get home sooner," said Alene. She slipped back into her father's room.

Just moments later, Ruthie showed up, which gave Alene a reason to smile. Ruthie always made Alene feel better about everything.

Chapter 7

Ruthie hugged Alene, saw that Cal was asleep, and plopped onto the chair where Blanca had been sitting. "It won't bother him if we talk," Alene said, "because he's been drifting in and out the whole time."

Ruthie told Alene about how the day had gotten off to a rough start when Jocelyn didn't show up to open in the morning with Edith. Edith had immediately called Ruthie, and she deserved praise for that, but then she complained bitterly because she still didn't have the codes to get in or turn off the alarm. Ruthie had reached Olly, and he managed to wake up, get dressed, and race his bike over to the café within fifteen minutes.

The good news was that nothing horrendous happened and they were only fifteen minutes behind schedule. The bad news was that while Olly was setting up in the café, Edith hadn't managed to turn on the ovens or take out all the doughs that needed to get to room temperature, so they'd been set back in their baking. The dessert case hadn't been fully stocked when the café opened at seven, and some customers had been disappointed.

Alene said, "Jocelyn has never been late or missed a shift before."

"That's the thing, Six," said Ruthie. "Olly thought she might have met someone cute at the police station yesterday, which would explain why she didn't go home. But that doesn't explain why she never came to work today."

Alene felt her stomach flip. There might be a murderer loose in the neighborhood and trans people suffered more violent attacks than most other groups. She texted Jocelyn and tried calling, but there was no answer. Alene said, "What if she's lying on a floor somewhere?"

Ruthie reminded her that there was usually a logical reason when an employee failed to show up, mostly having to do with not waking up in time or screwing up their schedules. "Yeah, but she lives with Olly," said Alene, thinking that she should have had him accompany Jocelyn to the police station and then walk her home. If Olly was busy, Alene could have asked Jack Stone, who might have felt honored to be trusted with the task.

Cal, his eyes momentarily open, waved at Ruthie before falling back to sleep. Blanca returned to the room, Ruthie left, and Alene let herself cry. There was so much to worry about. Blanca gave her a lavender and vanilla scented hug. "Your daddy comes soon home. He's gonna be okay."

"No, it's not that," said Alene, although really, that's what it should have been. She told Blanca about Jocelyn.

Blanca said, "You call Frank now."

That was exactly what Alene should have done the minute Ruthie told her about Jocelyn missing work. Frank answered on the second ring and she blurted into the phone, "Did you arrest Jocelyn?"

"Whoa, Alene," said Frank. "Why are you asking?"

If he gave her a runaround, she wouldn't waste another minute of time on him. She told him that Jocelyn hadn't shown up at the café. "You'd tell me if you arrested her, right?" She was building a worst-case scenario, the kind that derailed her common sense.

"Of course, I'd tell you," Frank said in what she recognized as his soothing tone. She plugged in ear buds and tucked her cellphone in her back pocket. "I promise you that

Jocelyn walked out of the station after we'd finished talking," he continued.

"Then where'd she go?" asked Alene, not at all soothed. The last time he spoke that softly, it had felt like a caress. They'd been walking on the bike path just the week before, holding hands and talking about their relationship. He'd said all the obstacles were surmountable, but it had been six weeks and they still hadn't managed to be alone in a bedroom. Alene walked towards the nurse's station and found a bench near the window. "Did she tell you anything, Frank? Was she planning to meet someone? It would be just like Jocelyn to arrange a meeting with a murder suspect."

Frank, in a lighthearted voice, said, "I keep forgetting that your side gig is investigating crime."

"It's not funny, Frank." Alene said, although she usually liked his jesting. She looked out the tenth-floor window at the expanse of lake, the green edge formed by Lincoln Park, and the striking Chicago skyline. It was better than the view they had from her dad's apartment.

Frank said, "I'm definitely taking this seriously. We questioned Jocelyn, but we didn't ask her where she was heading after we finished our meeting. I would have called you if I thought something was wrong."

Alene looked out at the calm lake and thought about how to phrase her next question. "You'd wanted to know what she'd been doing in Stanley's office after Kacey found him on the floor. Can you tell me what you learned?" If he wasn't going to help her find Jocelyn, how could they have a relationship?

"She told me that while she was in his office," said Frank, "she took some of her father's files."

That was foolish of Jocelyn, but Alene wasn't going to let Frank hear her falter. "Could they have been her own files, under her name?"

"Maybe," said Frank. "We're still collecting information."

It would have been so much better to talk to him in person rather than by phone. An elderly woman waiting for the elevator turned and smiled at her just as the elevator door opened. "I'm sorry, Frank," she said. "I'm just so worried about her."

"Jocelyn is a potential witness," Frank responded. "We've asked her not to leave town in case we have more questions, and if we can't get hold of her, we'll do something about it."

"Thank you," she said, feeling better, but not much.

"Question for you," Frank said. "Did she tell you she thought someone had been following her?"

"Jocelyn always thought she was being followed. I think something dreadful happened to her, maybe when she was in the military, but she doesn't talk about it."

She heard Frank breathing. "I get it," he said. "I'll let you know when we learn something." He paused, and added, "How's your father?"

"He's asleep most of the time," she reported. Frank sounded sincere, but she wasn't about to let him change the subject. "Just tell me if you feel like Jocelyn could have, you know, done it," she said, lowering her voice as two white-coated doctors and a woman with a leg brace got off the next elevator.

"My personal feelings aren't the issue here," he said.

"I know," Alene said, grouchier than she'd intended, "but Jocelyn is a sweetheart. She wouldn't hurt anyone."

"Jocelyn knows how to shoot several kinds of weapons, Alene," said Frank, all business now, "and she practices Krav Maga. It's an extremely effective method of fighting."

"Right," said Alene, "she needed to protect herself, for obvious reasons."

"I can't tell you everything," said Frank, "but there was no sign of a forced entry at Better Be Fit."

Alene scoffed. "Stanley might have left his door unlocked."

"Or he knew his attacker," said Frank. "And that person might have been seen hovering in the alley near his door."

People hung around in that alley all the time; employees from Tipped, Brianne's bar, other neighbors, Kacey's boyfriend when he was scavenging materials. She interrupted before he could say anything else, "Jocelyn wasn't hovering."

"Alene, nearly everyone in your kitchen saw Jocelyn in the alley beforehand, and she was in the office with Stanley after Kacey found him." Now Frank sounded like a cop, not at all soothing.

"But he still might have had a simple heart attack." Alene wiped her eyes with her sleeve and wondered why Frank was so intent on making Jocelyn sound guilty.

Frank said, "He had broken capillaries and bruising, Alene. You know what that could mean."

"He always had broken capillaries," said Alene. "He probably had rosacea or something."

Frank took a moment to respond. "Look, I'm sorry I've upset you. My guess is that Jocelyn is innocent. She didn't even ask for a lawyer." Alene held her breath. Maybe Jocelyn hadn't felt the need for a lawyer until she realized that they suspected her. Maybe she ran away because of it. Frank added, "Let's not argue about this, Alene. This is my job, but you're the best thing to happen to me in years."

Alene wished she could have recorded that. It was old-fashioned but sweet. "Me too," she said, walking back up the hallway and into her father's room. She waved at Blanca, who'd put her feet up on the empty bed next to Cal and was leafing through a fashion magazine. "Can we talk again later?"

Frank said, "Call me anytime, Alene." They said goodbye and Alene put her phone back in her pocket. She looked at the fine veins across Cal's face, which was calm as he slept. She should stop thinking about Frank and concentrate on her dad.

Blanca looked up from her magazine and said, "I'm gonna tell Frank you not gonna wait forever."

Alene shook herself. "I'm not sure about him right now."

Blanca said, "Never mind. I'm telling you story." Alene leaned back in her chair and listened to Blanca describe how her grandmother kept the family alive during the Second World War by making soups out of potatoes she buried in the cellar and herbs she found in the forest and dried. Cal slept on, even though he enjoyed stories about food and war. Blanca talked about how her grandmother had once smashed the head of a German soldier who'd tried to rape Blanca's fifteen-year-old-aunt. That somehow turned into a story about how her grandmother topped her paczki with a milk glaze for Easter and powdered sugar for Christmas.

Alene, half-listening, asked what Blanca's grandmother used for the filling. Maybe Ruthie could use fresh fruit and figure out a way to bake instead of frying the stuffed donuts. They could substitute oat or coconut milk for the glaze.

Cal's breathing seemed even, but his skin looked clammy, his thinning gray hair was plastered to his scalp, and the intravenous steroids had already made his face puffy. Alene had to remind herself that Cal was going to have these occasional flare-ups. When his eyes fluttered open, Alene asked, "How are you feeling, Dad?"

"They haven't gotten me yet," he said with a brief smile. "And I want to go. Hiking in Colorado. Or Utah."

Alene smiled. "Hiking sounds fantastic, Dad."

Blanca crocheted while Alene checked email, worked on the kids' camp calendars, and texted Neal to ask about the coming weekend. She'd bring her laptop if Cal wasn't released that afternoon, and work on café scheduling for the following week. She'd have to shuffle people around if Jocelyn wasn't going to be available.

Then she stepped back out into the hallway to call her sister. The walls were painted light mustard-yellow, and between every few rooms there was a framed watercolor of flowers, fields, or streams. Whoever cleaned the glass had left streaks. Doctors in white jackets, nurses wearing green scrubs, and a variety of other hospital personnel dashed up and down the hallway. Patients and food trays were being wheeled in and out of rooms and a white-collared priest passed Alene with a slight bow. She hoped he wasn't planning to visit Cal, who if he felt well enough, couldn't resist a good priest joke. Her dad had always been virulently anti-religion.

Alene's call to Lydia went directly to voicemail. Leaning against the wall opposite Cal's door, she debated leaving a message. Just then Julian Evans walked out of his mother's room, his hair a frizzy mess, wearing baggy jeans and a t-shirt with the insignia of a fast-food place that sold only roasted chicken and side dishes. Alene asked, "What do you know about Jocelyn DeVale?"

"Not much," said Julian, looking a little taken aback, "although I've heard that she's really good at Krav Maga. It's a kind of self-defense method. And she's usually at the café when I come in. Why are you asking me?"

"I was wondering," she said slowly, "if you recognized her when you first saw her working at the café. I mean, you were stepbrothers at one point. I don't know if you ever lived in the same house, but your mother was married to Jocelyn's father."

"We weren't close or anything, and we never lived in the same house, but yeah, I recognized him. He looks basically the same," said Julian. "Except for the hair, and the clothes and jewelry."

"You mean 'she,'" said Alene. "Does Phyllie know that Jocelyn was Jonathan?"

"Yes, Phyllie knows," said Julian. He grimaced as though she'd shown him a bloody wound. Was he one of those people who felt the need to dictate how everybody presented themselves to the world? "I feel bad for Jocelyn," he added, "but I'm a decade older, and we never had much to do with each other, mostly because of Stanley and my mother. Once, I heard Stanley tell Jocelyn that if he ever wrote a will, he'd cut her out of it." Alene sucked in a breath. Frank would see that as a motive.

"She just wanted Stanley to accept her," said Alene. Cal wrote an annual Father's Day letter telling Alene and Lydia how proud he was of what they'd become, the way they behaved, their professional successes. Every year his letter concluded by reminding them to love and take care of each other. She always hoped Lydia would take Cal's advice seriously. Jocelyn had said that she wished her family supported her choices, and Alene wondered if that meant nobody in the family did. Jocelyn rarely mentioned her mother, who'd remarried and moved to the West Coast.

"I don't know anything about their current relationship," Julian said, "but the few times we saw Harrison and Jonathan when they were young, Stanley was always yelling at them. Harrison would stiffen up, but Jonathan was a sensitive kid. Stanley had no patience for Jonathan's crying. Harrison used to protect him when Stanley got on Jonathan's case, and one time I saw Harrison yell at Stanley to leave Jonathan alone. Stanley listened to Harrison. Really, I was surprised when Jonathan grew up and went into the navy. And then he came home and suddenly he was Jocelyn. None of it made sense to me."

That was probably the most honest thing he'd ever said. She imagined Jocelyn as a child, struggling with her identity and suffering every time Stanley opened his mouth. Alene was about to respond but then she heard heels tapping in the hallway and looked up to see her sister. Lydia was beautifully dressed, in black slacks with a crisp white blouse, wearing a mauve lipstick, but her hair was swept back into an atypically sloppy, low bun. She lacked the usual Lydia panache.

"Thanks for coming," said Alene, kissing her sister on the cheek. As usual, Lydia didn't reciprocate and just stood there unmoving. "Is everything okay?"

Lydia gave a brusque, "Yes," while checking the expensive Bulova watch on her left wrist. Alene remembered moving home after college, not long after their mother died. Lydia always retreated into herself when she was upset, hardly speaking and terse unless she needed to cry. Alene had learned that the best way to handle her sister's stress was by distracting her.

"Have you met Julian Evans?" Alene asked. "His mother's in the room next to Dad's, which I thought was a weird coincidence until I overheard someone say that the

11th floor is closed and they're packing patients here on the 10th." She reminded Lydia that Stanley Huff had been murdered, that he'd been a neighbor in Cal's building, and that he'd been Julian's stepfather.

"Hello Julian," Lydia said, abrupt in a way Alene recognized. She was probably worried about Cal. "Sorry about your loss."

Alene gave Lydia's arm a squeeze and said, "Julian, did you know that my sister does estate planning? She has a lot of legal expertise."

Lydia lifted her head and perked up. Nothing like a potential client to light a fire in her. Alene added, "Do you happen to have a business card with you, Lydia? Maybe you could give one to Julian, just in case."

Julian had a befuddled look on his face. "I don't know much about it, but knowing my mother, she probably left all financial and legal matters to Stanley."

That did it. Lydia whipped out a little leather case and handed a card to Julian. "I'm sorry to hear about your stepfather. If you or your mother need help navigating through the complexities of estate law, I'm happy to do what I can." Alene was relieved to see Lydia standing with her shoulders back and her chin jutting forward now that she was in her can-do, lawyer mode.

"He's not my stepfather. He's my mother's husband," said Julian, scratching his head. "My mother inherited property from her parents, and it's in her name, but Stanley took over and she probably doesn't have much of an estate left."

Lydia smiled and said, "Please feel free to call me if you need any help. It's complicated, but I've gotten that sort of thing straightened out for dozens of clients." Julian and Lydia continued talking as Alene walked back into her father's room, feeling like she'd accomplished something.

Cal kept tossing and changing positions in the bed, trying to get comfortable. Having trouble sleeping was one of MG's side effects, and it had been happening to Cal more and more. Blanca handed her a cheese and tomato sandwich. Alene washed her hands and told Blanca about Lydia seeming so down until she started talking about estate planning with Julian. "It'll be better if she doesn't affect Dad with her anxiety."

Blanca said, "Everyone wants a sister to help through bad times." They nibbled their sandwiches.

After a bit, Lydia came in and greeted Cal with a kiss on the cheek. Blanca jumped up and offered her chair, but Lydia instead perched on Cal's bed and scrolled through her Facebook page. "Stanley Huff," she said, glancing down at Cal, who smiled weakly at his two daughters. "I wonder if he's related to a new client with the same last name?"

"Lydia! What if I know him?" asked Alene, wondering if Lydia, her thorny sister, would disclose privileged information. "I mean, what if I know your new client."

"It's not like I said her actual name or anything," said Lydia, standing up and heading to the door.

"Are you leaving already Lydia?" Alene asked, wondering if Harrison Huff's wife was Lydia's new client. Didn't Julian say that Harrison had been badgering Sylvie about Stanley's Last Will and Testament? Maybe Lydia had already known about Stanley's estate before she even met Julian. Maybe Stanley wanted to get his hands on the Better Be Fit building next door and a family member was unhappy about it. There were five floors of rental property above the ground floor retail space. Frank would probably want to know. "You just got here, Lydia," she added, trying to be understanding, but still a little disappointed.

"I'm sorry," said Lydia, "but I've been under a lot of pressure and Theo and I have been working really long hours." She stood and pulled her purse strap over her shoulder. "At least Dad knows I was here."

"That's true," said Alene, glancing at Cal as Lydia marched out the door. She wished her sister realized that she wasn't the only one whose father was ill. When had it become so difficult for Lydia to express her feelings? When was the last time she initiated a hug or conveyed some warmth? Was it her own fault for not being a better big sister? Alene dozed off in the chair next to Cal's bed and woke from a dreamless sleep when a nurse came in to change his intravenous bag.

She stepped into the hallway and Sylvie spotted her before she had a chance to rush past. "Alene," Sylvie shouted. "I need help."

"Did you try the call button?" asked Alene. Where had Julian gone? Up close, Sylvie's eyes, half closed like Heather's, were magnified by her distinctive red eyeglasses. She reminded Alene of one of those strange nocturnal primates. Why, when there were five hospitals within a few miles, and hundreds of rooms at St. Darius, had Cal ended up in the room next to Sylvie Huff? Even if the 11th floor was closed, she should have been placed on a floor for mentally unstable patients who yelled and demanded attention.

"No, these nurses are useless," said Sylvie, her matching red glasses and nails contrasting with her pale arms, the washed-out blue hospital gown, and over-washed, colorless blankets. "And my children don't have the time of day for me." Just then, Julian slipped back into the room.

Sylvie reached out and grabbed Alene's hand. "My children never liked Stanley, but what could I do? He made me happy, and he was fantastic in bed."

"Nobody needs to hear about that, Mom," Julian said. He sat in his usual chair next to Sylvie's bed.

Sylvie said, "Stop being such a prude. It's not like you don't have sex with your wife, I hope. Sit down, Alene, you're making me nervous."

Did Alene want to be more like her sister, who was so absorbed in herself that she didn't even consider anyone else's feelings, or like Ruthie, who cared about other people? She perched on the chair closest to the door. Julian said, "I know that Stanley tried to grope my wife. He was a sexual predator, and nobody needs to hear about his bedroom prowess."

So, Julian knew about Stanley putting his hand up Phyllie's skirt. Would he have waited all this time to get revenge?

91

"Don't be disrespectful to the dead, Julian," said Sylvie.

Julian looked disgusted. "He pulled you out of a marriage and wrecked our family." Alene knew nothing about Julian and Heather's father, but she guessed he dodged a bullet by divorcing Sylvie back then.

A nurse entered the room at that moment and Julian stomped out before Sylvie had a chance to respond. Alene left too, turning back into her father's room. She should tell Frank what Julian had said about Stanley trying to grope his wife. She stood at the foot of Cal's bed as he looked groggily around the room.

A white-coated doctor with caterpillar eyebrows entered, mumbled a greeting, and began scrolling through the mounted computer screen, looking at Cal's chart. He asked questions that Cal answered slowly, still half asleep. The doctor said something about his lethargy. Alene asked, "Do you think he can come home tomorrow?" She wanted her father sitting in front of the television watching a ballgame and yelling at Leury Garcia for not hitting the cutoff man.

"Probably not," said the doctor. He wore identification, as they all did, but Alene wasn't close enough to read his name, and hadn't heard him clearly. "He's still presenting with MG symptoms."

The doctor swept out of the room, briefly stopping, as they all did when they traipsed in and out, to rub his hands with antibacterial foam from the wall container. It was a good thing Cal was on Medicare and didn't have to pay separately for all these doctors. "Doctors. Wear me out," he managed to say before his eyes fully closed.

Alene could hear Sylvie screeching at Julian again, so she stood up, and shut her father's door.

Chapter 8

Alene pulled her chair closer to Cal's bed when his eyes fluttered open. He croaked in a hoarse voice, "Hello, Sweetheart."

"How are you feeling, Dad?" She kept hoping he was going to toss off the sheet and jump out of bed.

He didn't move, and his smile looked more like a scowl. "That woman. Is too loud," he said slowly. She hated how much exertion it took for him to speak. Alene had always thought of her father as robust. Just a few months before, he'd carried eight-year-old Noah, who'd fallen asleep, all the way from the garage up to the apartment. And now look at him. Sixty-five was too young to be so debilitated. "Tell her. To shut up."

Alene could see pink scalp where his once-thick hair was thin and silvery. "I know, Dad," she said. She watched as he tried to form the next sentence. Sierra had inherited his straight nose and his pale blue eyes. "Are you feeling any better?"

His reply was a grumpy face. "How many. Next door."

"Just the one," she said. "It's just Sylvie Huff." She hoped disgruntlement was a sign of improvement, and glanced out the window at a million shades of green. Beyond the park, the lake, dotted with what looked like toy sailboats, glittered in the sun. At least the second bed was empty, and Cal was alone in the room.

"She's loud," said Cal. "I'm sick. Not Deaf." He stopped to hold up a finger the way he often did when he wanted to tell a joke. "Doctor sees a guy. Walking with. Curvy woman. You know?"

"Yeah, Dad. I know this one."

Cal closed his eyes but continued with the joke. "Doctor says. Glad to see you. Doing so well." Alene waited, hoping she'd be able to remember jokes when she got old. "The guy says. 'You told me. Get a hot momma. Be cheerful.'"

The pause lasted too long. Alene asked, "And then what, Dad?"

"Doctor says. 'No. I said. You've got a heart murmur. Be careful.'" Cal let his head fall back against the pillows. His eyes closed and his mouth dropped open. So much effort, but he loved telling those old jokes. Twenty minutes later, he woke again and asked, "What were we. Talking about?"

"You asked about the room next door, Dad. It's Sylvie Huff, from our building," said Alene. He'd been asleep when she'd told Blanca. "She doesn't stop making noise."

"Loudmouths," he said, coughing. "They don't care. About anyone else. We taught you girls. To be considerate. Not everyone. Knows how."

"No, they don't, Dad," said Alene, guessing that he was alluding to her marriage. He'd questioned Neal's character and had continuously reminded her, until the morning of her wedding day, that she could change her mind. During all those months leading up to the wedding, she'd convinced herself that her father just didn't know Neal like she did. Now, whenever she thought of her marriage as a mistake, she recalled that if she'd heeded her father, she wouldn't have Sierra, Quinn and Noah. She wondered what they were doing right now.

Cal said, "Too late for some. To learn." He fell asleep and his breathing evened out. Alene tiptoed out to the hallway and called home to discuss the kids' dinner with

94

Zuleyka. There was a spaghetti squash sitting on the counter that needed an hour in the oven. Alene reminded her to heat up the homemade sesame sauce from the fridge and serve it alongside the vegetables Quinn loved cutting into tiny pieces. Noah would need supervision when he sliced the homemade sourdough bread and Sierra was supposed to set the table. Alene told Zuleyka that she'd come home after Cal fell asleep for the night.

She spoke next to Noah, who told her about the frogs and toads they'd seen at camp. He would have continued talking, but Quinn grabbed the phone. There was some shouting until Zuleyka pulled Noah away to take a bath, and Quinn then told Alene about a girl who'd called her a mean name. Quinn had handled it like a mature person, she reported, by telling the counselor instead of getting into a fight. Alene commended her.

Next, Sierra mumbled a greeting and launched into a complaint about not having anything to wear to the birthday party of a girl who was probably going to be the most popular person in seventh grade. Alene reminded her that Cal was still in the hospital, and Sierra responded by asking if Aunt Lydia could take her shopping instead. Alene wondered if she was doing enough to teach her children about compassion.

She rose to straighten Cal's blankets and rub his forehead the way he used to rub hers when she had trouble falling asleep as a child. Then she sat back down, opened her laptop, and began to work on the café's accounts and employee schedules. Ruthie called to ask about Cal, and wondered if there was any news about Jocelyn. Alene had hoped to hear that Jocelyn surprised everyone by showing up at the café and was sorry to report that she hadn't heard anything new. Then Lydia called to say that she wasn't going to make it to the hospital until the next day.

"I wish you could just come by for a quick visit. I know it upsets you to see Dad like this, but he loves having us both here, Lydia," said Alene. "And Theo too."

"Not going to happen," said Lydia. Alene imagined her pursing her lips the way she always did after stating a firm opinion.

Alene let her chin fall to her chest. As the older sister, it was probably her fault that her relationship with Lydia was strained. All those years ago, she shouldn't have left her sister alone at home. She should have invited Lydia when she and her friends went to the beach, or the park, or the movies. She should have helped Lydia more when their mother was sick and dying. She could have come home more often and stayed longer when she saw how paralyzed with grief their father was. Lydia had spent her senior year of high school grappling with their mother's decline, a heavy course load, and college admissions. By the time Alene thought to ask about her plans for the coming year, Lydia had already made all the decisions by herself. Was it so surprising that Lydia didn't share feelings or turn to her when she needed help now?

At least their lack of a close relationship hadn't affected Lydia's dealings with the kids. She and Theo were incredibly magnanimous. They invited each child for a birthday sleepover that included a fancy restaurant dinner, a show or special event, and a generous gift. Sierra loved the makeup and nail polish collection she'd gotten when she turned twelve. At ten, Quinn was presented with the personalized rolling suitcase she'd coveted. And Noah was still contentedly constructing the huge Lego set they'd given him for his eighth birthday.

Lydia was even generous with Alene. It seemed like it was easier for her to whip out her credit card than to spend an evening together. Alene gave Lydia nice presents too, and the last three birthday gifts had been spectacularly successful. Alene's former-mother-in-law, Mitzi Dunn, who worked at Neiman Marcus, had helped her choose and had given her a discount on a special face cream, a small evening bag, and a tiny but stunning brooch. Still, gifts didn't bring them closer or convince Lydia that Alene would always be on her side.

"Dad's asleep most of the time anyway," Alene said, "so don't worry about it Lydia. I'll just see you tomorrow." She tucked her phone away, straightened her father's blankets again, kissed his forehead and whispered goodnight. He was asleep and didn't respond.

The evening air was sticky and still. As she walked home, Alene inhaled a summer blend of barbecue, blossoming flowers, and traffic. The Cubs game must have just ended because the streets were packed and overflowing with cars and people. She passed a gaggle of laughing twenty-somethings who vaped as they walked. They reminded her of Jocelyn.

After vaping in the alley, Jocelyn could have stopped at her father's office to confront him about his will, and someone could have slipped in after her. Maybe she'd seen her father's attacker and feared that she was next, so she'd gone somewhere to hide. Worst case scenario, what if the murderer, who'd already managed to smother Stanley, had found Jocelyn, and silenced her? Maybe Jocelyn hadn't only imagined that someone was following her for some reason other than admiration. What if someone, like Miles, or Harrison, was trying to unsettle her. It could be something Phyllie might do to throw Jocelyn off her game. Even Lawrence, who seemed so harmless, could be trying to find a way to get rid of her. What if he'd only started dating Lillian to get close to Jocelyn and anyone else who might get in the way of whatever he wanted? Even an old guy like him could have taken Stanley by surprise.

Alene frightened herself into running the rest of the way home. What a relief to lock the door of her apartment and take a few calming breaths. She was glad to be able to kiss her children goodnight and grab a few forkfuls of dinner before going to bed. That night, she dreamed about Jocelyn, who kept disappearing around sharp corners, and was always just out of Alene's reach.

Finally, the alarm rang at five and Alene woke up, feeling congested. It was not a good time to get sick, with Jocelyn missing and a murderer in the neighborhood.

Maybe Jocelyn had returned home the night before and was planning to open the café as expected this morning. As she got ready to leave, Alene thought about adding more positive thinking and less negativity to everything she wanted to change about herself.

What a pleasure to be outside running before the heat of the sun sapped all her energy and the heat index inched up. It was just a warm-up to working out at Michael's gym, but she started feeling stronger as she headed south toward the twinkling lights and hazy buildings of the city. Thanks to the second wealthiest billionaire in Illinois, the city had finally repaved the bike path last summer. If they'd done it eight years before, Brianne's husband wouldn't have died of a fatal heart attack triggered by a speeding bicyclist on the path. All that negative thinking made the endorphins rise like mist and scatter in the breeze. Instead of feeling reinvigorated, by the time she got to her workout, Alene was sweaty and enervated.

"Are you always going to come in here looking like someone just drowned?" Michael asked with a penetrating look. She filled him in while lifting, pushing, and punching. He thought Jocelyn had acted guilty. "Why would an innocent person run away?"

Alene said, "Maybe she was frightened."

Michael shared more negative theories in between reminding her to focus on breathing, keep her shoulders back, and slow down. But then he apologized for rattling her so much about Jocelyn that she couldn't lift a ten-pound weight, and she spent the last fifteen minutes stretching while she told him what she liked about Frank.

Michael said, "I guess you can't talk about the guy without a smile on your face." On the spot, he invented a long, scientific-sounding title for a study that indicated smiling at least once a day had been proven to extend the lives of single mothers in their thirties. Alene challenged him about how that study had been scientifically conducted. Michael assured her that at least half of what he said could be scientifically proven, at which point, Alene left for home.

Less than two hours later, after the kids were picked up for camp, she headed to the café. Ruthie and her baking team were already up to their elbows in flour and Jack was scrubbing pans in the sink. Jocelyn was still missing. Other employees were making sure the trays were full and keeping up with a steady line of customers. Edith seemed unusually cheerful, but Olly was uncommonly morose and still. Not a single melody or whistle. Alene put an arm around him and said, "Frank's got guys looking for her, Olly. She'll be back before you know it."

Olly said, "It's just not like her. We usually text all day, even when we're here, and now I haven't heard from her in two nights." Alene spent some time reassuring him and tried to call Frank while Olly cracked his knuckles.

Frank didn't answer. She texted him while Olly pulled up a picture on his phone of two lanky teenagers, one with red curls and the other with jet black hair. He held it in front of Alene until she smiled. The two boys wore steel-tipped boots and torn jeans. They were leaning against an old car, and it all looked a little too studied, as if they were in a photo shoot. Olly looked nearly the same, with shorter curls, but it took her a minute to recognize the other boy. It was Jocelyn. Had Stanley already kicked her out of the house then?

Alene asked Olly to send her a copy of the photo and went back to the kitchen to help Ruthie. An hour later she was spinning around the café greeting regulars and helping at the counter when the line got too long. She stopped to greet a young moms' group. She chatted with a sweet-faced woman named Ella, who always wore a backpack carrying her support dog, Bella. Then she talked with Toula Savas, who told Alene that she worked as a speech therapist and that she was obsessed with working out. Alene admired her muscular arms, slightly bruised from all her weight training. She had violet-hued eyes, smooth skin, and a long braid, a style Ruthie often wore. Alene wondered if Toula had ever professionally helped anyone who spoke in short bursts, like Cal, but decided to ask about it some other time.

It was after nine by the time she got to the hospital. On Cal's floor, the nurses and technicians were moving in and out of rooms. Alene passed Sylvie's open door and saw Julian sitting in the chair next to her bed, slumped over his laptop as if he'd never left. He was probably writing another story about post-apocalyptic technology. Sylvie was abnormally tranquil, probably sleeping. Julian looked up with his odd, half-closed eyes and waved. Alene gave him a quick nod before hurrying into her father's room.

Cal grinned as she approached his bed. "You again!" He lifted both arms but dropped them before she could get close enough for a hug.

"So good to see you smiling, Dad." She leaned over to kiss the top of his head. He still smelled like a combination of cigars and coffee even though he hadn't smoked in fifteen years. Now he didn't look as fatigued or floppy. She'd brought pastries and a thermos of coffee from the café, a dark roast prepared just how he liked it, with milk and sugar. She poured it into his ceramic cup. "You ready for a sip?" she asked, holding the cup close enough for him to enjoy the smell.

"Please, Sweetheart," he said, hoarsely. "Noisy here. If I don't get out soon. I might murder someone." Alene quickly looked up to see if anyone was in the doorway. Between Stanley's death and Jocelyn's disappearance, she wasn't sure joking about murder was a good way to start the morning.

"I'll keep the door closed and won't let anyone bother you, Dad," said Alene, stroking his hand.

Cal nearly snorted. "Can you shut them up?" He used to yell a lot when Alene was growing up, but it was mostly at the television, or in the car, when the clueless driver who'd upset him couldn't hear Cal's foul name-calling. Vivian, Alene's mother, had only raised her voice when she or Lydia did something dangerous. Otherwise, when one of her daughters disappointed her, she'd sit them down and talk to them about how their choices always had consequences. Alene hoped she was doing enough discussing of choices and consequences with Sierra, Quinn, and Noah. She said, "Remember I told you that it's Sylvie Huff from the twelfth floor, Dad?"

Cal stared blankly. Alene felt like crying. Where was her usually sharp-witted father? She reminded him about Stanley's heart attack and how she and Ruthie had taken voice lessons from Sylvie when they were about to become mothers.

"You didn't need. Voice lessons," Cal said, "you always had. A sweet voice."

"You're exaggerating, Dad," said Alene. "Anyway, Sylvie wants to tell me the story of her life because she thinks that her children never listen to her."

"You've always been. A good listener," said Cal, nodding off again.

He'd always been her biggest fan, and it still felt good to get a compliment from her father. She pulled out her cellphone and checked in with Ruthie. Everything was fine at the café, so Alene sat down and removed a book from her backpack. She'd already finished the clever paranormal mystery written by a retired Birmingham cop, and now started the third in a delightful series about a psychologist who sings in the Lyric Opera chorus, eats enticing pastries while sipping coffee, and helps the Chicago police, who are unexpectedly cheery and open-minded, in solving crimes. The next time Alene looked up, Frank Shaw was standing in the doorway, holding a small potted kalanchoe plant with tiny yellow flowers.

"Hi," she said, her thoughts suddenly scattered and disconnected, although she couldn't help admiring his shoulders again. And his thoughtfulness. That was one of the main reasons she was drawn to him. Neal had been fun and spontaneous during those early years, but he'd never been all that thoughtful. Then they'd had the girls, and it wasn't so easy to be spontaneous. Between both their jobs, the children and the house, Alene remembered walking around in a state of exhaustion. It was a surprise when she got pregnant a third time, and their lives got even more complicated. Neal hadn't wanted another child and accused her of getting pregnant on purpose. It wasn't true. As the months passed, she realized that they weren't spending much time together, but never thought he'd handle his frustration by having an affair.

The very first time she met Frank was when her water suddenly broke while out walking with the girls. He'd rushed her to the hospital in his squad car. He'd also stayed through Noah's delivery when Neal failed to show up. A few weeks later, she learned that he'd been having an affair, and with Lydia's encouragement, had started divorce proceedings. Alene didn't ever want to be with someone who lied to her. She wanted someone she could count on.

Would Frank have come up to her father's room if he didn't want a relationship? Maybe he'd found Jocelyn. Or maybe Chicago cops were being told to buff up their current image by bringing plants when they visited people in the hospital. Or she was confusing the real CPD with the overly accommodating police department in the book she was reading.

"I hope it isn't a bad time," he said, stepping forward and kissing Alene in a friendly way on her cheek. He lingered for just a moment and she breathed in his scent of orange peel, chocolate, and aftershave. Should she ask if he'd really come just to visit her dad? She'd recently read about a detective's girlfriend who'd asked too many questions and ended up dead.

"Hello there," said Cal, awake again. Either he remembered meeting Frank, or he was just being friendly, as usual.

Frank asked, "How are you today, sir?"

Cal answered slowly in his raspy voice, "The doctor gave me six months to live. But I couldn't pay. So, he gave me. Six more months." Frank laughed and gave him a thumbs-up.

Alene had heard that one a thousand times. As her father drifted off again, she led Frank out to the hallway. "His disease makes little naps easier than long periods of deep sleep."

Closing the door behind him, Frank commiserated, and said, "I thought I could count on seeing you when I picked up my coffee every day." Alene's eyes promptly filled with tears, and Frank, misinterpreting, put his arms around her. "How's your dad doing, really?"

Sylvie's bed was just steps from the hallway and her door was wide open. Before Alene could respond to Frank, Sylvie called her name with the flat nasal sound she'd come to dread. Julian was still immersed in his laptop and didn't look up. "Alene," Sylvie demanded a second time. "Don't just stand out in the hallway. Introduce me to your handsome friend." She patted the bed, as if anyone was going to sit on it. "Come talk to me, both of you."

Alene rubbed her suddenly aching neck. Frank had certainly already interviewed Sylvie and Julian as part of his investigation. Alene was glad he didn't step closer to Sylvie or try to shake hands. She hated touching anyone in the germy air of a hospital room. "Hello again, Mrs. Huff," said Frank as Sylvie appraised him. She'd found time to put on a salmon-colored lipstick. "I hope you're feeling better since we met earlier this week."

Sylvie either pretended not to recognize Frank, or she was too vain to wear her glasses. Alene's stomach clenched as Sylvie started on her litany of complaints.

"I'm sorry you're having such a difficult time," Frank interjected when Sylvie paused, glancing at him as if he were a gentleman caller from another era.

"Don't even let me get started about my joint pain," she continued. "I have fibromyalgia, probably one of the worst, most difficult diseases to treat, and there's no cure." Sylvie touched her hand to her hair, as though it was done up. She wore a fluffy pink robe over her hospital gown. "Also, my husband had a heart attack and died last week."

"Again, my sincere condolences," said Frank, who'd edged forward. Did Sylvie know the police suspected more than a simple heart attack? Or that she was number four on Alene's list of suspects, after Miles, Harrison, and Phyllie?

103

"Thank you, but Stanley was a jackass," said Sylvie, now studying her nails. "He had a bad heart and a rotten personality. He was mean, he didn't say anything nice to me for years, and I should have left him long before now. I don't plan to have a memorial service. He doesn't deserve one."

Alene tapped Frank's elbow, hoping he'd get the hint and back out of the room. He said, "I heard you've been telling your life story to Alene."

"It's a favor to Ruthie's mother," Alene whispered.

"Lillian Blum has been my best friend for a hundred years," said Sylvie with the sudden drawl of a Southern belle. She straightened the thin blanket and smoothed her fluffy robe. "Unlike my children," she stopped to point a finger at Julian, who didn't react, and then at Alene, "this girl doesn't try to shut me up. Good to see you again, Officer Shaw, because I neglected to mention something."

Ah, thought Alene, so she recognizes him.

Julian said, "Enough, Ma." He might not succeed as a sci-fi author, but he sure was a dedicated son. "You don't have to say anything else."

"Don't tell me what to do, Julian," Sylvie said. "Stanley hasn't been a real husband for years," Sylvie paused. Alene was riveted by Sylvie's transformation from irrational to coquettish and back again, but hoped Sylvie wasn't planning to repeat the stories she'd already told.

"He humiliated me and made me do unspeakable things," Sylvie began.

Frank's face was blank. Maybe he'd gone into cop mode. Alene studied the floor, hoping Frank would come up with something official that a detective might say.

Sylvie said, "I did what he asked because I was trying to save our marriage." Julian concentrated on his laptop and pretended not to listen. "Stanley didn't want to be married to me. He said I disgusted him." Alene empathized with Sylvie but wished she could slink out of the room.

"Last week his older son came over to the apartment, with his custom-made shirt and pointy designer shoes. Maybe I got heavier, and Stanley and I drifted apart, but we're still married. I think Harrison could have at least been polite. He sells expensive houses and knows how to talk to people, but he barely said hello to me, and he didn't even bring anything – a bottle of wine, chocolate, flowers. Those boys were young when Stanley and I got married, and we had them every other weekend. We taught them to bring a gift whenever you visit someone.

"Anyway, then Jonathan came too and brought a box of cookies made with sunflowers seeds and all kinds of crazy combinations like what you sell at your café, Alene. Jonathan is the one who turned into a woman, and I've got to tell you, he was a lot more polite than he used to be. At least he got the message about bringing a hostess gift. And I was pleasantly surprised at how good those cookies were."

"Thanks, Sylvie," said Alene. "Those are Ruthie's recipes. And I'm sure you meant to say, 'SHE was a lot more polite than she used to be.'"

"Whatever," said Sylvie. "The point is that Harrison should know better. He's a thirty-two-year-old, married man. Stanley, by the way, talked to them about his Last Will and Testament. He was obsessed with talking about his estate, which, by the way, is actually my estate."

"You've seen Jocelyn dozens of times, Sylvie," said Alene, starting to lose her patience. "She works for me in the café."

Sylvie focused only on Frank. "I never noticed," she said, sounding disingenuous to Alene. "Anyway, the three of them talked for a long time, and I just sat and listened."

Alene didn't believe a word of it. Maybe Sylvie was trying to deflect attention because she was the one who murdered her husband. If she'd shoved Stanley, he could have hit the desk hard enough to knock himself out. Sylvie might have planned to murder him beforehand, but it could also have been a crime of opportunity.

"Why didn't you tell me about this before?" Frank's mistake was to expect rational behavior from Sylvie, but Jocelyn had probably told him about the conversation with her father and brother. "And why are you telling me now, Sylvie?"

Sylvie mumbled with another sweep of her hand. "She's really not that pretty with that neck and those hands. And it's obvious that she's had work done, not to mention the fake eyelashes. Although maybe she uses that whatever-it's-called product to help thicken your eyelashes. I heard you can get it much cheaper in..."

Frank interrupted her. "I asked you about the meeting."

"I'm getting there," Sylvie said, as if Frank was being unreasonable. "Stanley never looked at Jonathan, but he doesn't look at me either. You have no idea how hard that is for a woman." She clutched her chest, suddenly lying back weakly against her stack of pillows.

Julian said, "Maybe you should go now."

"What did you want to tell me about that conversation, Sylvie?" Frank asked in a firm voice. Alene started to slide back out to the hallway, but Frank looked at her and blinked. She took it as a sign that he wanted her to stay put.

"Stanley only cared about money," said Sylvie, her hand delicately hovering as if she were starring in a Tennessee Williams play. "But I brought all the money and property into the marriage and my children are going to prove it.

"Thank you for your time, Mrs. Huff," said Frank. He lightly tapped Alene's elbow and turned to the door.

"You're a cute couple," Sylvie said as they walked out, "but make sure to get a prenuptial agreement. And Alene, honey, never sign your name to anything without showing it to a lawyer first."

As soon as they were in the hallway, Frank leaned down and whispered, "I learned something from her rant, so thank you."

What had he learned? His breath was so sweet, she stopped thinking about it.

Chapter 9

Alene led Frank back into her father's room. She hoped they'd both forget Sylvie's relationship advice. "She could have killed Stanley in a psychotic fury," said Alene as she sat in the chair to the left of Cal's bed.

Frank, looking calm, shrugged, and said, "Sometimes people snap." He told her about a case that had given him nightmares for years. He and his partner at the time had been called to a house from which neighbors reported hearing screams. When they arrived, the husband explained that his wife had been attacked by a bat inside the house. The wife had agreed and showed them where she'd smashed up against the walls, trying to avoid the bat. They'd received several calls about bats and rodents recently, so it made sense, and they left after a quick survey. Two weeks later, they were called to the same house, but by the time they arrived, the husband had already beaten his wife to death, with a baseball bat.

Alene gasped, but she recalled several Tribune articles about the police failing to protect an abused spouse. Frank concluded, "I'm no longer in that division, but we take those claims seriously."

Alene said, "I think men who hurt women should be castrated." She put her feet against the edge of her dad's bed.

Frank gave her a look. "That's not legal," he said. "And what do you suggest for wives who abuse their husbands?"

"Therapy," she said, shrugging. She could see that he was about to give a logical argument opposing her biased view, but that was a discussion for another time. She asked, "So, what do you think about Sylvie?"

Frank's forehead crinkled. "She's an undependable witness," he said. "It's hard to believe anything that comes out of her mouth."

"My dad always says, 'Whoever profits by the crime is guilty of it.' Doesn't that describe Sylvie?"

"Possibly," said Frank, "but we interviewed the neighbors, viewed footage from whichever of them had cameras, and talked to employees at nearby businesses. Nobody remembered seeing a person resembling Sylvie Huff."

He had a way of making her think she could be right while simultaneously refuting her answer with facts. Alene pressed on. "How many people really pay attention to their surroundings, Frank? Maybe nobody saw Sylvie, but that doesn't mean she wasn't there."

"You're right, but what would she have done?" Frank asked, his eyes twinkling. "Talk him into having a heart attack?"

Alene looked at her father, who'd flung his hand off the bed. Alene held it in both of hers. "She could have knocked him out and then somehow prevented him from breathing. She always wears stretchy pants and microfiber shirts, so there wouldn't be any evidence of her suffocating him." Alene had read at least two mysteries in which fiber on the victim's clothes or inside his or her lungs had led to a suspect.

"It's possible," said Frank, "but she checked herself into St. Darius at 9:15 on Friday night."

"Yeah," said Alene, "because she was exhausted. Her heart was racing after she smothered her husband." Now Cal was starting to fidget in his sleep. "Clever of her," Alene went on. "Then she could have left Stanley on the floor in his office and taken the 77 bus straight to the hospital."

Frank leaned forward. "Alene, I value your opinion, but I've been working long hours sifting through evidence. And we're still waiting for lab results."

Jack Stone appeared in the doorway then. Alene was startled for a moment, but maybe he was starting to pick up on all the training she and Ruthie had been doing, about how to be a nice person. "Hi, Jack." Alene smiled, gesturing for him to enter. "You remember Frank Shaw, don't you?"

"Yes," Jack glanced at Cal and mumbled towards his shoes. "Hello Officer Shaw. I guess it's a bad time since Mr. Baron is sleeping."

Alene said, "Don't worry about it, Jack. He's in and out of sleep all day. I was just about to ask Frank if he's been able to find Jocelyn."

"She'll turn up, Alene," said Frank. "There are lots of reasons why someone like Jocelyn would disappear for a couple of days. But she's tough and she knows how to take care of herself."

Jack said, "Damn right, she does."

Cal's eyes popped open. "Jack Stone? What are you? Doing here? Did you bring? Ruthie's brownies?"

"Hi, Mr. Baron," said Jack. "I meant to bring something, but I forgot. Everyone is worried about you. How are you doing?"

"Better, I think," said Cal slowly. "I'm not hungry. Anyway. You're kind. To visit."

Jack said, "That's what neighbors do, Mr. Baron. You're the one who taught me that."

So, Alene and Ruthie couldn't take credit. Cal had always loved dispensing advice. The surprising part was that Jack had started listening to him. "I also taught you. Cribbage. Did you bring. A deck? A board?"

When had Cal taught Jack how to play cribbage? He'd never taught her or Lydia. Jack said, "I'll bring them next time. You'll probably be home soon." That was one good thing about Jack being across the hall even though he was a thirty-four-year-old man who still lived with his mother. She'd been at a rehabilitation facility for nearly two months, so Jack Stone and Kacey Vanza had been temporarily on their own. Alene hoped they'd both move out one day soon.

"Good man," said Cal. He turned to Alene. "What'd I miss. In the world?"

That was the question he always asked when he came home from what he used to call a "business trip." Years later, he told her that those were actually golfing weekends. He'd tried to get both her and her sister to love golf the way he did, but they both thought it took too long to play. She knew how much he loved the sport and was sad that he hadn't been strong enough to play or even just hit balls at the driving range all summer. She said, "We're talking about Jocelyn DeVale. You know, Dad, she's the one who was in the navy. She shares an apartment with Olly Burns."

Cal nodded and gestured with one hand. "Mop-headed kid. Helped build shelves."

"He's kind of gay," said Jack. Alene gave him a look, and he added, "Well, he is."

Alene turned to Cal. "Jocelyn and Olly were good friends in high school, and she moved in with him when she came back to Chicago. She didn't show up to work today."

"So, are you going to fire her?" Jack asked. "You'd probably fire me if I didn't show up."

Alene said, "No, I'm not going to fire her."

Frank said, "You told me that Jocelyn always thought she was being followed. Can you say more about that before I go?"

Alene thought for a moment. "She never said who she thought was following her. It was more that she never wanted to go anywhere by herself. She'd ask LaTonya or another one of my employees to go running together, and she scheduled her Krav Maga classes around Olly's schedule. As I might have mentioned, I think it was because of something that happened when she was in Afghanistan."

110

"I've already taken two of her classes, so we're starting to be friends," Jack said. He was just a fountain of surprises. She felt like Geppetto finding out that Pinocchio had turned into a real boy. "I like learning how to defend myself, but I'm not sure it would help if someone pulled a gun on me."

Alene said, "That doesn't happen as much when you work in a regular job, Jack. In fact, it's never once happened at the cafe."

"And I hope it never does," said Frank. "Let's get back to Jocelyn."

"You should see how fast she can get someone on the ground before they know what hit them," said Jack. "Anyone who follows her is in for a big surprise."

"People always follow. Beautiful women," said Cal.

With her height, her dark hair and greenish blue eyes, and those cheekbones, she was certainly beautiful. "She's been even more anxious since we found Stanley Huff's body, but that's understandable," Alene said.

"Wait," said Cal. "Is that Stanley? From our building?"

"Yeah, the dude with the perfume," Jack said, pointedly looking away from Frank. "He just got whacked."

"We talked about this already, Dad," said Alene. She massaged Cal's cold hands and wondered how he could feel chilled in such a warm room. "What do you think Jack, did someone murder Stanley for the money?"

"I think a lot of bad things happen because of money," Jack answered, looking pleased to have been asked. At least he showered every day now that Alene told him that's what she expected of employees. He used to have greasy hair and his jeans were always stained and ratty, like a rebellious teenager. Now he wore clean clothes and was starting to look more like a man. He had nice enough features, and that thick blondish hair, but Alene thought he'd look even better if he stopped slouching like an old guy.

"You might be right, Jack," said Frank, walking around the bed, stopping to shake Cal's hand and wish him well. He smiled with little creases edging his gray eyes and then walked Alene out to the hall.

"I'd be okay with the Whipped and Sipped crew figuring this out before us," he told her, his hand cupping her chin.

"We just might, but I wish you'd find Jocelyn," said Alene. "I'm worried about her."

"I know, Alene. The thing is," Frank whispered, "I think you and I have something here, you know? But I've got to run." Alene was speechless. Frank put his head back inside Cal's room and said, "Good to see you, Jack. You too, Cal, and I hope you get out of here soon."

"Thank you," said Cal. "And don't forget. Life's tragedy. We get old too soon. And wise too late."

Frank said, "Good one." He turned to Alene, who stood behind him in the hallway. "I'll have to work late today but how about dinner or something tomorrow night?" She nodded and watched him walk up the hallway toward the elevators. The next day was Friday, and Neal was supposed to take the kids again. Unless he cancelled. Again.

"Was that Mark Twain?" she asked as she walked back into the room. "About getting old too soon and wise too late?"

"Nope," said Cal, "Benjamin Franklin. You should read what he wrote. Jack. Worthwhile."

Jack nodded. "I will, Mr. Baron. And feel better. I'll see you when you get home."

Cal smiled and closed his eyes. Alene waved at Jack, thinking that she'd underestimated him. Then she thought about the shiver she felt when Frank ran his fingers down her arm.

An hour later, she looked up as her father's neurologist, a petite woman whose mouth seemed frozen in a constant frown, rushed through the door. This was the neurologist who'd diagnosed Cal with myasthenia gravis. She nodded to Alene and said, "Hello. I'm Dr. Truong."

Alene said, "We met last year. I'm Cal's older daughter." The doctor nodded and proceeded to review Cal's chart and medication history while painstakingly describing the symptoms of MG as though Alene had never heard of it before.

Cal woke up and said, "Hello, Doc. Have you? Met my daughter? She owns the Whipped. And Sipped café." It was still embarrassing when he bragged about her as if she'd accomplished something noteworthy. He sometimes told random strangers in medical offices, taxicabs, and the lobby of their building, or whenever else she was with him and he found the opportunity. Sometimes he'd also mention that his younger daughter was a lawyer.

"How nice," said Dr. Truong, glued to the computer screen. "You must be very proud." Alene wondered if she ever looked anyone in the eye.

After a few moments she announced that Cal wasn't ready to go home. "He's unable to get in and out of bed by himself, his reflexes are slow, and his numbers aren't optimal."

What numbers? Alene wished her father could have gotten out of the bed and stood up straight while sharing one of his corny jokes. Then the doctor would realize that he was much improved and ready to go home. The previous year at his check-up he'd told Dr. Truong, who had a limited sense of humor, about an older man who tells his doctor that he wants his sex drive lowered. The doctor tells him that it's all in his head, and the old guy responds, "That's exactly why I want it lowered!"

Dr. Truong had smiled politely, but Alene remembered blushing at her dad's inappropriate joke. Now she asked, "Do you think he'll be ready to go home tomorrow?"

Dr. Truong said, "We'll have to see." She spouted more information about Cal's disease that Alene already knew, ending with a warning that these crises could become more frequent. He'd need a lot of attention and at some point, he might require more help. Alene worried about that point. They couldn't afford 24/7 caregiving, but there was no way she'd put him in a nursing home.

Cal was asleep before the doctor left the room. Alene walked out to the hallway. It felt so industrial with the fake tile floors and the pale walls with soothing artwork in matching frames. At least there were windows in the rooms,

113

providing patients with natural light. She felt chilled by the air conditioning and upset that she'd used her limited time with Frank talking about murder. If they could finally have their date the next night, she'd force herself to stop thinking about it.

In the room next door, Julian sat next to his mother, looking dejected. Sylvie was speaking loudly, as usual, and Alene heard her say, "She can't even wear normal clothes with those shoulders."

"She's a swimmer, mother," said Julian. "Swimmers get big shoulders." He looked up and nodded at Alene. "My mother is worked up about Rhea Huff. That's Stanley's daughter-in-law who is married to his older son, Harrison."

Alene waved but didn't stop to chat. She didn't need to know anything else about anyone in that family. Her phone chirped as she walked toward the elevators. She answered Ruthie's call and complained briefly about having Sylvie in the room next door to Cal. Ruthie said, "Don't let her September you, Six."

Alene loved when Ruthie used the secret code that they'd invented back when they were studying for history exams in college. 'September' referred to the 1939 invasion of Poland, which, in their code, meant to not let Sylvie barrel over her.

"Roger that," said Alene. They chatted about the café before hanging up. Then Alene walked back to Cal's room. He seemed to be asleep for the night, so she left the hospital and headed home. She couldn't stop thinking about Julian, and how he'd felt when his mother married Stanley. What if he'd harbored a grudge for the past twenty-two years and kept trying to get rid of Stanley until something finally worked? It would mean that her daughter had learned sixth-grade science from a murderer.

At home, Alene relieved Zuleyka, grabbed some leftover dinner, got the kids to help her clean up, and spent as much time as she could with each child before kissing them goodnight. Finally, alone in bed, Alene thought about who had the most to gain from Stanley's death.

What if Stanley had treated Miles Taylor like he'd treated Alene's trainer, stealing his clients and then threatening to take him to court if he left Better Be Fit? Maybe Miles had been trying to remove his client list out of Stanley's database, and Stanley caught him hacking into the office computer? Or, what if Jocelyn was right, even though Alene thought it unlikely, and Stanley really had tried something with Heather, even though she was his stepdaughter, and she snapped. It had happened in Nabakov's Lolita, and in a depressing novel Alene had read about a twenty-two-year-old woman who then had a psychotic breakdown.

But, thought Alene, there's still a possibility that Stanley put the moves on Phyllie Evans again, and this time she fought back. Julian and Phyllie lived just moments away from the café, so Phyllie could have snuck out anytime. Julian might have thought she was taking a long bath when she was busy fighting with Stanley, who got knocked out when he fell against the desk or the wall. Or Julian might have been sickened that Stanley assaulted Phyllie, and even though he said he'd been at a tournament of some kind that Friday night, he could have gone to Better Be Fit. Maybe the two of them did it together.

And Alene wasn't ready to cross Sylvie off her list, thinking she could have managed to walk home after killing Stanley, and then realized what she'd done. If she flagged a taxi and paid cash for the five-minute drive to the hospital, there was probably no record of it.

Then there was Jocelyn's brother, Harrison Huff, who might have thought his father cut him out of an inheritance. He could have gone over to Stanley's office just to talk, and Stanley could have upset him. Maybe the two of them roughhoused a little, something they'd done hundreds of times, but Stanley's heart suddenly gave out. Harrison might have been too distraught and frightened to call an ambulance. Even if he hadn't killed his father on purpose, thought Alene, he didn't come off all that well.

And what about Lillian's boyfriend, Lawrence Habern? He seemed like a nice guy, but what if he'd helped Stanley engage in tax evasion or some other illegal business dealings. Why had they stopped working together, did Stanley fire Lawrence for a specific reason? Maybe he'd gone over to Better Be Fit to tell Stanley that he was turning himself in and exposing their misdeeds, and Stanley couldn't allow that, so they started fighting. Again, Alene assumed that Stanley knocked himself out by accident, but Frank said he'd been smothered. Had that also been an accident?

Jack Stone wanted her to consider Kofi Lloyd a suspect, but that just seemed too farfetched. Kofi dreamed of creating art, and just because he cruised around town looking for garbage to convert into art didn't mean he was looking for trouble. He was not the kind of person to be sidetracked into bickering with an old white guy who owned a gym.

There was a small voice in Alene's mind telling her that her suspicions were silly, because maybe an unknown stranger happened upon Stanley's open office door and tried to steal something. Stanley might have gotten knocked out trying to protect his business. The intruder might have fled, leaving Stanley collapsed on the ground, his heart slowing down until it stopped.

Alene woke up on Friday morning feeling drugged. After a desultory workout at Michael's gym, she dragged herself into the café. Olly just hugged her without saying anything. She missed his goofy energy, and it was probably the first time he'd left his apartment without calming down his curls. "She didn't come home yet?" Alene asked.

Olly shook his messy hair. "I'm hoping she checked into a spa or something," he said, "and her phone battery must have died, because she hasn't texted me." He didn't sound convinced.

Ruthie and her team had already started baking. The rest of the Friday staff staggered in and got busy. The breakfast rush went smoothly, nothing was burned, not a single drink spilled, and Edith didn't start any arguments. Maybe she was behaving better because of Olly's uncharacteristic reserve.

Instead of serving food with the dramatic flair of someone auditioning for the part of a waiter, Olly slouched to the tables and silently handed over plates. He served the guy who always showed his belly button, and two sleekly white-haired, bespectacled women who were too immersed in conversation to thank him. He handed the usual plates to Toula Savas, again wearing a long-sleeved, shimmery blouse despite the heat, and Royce, who sniped at Toula without touching his food while she began nibbling on her omelet. Alene needed to grill Olly when things slowed down, ask him detailed questions about Jocelyn's other friends and if any of them might be harboring her.

Frank and Lee arrived and sat near the door. Alene liked how Frank took in his surroundings without staring. He could probably draw a picture of everyone in the café. Alene imagined that he remembered each person he saw, what they wore, how they looked, what they carried.

Royce got up from his chair and stormed out of the café, leaving Toula sitting by herself with her omelet. She looked miserable, and Alene debated walking over to offer a friendly ear. Sometimes people needed commiseration, but Toula was dabbing her eyes with a tissue, and Alene decided to respect her privacy. It wasn't the first time she'd seen a marriage fall apart in front of her, although, for all she knew, she was misinterpreting the whole situation. A moment later, Royce stomped back in, sat at his place, and took a sip of his coffee. Toula didn't look thrilled to see him, although a small smile flickered. Alene was glad she'd made the right decision not to meddle.

Kacey's boyfriend locked his bicycle in front and limped into the café with an ugly gash on his leg. Great. Who didn't enjoy seeing blood while sipping a cappuccino? Alene asked Jack Stone, now clearing tables, to guide Kofi back to her office and bring paper towels, antibacterial spray, and a roll of gauze tape.

Edith, who was working at the smoothie counter, immediately started protesting in a loud voice, "You need to send Kacey's boyfriend straight back out the door, Alene. We cannot have wounded bicyclists wandering in off the street as if we're a clinic." Several people got up and left, either because they'd finished, or because they didn't want to hear Edith grousing.

"I'd be so grateful if you could take over for Kacey in the kitchen, Edith," said Alene, turning away before Edith could respond.

Jack ran from Kofi back to Alene, and said, "He doesn't want to go to your office," just as Kofi sat himself down at the closest table. At least he chose a table next to the wall, so he wasn't sitting in the middle of the cafe. Before Alene could reply, Kacey ran out of the kitchen, pulled a chair close and held onto Kofi as Olly blotted, sprayed, and wrapped his leg.

"You should get it looked at, Kofi," Alene said a few moments later, now sitting with a latte at Frank's table.

"It's no big deal," said Kofi.

"You need a clinic," said Kacey, handing him his iced tea. "I can't believe you got hurt again." The city had put in more bicycle lanes, but they should have put them on the other side of the parked cars. And drivers needed more training about looking out for bicyclists.

Kofi glanced at Frank and Lee, and said, "Some fool turned right on a red without looking. He could have killed me."

Kacey squeezed his hand. "Why didn't you call me?" she asked.

Kofi sat stoically in his chair. "I don't know, K," he said. "Sorry."

Frank was sitting close enough to tell Kofi that he should get it looked at. Lee scowled in a way that made Alene think he'd already decided that Kofi was guilty of something or other just because he was Black. Kofi pivoted toward the detectives and said, "It was just down the block. If you weren't so busy enjoying your free coffee, you might have

118

been able to catch the guy who did this to me." Alene wanted to jump up and defend Frank. They weren't beat officers who drove around looking for bad drivers. They didn't even wear uniforms.

Lee looked like he was reaching for his handcuffs, about to arrest Kofi for provoking him. "I'll make sure to pass that along to the next traffic cop I see," said Frank, smiling cheerfully. "Thanks for your input. Kofi, is it? And your last name is what?"

Alene could tell that Frank was joking, but Kofi's face slackened, as if he'd just realized he was now known to two Chicago cops. Kacey tried to divert him, but Kofi looked like he was about to faint.

Lee rose from his chair. "I can drop you off at the clinic on Belmont," he said. "They're good."

Maybe Alene had misjudged Lee. Kofi was hesitant but with Kacey on one side and Olly holding him up on the other, he followed Lee out the door. Now Alene could hear Royce almost hissing at Toula. His voice was low, but something about the way he punctuated made each word sound like a canon shot. Frank leaned closer and whispered, "Do you know those two?"

"She comes in nearly every day, but I've only seen the husband a few times," said Alene.

Frank said, "You know how we were talking about abusive spouses the other day at the hospital? Sometimes, it's hard to know when it's gotten past normal bickering." Toula and Royce stood up then and put their dishes in the bin.

"Are you like a hammer to whom everything looks like a nail?" Alene asked as they watched Toula follow her sullen husband out the door.

Frank laughed. He kissed her goodbye, and she stood for a moment, wondering if anyone could tell that she was tingling all over. It felt good to be falling in love. More customers had come in. Some sat alone, slowly nursing their drinks, focused on their cellphones. Three older women shared breakfast cake and orange-tahini cookies. Two younger women with heavily tattooed arms bent their heads together over what looked like a manuscript. A group of five high school students came in tussling. Alene helped serve them, and at the next lull, checked her phone for an update on her dad. Blanca had texted: "Still no doctor comes."

A while later, Olly, who had been oddly silent while he bandaged Kofi's leg, said, "So, what are the possibilities, and just hear me out on this, that Kofi's accident is somehow connected to Stanley's death?" He picked up an empty tray to bring back to the kitchen.

"I don't know, Olly," said Alene, not seeing it. Maybe this was how Frank felt when she threw scenarios at him. "We live in a big city where people have accidents all the time. It's seems like a stretch to think that there's a connection between two random events."

"Yeah, maybe," said Olly, "but we all just saw Kofi get into a police car with Frank's partner. That's strange, don't you think?"

Alene took a rag to the espresso station. "There's nothing strange about it," she said. "Lee, Frank's partner, saw that Kofi needed medical attention, so he offered to drive him to a clinic."

Olly hugged himself. "I don't believe in coincidence," he said. "Stanley dead. Jocelyn missing. Kofi injured. And I'm not even including rising sea levels, earthquakes, or the melting ice shelf. If I start worrying about everything, I won't stop."

"Those things might have nothing to do with each other," said Alene. She wished people didn't see hidden forces in everything bad that happens.

"It's still weird," said Olly. "And scary."

"I think that the world has always been a precarious place," said Alene, thinking about losing her mother, the failure of her marriage, her dad's autoimmune disease, and her sister not being able to get pregnant. "Jocelyn's going to come back, Kofi is going to be fine, and if the state of the world bothers you, then do something about it. Volunteer to help people who have less than you, help with voter

120

registration, join organizations that are doing good things. But right now, you should be the one cleaning this espresso machine." If only she felt as confident as she sounded. She gave Olly the rag and turned around to serve a statuesque woman with a beaky nose.

"Jocelyn has gone on little walkabouts before," said Olly, just holding the rag. "For all we know, she could be snuggled in someone's bed eating Chinese takeout and watching old movies." That sounded exquisite to Alene, but she wanted to know more about Jocelyn's previous walkabouts.

Jack had come back into the café with the mop and said, "Maybe she doesn't feel the need to tell you every little thing that she's doing, Olly."

He kept surprising Alene. It was a good point. "Isn't it possible that Jocelyn keeps secrets from you?" Alene asked. She pointed to the rag in Olly's hand and gestured to what needed cleaning.

Edith started to speak, but instead turned abruptly and busied herself with cleaning up the smoothie section. She was probably distressed about Jocelyn's disappearance, but wasn't being very vocal about it.

Alene suddenly stopped in the middle of filling a box with apple and blueberry mini pies. "What about Jocelyn's cat? Are you taking care of him, Olly?"

"No," said Olly, dejectedly. "And I'm her best friend. I can't believe she left me hanging like this. Her cat hasn't shown up either."

"Cats only show up when they feel like it," Edith said, "and I can tell you that it never works to beg them. They won't come in until they're good and ready."

Jack said, "I'm sure the cat is okay, Alene." When and how did Jack learn to say exactly the right thing?

Chapter 10

The Sweet Potato Black Bean Soup sold out even though it was the middle of summer and Friday was sweltering. Alene put the pot in the sink and showed Ruthie the text from Frank, who'd written: "Still on for later tonight? Drinks or a walk?"

"Wait just a minute," Ruthie said, glancing at her watch. She always left at 2:00 on Fridays. "Why isn't Frank taking you out to dinner? Why is he suggesting drinks or a walk?"

"Neal is coming to get the kids after work, at nine," Alene said, "and I think a walk sounds great."

"You could bring them to our house for dinner," said Ruthie. "Neal can pick them up whenever he wants. It's never a problem adding a few more to our table."

That was another amazing thing about Ruthie, the ability to feed whoever appeared. Alene said, "You don't mind Neal interrupting your dinner when he comes to get them?"

Ruthie said, "Not if it makes your dating life better, Six."

If only Alene could learn to prioritize doing things for other people in her life. She thanked Ruthie. "I owe you, Nine," she said.

Ruthie squeezed Alene's arm. "You don't owe me anything. It's what friends do." Alene knew she was saying it out loud so the young employees would hear. She was always teaching them how to be more empathetic, and kinder.

Alene left shortly after Ruthie and walked to the hospital. In his room, Blanca was smoothing down Cal's blankets. She wore a long, pale-pink tunic and her hair was held in place with a coordinated scarf. Cal, looking way too thin and colorless, smiled at Alene.

"Cal stays here in hospital," Blanca said, "He needs more steroid."

Cal, his eyes following Blanca's sparkly earrings, said, "You just missed. Dr. Truong. She won't let me go home."

If only she'd left the café earlier. "I thought you were going to call me, Blanca." At least her father had remembered the doctor's name.

"Now I am calling if you don't come," said Blanca, tucking him in and making sure Cal was comfortable. Alene sort of knew what she meant.

Alene texted Zuleyka about meeting the children after camp. Blanca left soon after, and Alene waited until Cal opened his eyes to ask if he wanted his coffee. She'd brought a piece of Ruthie's blueberry cake and another thermos.

"Coffee here is bitter," said Cal. "And the food is terrible. The portions are too small."

Alene wished she had it in her to laugh out loud. Everything was starting to pinch at the edge of her nerves. "You're still sharp, Dad," she said, unwrapping the cake.

Cal said, "Sorry I'm such. A bother. I know you're busy."

She cuffed him lightly on the arm. "But I got all the time in the world for you." It was something he used to say when Alene and Lydia were growing up.

Alene's cellphone rang. It was her sister, calling to ask about Cal. Alene answered, "He's keeping the jokes coming, so he must be feeling better."

Lydia said, "I assume he's going home today."

"No, he's not going home today," said Alene, rubbing her forehead.

Big sigh. "All they do over the weekend is warehouse the patients. Maybe you're not arguing persuasively enough about why Dad should recover at home," said Lydia.

Right, thought Alene, interactions with the doctor should be like a lawyer in court. Cal would probably recover more quickly if he could sleep in his own bed in the hushed apartment without all the buzzing in the hospital. "You're so much better at that than me, Lydia," she said. "Why don't you come and make it happen?"

Lydia said, "I'll have to check with Theo. We might be fully booked all weekend."

"What are you, a hotel?" Alene felt guilty the moment she said it. She really needed to be a better sister if she wanted Lydia to act differently.

"Very amusing," said Lydia, "and by the way, I thought you'd be interested to know that I got a call from Sylvie Huff."

"So, you have two clients whose last name is Huff?" Alene recalled that Lydia had passed a business card to Julian. "What does Sylvie want from you?"

"Legal help, obviously," said Lydia. "I mean, I can't give you all the details, but apparently Stanley rewrote his will so that his oldest son inherits everything. It's complicated. Sylvie thinks everything is in her name, but I'm not sure where she got that idea from. I'm going to have to be very patient in explaining how inheritance law works in the state of Illinois."

"Can you explain it to me too? Alene asked. "I don't understand what happens to Harrison and Jocelyn if Sylvie is the one who gets to make all the decisions about Stanley's estate. Could she give everything to her own children and leave Stanley's kids with nothing?"

"That's obviously not what worries Sylvie," said Lydia. "She's afraid Harrison will force her out of the condo, but you can't throw a surviving spouse out of her home just because the dead spouse wants you to get all of his money. I'll figure it all out and make it clear to all of them."

Alene said. "It's nice of you to help."

"It has nothing to do with being nice," said Lydia. "Sylvie is going to pay me and I'm going to do my job." Lydia explained more legalese to Alene without giving her a chance to ask questions before she abruptly said, "I've got to run but I'll get back to you as soon as I talk to Theo."

Alene dutifully reported everything Lydia had told her. Cal smiled and said, "Lydia will know. What to do." He held up his arms to prevent Alene from smoothing down his hair. He'd never liked being groomed.

Alene was glad that Sylvie wouldn't be kicked out of her home. "Lydia said unless there's an original, notarized copy of a last will, the surviving spouse gets one half of the estate and the children get the other half."

"I know. The lawyer keeps a copy," said Cal.

"That's the problem. Lydia told me that a copy of the will won't count because it has to be an original, but Sylvie doesn't know who has the original," said Alene. She'd forgotten to tell Lydia about Lawrence Habern. He'd probably drafted some of Stanley's legal documents. And why hadn't Stanley kept Sylvie informed about all that? Alene should have realized that something was wrong in her own marriage when Neal stopped sharing financial and business decisions with her. It had been Lydia, who'd represented Alene in her divorce, who'd uncovered shady and illegal financial dealings at Neal's auto dealership. And she'd used that information to get Alene a substantial settlement.

Cal said, "Stanley had money."

Alene wasn't sure if that was a statement or a question. "I don't know, Dad, but Lydia said that if he had more than $100,000 of personal property that's not in a trust, Sylvie will have to go through probate court, which is a big production. At least I think that's what she told me."

Cal said, "Lydia likes explaining things."

"Yes, she's quite the formidable lawyer," said Alene.

"Formidable," said Cal, mumbling a quote about women being like library books.

Alene googled probate court and asked absently, "Who said that, about women being like library books?"

After a few moments, Cal responded, "Who said what?"

She couldn't get him to eat his dinner. It reminded her of when the children were babies, and she'd try to get them to open their mouths so she could shove in a spoonful of mashed peas. Cal just wanted to sleep, so she kissed him goodbye and walked back home, inhaling the summer smells laced with exhaust from Lake Shore Drive. The sun was on the edge of sinking, and the sky was the color of Chagall's America Windows at the Art Institute. That would be a nice place to visit with Frank one day.

Alene called her sister again, wondering if Lydia was going to help with Cal once he got out of the hospital. "I'm in the middle of a million things and trying to get out of the office," Lydia answered. It was after eight o'clock on a Friday night.

Alene felt bad that Lydia was so stressed about her work, her infertility, and who knows what else. "Sorry," Alene said, slowing her pace. She always apologized, even when Lydia was being selfish. What if one day Lydia needed help and Alene was so immersed in her own life that she barely had time to talk on the phone? "Lydia, can you please hang out with Dad tomorrow morning"

Lydia said, "You know Theo and I do all our organizing on Saturday mornings and I can't give that up."

"I understand," Alene said, stopping to take a deep breath, "but I need your help with Dad." Everyone had to find a balance between what they wanted to do and what they needed to do. But Lydia hadn't let Alene help her in any way while she'd endured all those fertility specialists, hormone shots, and failed procedures. "You know I'd help you if you asked, Lydia, even though you don't even keep me in the loop about what's going on with you."

Lydia didn't respond right away. Alene thought she might have been crying. Finally, Lydia said, in a less combative tone, "You're right. I'll be there."

"You'll sit with Dad tomorrow morning?"

"And I'll try to keep you in the loop," said Lydia, already a little impatient.

"Thank you," said Alene, relieved. She could almost see Lydia rubbing her face and moving the palms of her hands down the front of her body, as if she were wiping them off. It was a gesture she'd always used when she was trying to readjust her thoughts. "I promise I'll get to the hospital as soon as I can."

Lydia said, "Don't worry about it. I'm sorry I've been so, I don't know, so unreachable. It has nothing to do with you, Alene, it's just my own stuff. And I just realized that August 6th is coming up. I hope you're going to let Theo and me take you and your new boyfriend out for your birthday dinner."

Just when she'd been thinking that she'd never have a normal relationship with her sister. "That's a sweet idea, Lydia, I'd love it."

"It'll be fun," Lydia answered, "but give me enough time to make good reservations. Okay, I'm going to ..."

"I also have a couple of questions about the law," Alene interrupted, as long as they were getting along so well.

Lydia said, "Fine, but I'm not in the practice of giving out free legal advice."

"Someone's been murdered, Lydia," said Alene, thinking that her sister's transformation had its limits. "I just want to know, could Stanley have made Sylvie sign everything over to him and then cut her out of his legal will?"

"Well, this is Illinois," said Lydia. Talking about the law, like discussing dinner reservations, always cheered her up. Now, she almost bubbled with enthusiasm. "In Illinois, the surviving spouse has the right to one third of everything, no matter what the will says. Even if Stanley wanted everything to go to one of his children, Sylvie would still get a third of his estate." Alene could hear her typing away at the computer. It was a mystery how she could simultaneously talk and work.

"But it was all her property to begin with, and when they got married, Stanley made Sylvie sign everything over to him," said Alene. "Are you saying that she would only get one third of the money or property that actually belonged to her?"

Lydia said, "Truthfully, Alene, the lawyers will take care of it."

"Okay, I guess," said Alene. Maybe Lydia knew all about the situation because she'd signed Sylvie up as a client. "And I forgot to tell you about Lawrence Habern, Lillian's boyfriend. He was Stanley's lawyer until about five years ago so maybe he still has some of Stanley's important documents."

"I know all about him," Lydia said. "Look, Alene, Sylvie could renounce Stanley's will, but it would be hard to prove that she was coerced into signing anything. What exactly are you worried about?"

"I'm worried about Jocelyn," said Alene. "Her father stopped talking to her and she never had a relationship with Sylvie. I'm worried she won't inherit a penny." Alene entered the building's lobby, waved at the doorman, and headed to the elevator, nodding on the way at a neighbor hobbling by on crutches.

Lydia said, "Isn't Jocelyn like twenty-two or something? You're almost old enough to be her mother."

As if age had anything to do with anything. This was her longest conversation with Lydia in ages. "Only if I started having children at fourteen, Lydia. She's twenty-four. And she might be a suspect in her father's murder, which would mean she could use money to hire a good lawyer. She's also trying to save up for more gender confirmation surgery."

"I could only help with her inheritance issues," said Lydia. "You should give her my name. And I know a good defense attorney." Lydia suddenly sounded animated. "He's gotten a lot of slimy characters off on technicalities. Jocelyn will need to mention my name so I can get a cut. I'll text you the exact language she should use."

"She's not a slimy character," said Alene, wondering how much she really knew about Jocelyn, who'd only worked at the café for six months. "She doesn't need the kind of lawyer who gets criminals off on technicalities, but I'll get back to you if she needs your help." She hadn't told Lydia that Jocelyn was missing.

"I'm serious, Alene, you could help me for a change. I've asked you before to give my name to your friends. They should all have legal wills."

"Okay, Lydia," said Alene, who didn't want to suggest post-death financial planning to anyone she knew. Maybe she'd just walk into the elevator and the call would drop without her participation.

"Or real-estate closings," Lydia added. "They're my bread and butter."

Alene said, "Got it." She needed to get cleaned up and changed before meeting Frank. "You should bring business cards tomorrow and I promise I'll get there as soon as I can leave the café."

"You're the owner," said Lydia. "You should be able to leave whenever you need to."

"It doesn't work that way," Alene said, hoping she still had enough time to shower, choose something cute to wear, dry her hair and apply some tinted lip gloss. "Anyway, I'll see you tomorrow." She clicked off and pressed the elevator button before Lydia could respond.

The doors opened, and Heather Evans and Miles Taylor stepped out of the elevator. Miles was carrying a banker's box. They both froze. Alene had often passed Julian pushing his stroller through the lobby, but she hardly ever saw Heather in the building. And now here she was, just when Alene needed to get ready for her date. If she kept being interrupted, her relationship with Frank could turn into one of the most chaste ones she'd ever had.

"Hello," said Alene. Miles had already been on her list of suspects, but what if the two of them did it together? And

If Miles had been able to smother a big guy like Stanley, it wouldn't be that difficult for him to snuff out Alene. She backed away, hoping they'd move along.

"My mother's condo is a mess," said Heather, still standing in front of the elevator, "so we came to help organize and clean up." Alene thought she looked more like someone who'd just gotten away with something than someone involved in doing a good deed. According to Julian, Heather was selfish and rarely did anything to help their mother, but Alene remembered Sylvie saying that her children were going to prove she owned everything before Stanley made her sign it over to him.

Alene said, "That was nice of you." They could have just smiled and gone on their way. Guilty people were the ones who felt the need to explain themselves. Maybe Frank should question them about stealing documents.

Heather noticed her looking at the box and said, "It's for my mother."

Alene, who couldn't wait to stop thinking about that entire family, stepped past Heather and Miles into the elevator and said, "Okay."

Heather nodded. "We were looking for Stanley's will."

Alene thought she'd scream if she heard anything else about Stanley or his frigging will. "Hope you were successful," she said.

"We weren't sure, so we just took a bunch of things," said Miles. "It took a long time to plough through all the drawers."

Yeah, I bet it did, thought Alene. She smiled, pressed the button, and said she hoped Sylvie was feeling better. The door closed before either of them could respond.

The elevator opened on a completely silent sixth floor. Alene's elderly neighbor was probably already in bed, Brianne was running her bar, Jack Stone was probably watching television, and his mother was still in a nursing home after her fall in the stairwell six weeks before. Kacey Vanza was probably perched at Brianne's bar, bantering with her boyfriend while he served drinks.

Alene turned the key in the door and dumped her purse on the table. Hopefully, Neal had picked the kids up from Ruthie's as planned, although worst case scenario, they'd just sleep at the Rosins'. She sent a text to Neal, and another to Sierra since Neal never responded right away. It felt strange to be alone in the apartment and there was stuff everywhere that needed putting away. What if, after walking her home from the bar, Frank took one look at the massive chaos, and changed his mind about her?

She flew through the apartment picking up the kids' toys, books, and clothes, and dumping them on their beds. Then she grabbed a few leftovers to pass as dinner. Sierra called and told Alene she was in one of the Rosins' upstairs bathrooms so nobody could hear that she was using her cellphone. First, she said, Alene needed to learn how to make sweet potatoes like Ruthie's. It was one of the best things she'd ever tasted. And second, Dad was going to pick them up in thirty minutes, but Quinn and Noah wanted to stay at the Rosins' and there was probably going to be a huge fight when their father came to get them. "Don't worry about it, Sweetie," Alene told Sierra. "Let Dad figure out what to do about Quinn and Noah." Alene clicked off thinking that it was good for Neal to learn how to solve the kind of child-related dilemmas that she had to deal with every single day.

Frank called after her shower while she was brushing her hair. "Ready for that drink?"

"Absolutely," she said, imagining how they'd lean into each other at the bar, talking about this and that, but both thinking about getting back to her bedroom. They'd hold hands on the way home, and hopefully not say a word about Stanley Huff. Better get that cleared up now. "And Frank, remind me to tell you about seeing Heather and Miles coming out of the elevator with a box of papers from Sylvie's apartment."

Frank said, "You've just told me, and I can be there in fifteen."

She put on a black skirt with a peacock blue blouse that Ruthie had once given her for her birthday. Frank had already complimented her on it once before. Her only concern should be whether this relationship was going to move forward. Alene finished her hair, put on mascara and lip gloss, made sure her fingernails were clean, and headed out the door.

Frank was already sitting at the bar chatting with the owner, Alene's good friend, Brianne. They could have met at a different bar or restaurant where they were unlikely to see someone they knew, but Tipped was Alene's favorite place. She noticed Frank's profile first, his chin jutting out just a bit, his high forehead and muscular neck. As Alene approached, he ran his fingers through his hair, looking relaxed. It didn't look like Kofi was working, but maybe he hadn't started his bartending shift. She touched Frank's shoulder and he pulled her closer to kiss her cheek. Even that made her a little lightheaded.

"So, what's happening tonight?" asked Brianne, offering Alene her usual stout and brushing light-brown bangs from her forehead with the back of her hand. She used the rag swung over her shoulder to mop up a spill on the counter in front of her.

Frank said, "We're finally out on the town."

"It's a start," said Brianne, adding wedges of lime to glasses that were whisked away by a curly-headed waitress who was the same height as twelve-year-old Sierra. "Have fun, kids." Alene wished Brianne wasn't still alone after losing her husband eight years before. She was in her fifties, petite and still beautiful, with smooth skin and her hair dyed a warm brown. Brianne once told Alene that since her husband, Dennis, died, she hadn't slept more than four hours a night. She was always tired, but that didn't stop her from running a successful business.

Now she turned to pour a couple of beers for two cherubic-looking kids sitting at the end of the bar. She said, for Frank's benefit, "Stand down, officer. I already carded them." They heard the word "officer," grabbed their beers, and scurried away from the bar, out of Frank's sight.

133

Alene followed him to an empty table, admiring his broad back and wondering if he'd notice her lightly touching one of his biceps. They sat in a booth facing each other, bathed in a flattering, low light that made everyone glow. She didn't recognize the music playing but it made her wish Brianne had a dance floor. Frank smiled at her and asked about her father.

"I'm hoping he'll come home on Monday," she answered. It was thoughtful of Frank to ask. They chatted, and she wanted to ask about Jocelyn, but it would break the mood. The bars closer to Wrigley Field were filled with kids in their twenties sloshing beer and yelling over a pulsing beat, but Tipped was the kind of place where you could go for a date. In addition to the soft lighting, the booths were comfortably private, and the background music allowed conversation. Frank started talking about Lake Michigan, and Alene asked if he ever missed having a boat. He'd sold his boat while going through a divorce. She could tell he missed it because every time they walked past one of the harbors, he told wistful boating stories and gazed longingly at all the other boats. Now, he admitted to missing time on the lake more than the upkeep his boat had required.

They'd almost finished their drinks when she finally asked if he had any cases more interesting than the one Olly had taken to calling, "Stanley-palooza."

"Yeah, about that," Frank murmured after a sip. "It's another one we would've solved already if we weren't so overworked. Our rate of solving cases is way lower than it should be." She wanted to caress the crinkles that edged his eyes. He didn't complain as much as present the situation. "Have you uncovered anything interesting in your own investigation?"

"What I do is closer to snooping," said Alene. "Especially since Sylvie's hospital room is next to my father's. That was an irritating coincidence."

"Did it feel like a personal invitation to participate?" He brought the glass to his mouth.

Alene took a sip of her mocha stout and tried to subtly wipe her mouth. She loved the dark, chocolatey taste, but it was even more delicious baked into a cake. "It was more like the world demanded it of me," she said, thinking about her dad being kept awake by Sylvie's booming voice. "I want to be there for people I care about, like Jocelyn. I know she didn't murder her father."

"It doesn't look good that she disappeared," said Frank.

Alene set her glass on the table. "Maybe not, but I'm worried that whoever murdered her father came after her. Or it could be even worse – suicide rates are high for transgendered people."

Frank shook his head. "We looked in her apartment, Alene, and we know that she took a suitcase." She stared at Frank with her mouth open. Why hadn't Olly mentioned that? It changed everything.

"She's going to show up," Frank continued as Alene closed her mouth, "but she ran away after a serious crime was committed. I'm sorry, but she's still a suspect."

Alene was about to argue that Jocelyn was probably afraid of being next, but Frank added, "I'm awed by how much you care about your employees."

"I do," she said. "They're so young, except for Edith, of course. Olly and Jocelyn have been friends since they were kids. Hold on, let me show you something." She took out her phone and pulled up the picture of Olly and Jocelyn as teenagers, leaning against a car. "Recognize these tough guys?"

He took a moment. "Yeah, Olly looks the same. Nice Mustang. A lot of us dressed like that in high school," said Frank, smiling. "We all thought we were tough guys. At least I did, until someone beat the crap out of me, and I ended up in the hospital."

Alene said, "I hope they caught whoever did it."

"It was my father," said Frank.

Alene covered her mouth with both hands, imagining the kind of person who would beat up a teenager. That was

135

the most personal thing Frank had ever told her. "That's horrifying," she said. "You must have been shocked."

"Yes, but I wasn't surprised," he said. "He pushed me around for years. I had a lot of time to think while I got back on my feet, and the police helped me a lot. That's when I decided to go into law enforcement." Frank finished his beer. She wanted to ask more questions, but he smiled at her and said, "Let's get out of here."

She liked that he wove his fingers with hers as they walked to his car. They left it with the doorman at her building. Alene's mind felt calm, but her body was on edge. She unlocked her door, he followed her down the hall to her room, and then he was gently holding both sides of her face and kissing her softly.

The night was exactly as she'd imagined, only better, and slower, with more caressing.

***

Alene woke up to her phone ringing. It was Lillian saying that she and Lawrence had been in a car accident. He'd been checked into St. Darius Hospital.

Chapter 11

Lillian was bruised, she told Alene in a thin voice, and Lawrence was bruised and cut up. At least he hadn't broken anything. "I'm sorry to bother you so early in the morning," Lillian said. She probably needed to tell someone and had nobody else to call, because Ruthie and Benjie never used their phones on Saturdays. Alene knew all about their sabbath observance and had always loved going over to their house on Friday nights or Saturday afternoons. She especially liked to bring her children, who were forced to interact with each other and the other children, because the Rosins' didn't use electricity or any devices on Saturdays. It was always a pleasure to work on puzzles, play board games, take walks, or visit with their other friends who popped in. Lillian was not as observant of the Sabbath as her daughter.

"No problem, Lillian, I had to get up anyway," Alene whispered as she tiptoed out of the bedroom. She quietly closed the door, glancing back at Frank, who pulled a pillow over his head. She could only see his broad back. "I'm so sorry. Was anyone else hurt?"

Lillian sounded weary. "The other car disappeared before I even noticed its color." Now Alene was wide awake.

Had it really been an accident or had somebody tried to hurt Stanley's former lawyer? What if one of Sylvie's kids learned that Lawrence had the original copy of Stanley's Last Will and Testament, and thought that they wouldn't get any money if it was revealed? Or, what if Harrison had a reason for preventing the original will from coming out? What if Lawrence had threatened Stanley or Sylvie's kids with what he knew? Had he brought the accident on himself? Lillian added, "It was unspeakably awful for Lawrence. They had to pull pieces of glass out of his face and stitch up his leg."

"How can I help, Lillian?" Alene asked, feeling uneasy as she walked into the kitchen. What if whoever murdered Stanley had been following Lawrence, waiting for an opportunity to strike? And why would anyone want to hurt Lillian?

Alene had loved Ruthie's mother since first being paired as roommates with Ruthie. Lillian had brought care packages to their Northwestern dorm, had taken them out for good meals, and opened her home to Alene. There'd been times when Alene had been overwhelmed with envy, and in the years after her mother died, she and Ruthie had plotted to bring her father and Ruthie's mother together, but it hadn't worked. They liked each other, but not in that way. "I have to open this morning," Alene said, "but I can get to the hospital by nine or nine-thirty. Can I bring you something to eat?"

"Thanks, Alene, but Lawrence is drugged up," said Lillian, sounding exhausted. "All I really need is sleep, and an extra phone charger for an Android."

"I'm on it," said Alene. She'd pack up some nourishing soup, a few healthy dips, and a selection of breads from the café, so that Lillian wouldn't have to eat any bland hospital food.

"You're a sweetheart," said Lillian. She abruptly clicked off before Alene could wish her well.

Frank came out of the bedroom wearing boxers and a concerned smile. She told him about Lillian's car accident. "It's too late to find someone else to open this morning," she said, "but Lillian sounded both depleted and distraught. I wish I could get the charger to her sooner."

Frank said, "I'm off today. I could bring it to her."

Alene inhaled sharply. When they were dating, Neal had been fun and spontaneous, but he'd never impulsively offered to help anyone. He was always about the quid pro quo, and she'd just glossed over his self-absorption. Frank might be someone she could count on. Lillian would probably enjoy having a real police officer to complain to. After Lillian got Frank to promise to find the hit-and-run driver, she'd grumble about potholes that hadn't been fixed since winter ended, and stoplights where drivers always behaved badly. Frank would diligently note everything she said, and Lillian would come out of the hospital feeling like she'd accomplished something.

Alene gave Frank a big hug and thanked him. Frank kissed her neck, and whispered, "It's what friends do for each other." If only they could have gone back to bed. It had been heaven to sleep for nearly six hours, much of it with his arm draped over her. But twenty minutes later, they were both in the elevator heading down, holding hands until the door opened in the lobby.

In the alley behind the café, Kacey was already leaning against the wall, a Mona Lisa smile on her usually passive face. Kofi had stayed the whole night, she said. Alene smiled. It was good to see Kacey looking so uncharacteristically content. "How'd it go?" she asked.

"Wonderful," said Kacey, her eyes dreamy. "We talked a lot, also. And at about eleven, we heard Jack open the front door, but he went to his room without noticing that Kofi was over." Jack's mother, who'd been married to Kacey's father, had been recuperating from a fall for the past six weeks and was still not back home. Kacey's father had recently died, and she was overcoming a tortured adolescence and drug dependence along with her grief, so Alene understood why she still lived in the apartment where she'd grown up. She was also a decade younger than Jack, who should have moved out long before. Jack and Kacey were both still living in their childhood bedrooms, but one day they'd both have to adult up and pay rent somewhere.

"You go, girl," said Alene as she unlocked the café door and turned off the alarm. She wondered where Jack spent his evenings now that he was sober and no longer selling drugs. He'd come far in the six weeks he'd worked at Whipped and Sipped. His mother, when she finally came home from the rehab facility, would be amazed at his transformation.

Kacey was smiling more than she'd smiled in a decade. "Kofi is really sweet and considerate," she said. "I can't believe this is happening." She gestured to indicate everything around her.

"I'm happy for you," said Alene. But Kacey had only known Kofi for a short time. Was he the kind of person who would go to the hospital to visit one of Kacey's friends? How did he spend his time when he wasn't searching for junk to turn into art, or working as a bartender at Tipped?

"How do you guys get around the city?" Alene asked, just to be sure that Kofi hadn't been involved in the hit-and-run that hurt Lawrence. "Does Kofi have a car?"

"We mostly take the bus," said Kacey, "but occasionally, when he needs to haul something big, he borrows a car from one of his cousins."

"Oh," Alene responded, relieved that Kofi couldn't have been involved. After Kacey's father, Gary, died earlier that summer, Alene had suspected everyone she knew of murdering him. Her suspicions and meddling hadn't accomplished anything. Frank would talk to Lillian and ask the right questions. Maybe he'd look up the official report and check the intersection. Maybe there'd been a traffic camera that had gotten the license plate of the other car, or a witness who'd seen the whole accident.

As they hurried to turn on the ovens and remove batters, eggs, and vegetables from the refrigerators, Kacey said, "In some ways it was a perfect night, but I felt bad for having such a good time while Jocelyn is out there somewhere, hopefully not lying in a ditch." She spoke in a hushed voice even though it was just the two of them. "We should be doing something, Alene, like searching for her."

"I've thought about it, but where would we start?" Alene asked. "I'm worried too, but Jocelyn knows how to take care of herself. She's had survival training, and maybe she decided to hide, you know, to lay low until they find the murderer."

She started another of Ruthie's vegan, protein-packed breakfast cakes. They had to come up with a tastier sounding name than Orange/Banana/Apple Cake. Something cheerful, maybe Sunshine Cake. "There's something else bothering me," Alene added. She told Kacey about Heather and Miles, the elevator, and the box of papers.

"What's up with these people who still use paper?" Kacey asked as she peeled and sliced cucumbers. "Old people like Sylvie don't seem to get the overall purpose of technology."

Alene looked at the floor. She still liked using paper sometimes. How else could she put loving notes in the kids' lunches? "Lawyers still use paper, Kacey," she said as she stirred together oats, slivered almonds, maple syrup and cinnamon to sprinkle on top of the cake. "I'm heading to the hospital after the breakfast rush and I'm going to ask Sylvie about those papers." She'd take care of it after she'd seen her father and stopped by to bring Lillian and Lawrence some food from the café.

"I'm sure Sylvie will give you a clear and lucid answer," Kacey deadpanned. Alene thought about saying, "As always," but she was trying to be less judgmental.

Kacey added, "Jocelyn thought Stanley and Sylvie were afraid of her. She said they acted like her gender dysphoria is contagious."

Of course, they made sure that Jocelyn knew how uncomfortable she made them, which no doubt made her feel even worse about herself. Maybe people have an obligation to avoid making others uncomfortable by their behavior, but what if the discomfort is caused by their very existence? Alene was reminded of The Elephant Man, a play she'd once seen, based on a true story about a man with a congenital condition that caused massive, terrible-looking deformities. The protagonist made people extremely uncomfortable, until his manners and erudition won them over. She said, "As Ruthie reminds me all the time, everyone has limitations."

"But Ruthie's not here," Kacey said, "so we can agree that Stanley and Sylvie are horrible." They both washed their hands and Alene divided, kneaded, and shaped a batch of dough into loaves while Kacey moved onto chopping onions. She could do it without crying, and they used pounds and pounds every day. On the other side of the kitchen, Alene inhaled the tantalizing smells of cinnamon and chocolate, but the calm moment passed, and her thoughts started churning again. Dad. Children. Jocelyn. Murderer.

The rest of the staff came in at seven and got to work. Alene asked Olly to take over the weekly story reading hour and got him a stack of books to choose from. She reminded Jack to set it up over by the crimson wall so the kids could sit on the floor and the parents or caregivers on chairs.

She was also going to mention that it was time for Olly to re-curate the wall, but he looked like he'd hardly slept, and his carrot top was a wiry halo. She'd never seen him so bedraggled. "I already texted Frank twice this morning," he said, his freckled skin nearly translucent. "I want to know what they're doing to find Jocelyn."

Alene gave Olly a quick hug. "He's off today, but he's going to call me the second he hears anything," said Alene. She told Olly about Lillian and Lawrence's accident.

Olly scowled. "I'd like to murder all hit-and-run drivers, not literally, but you know what I mean."

"Yeah, I know," said Alene. She kind of felt that way too.

Jack Stone set up the story hour and finished polishing the front window. Then he started scrubbing the bowls, utensils, and pans already dirty from the early-morning batches. He blushed when Alene told him that he'd won the award for most industrious employee of the day. She should complement her employees more often, especially those like Jack, who hadn't ever received much validation.

Edith Vanza cut up vegetables for the smoothie station while complaining loudly about the heat, and cats throwing up and crying in the night, until she realized that she wasn't going to get any sympathy. "Jocelyn is the only one who cares about me," she whined.

"We all miss Jocelyn," said Alene. Jocelyn's relationship with Edith made it easier for Alene to honor her promise to Edith's brother. Back when he sold her the café, she'd assured him that Edith would always have a job.

Alene unlocked the front door and headed back to the counter as the first customers, a spandex-clad, toned couple, came in. Then came four well-dressed women who worked at a nearby bank and showed up frequently. Alene greeted them by name. Toula came in still in her workout clothes and sat near the crimson wall, probably waiting for her husband to arrive before she ordered anything. Alene glanced at the bruises on her arms and legs and thought she'd better find a new trainer so she wouldn't keep hurting herself while lifting weights.

Toula's eyes lit up as she approached the table, so Alene sat down to chat. She asked Toula about her speech therapy patients, and at some point in the conversation, Toula started to tell Alene about her husband. He worked for a large construction company and they'd been married for nearly eight years. No children, but they fostered dogs from a private shelter. Alene shared a little of her own story, and they figured out that they shared a love of the impressionist rooms at the Art Institute, the new River Walk, and Lou Malnati's pizza. Then Alene told her about Cal, and how he didn't have enough energy to say a full sentence. Toula suggested vocal and breathing exercises that might help.

Toula mentioned that she missed training with Stanley Huff, who'd completely re-sculpted her body. She turned this way and that, so Alene could admire her flat tummy and muscular arms. Alene had thought they were about the same age, and gasped when she learned that Toula was forty-three. "You've got to stop doing those weights by yourself. Just let me know if you want my trainer's number," Alene reminded her before jumping up to help behind the counter.

After a while, she noticed a lanky man with hair plugs lined up like soldiers at the top of his forehead. Standing behind him was a woman with short hair and broad shoulders, wearing a sleeveless citrine-colored dress. The man was tall, with prominent cheekbones and the same startling blue eyes as Jocelyn's. It had to be Harrison Huff and his wife. Alene tried not to stare as she took their order. Sylvie had said he sold houses or something. This was the guy she thought was going to kick her out of the condo.

Harrison's hair plugs weren't that horrific. He shared Jocelyn's wide forehead and lush eyelashes, but he was heftier. Alene wondered if they'd looked alike as children, with those splendidly arched eyebrows and long faces.

Olly hurried into the kitchen and didn't come out until the Huffs left. Alene was busy at the counter, but she wished she'd had Olly follow them back to their car. Harrison was fourth on her list of suspects, after Miles, Phyllie and Sylvie. Olly could have inspected the front fender for evidence of a recent collision. Could Harrison and Rhea have been worried about Lawrence turning up with an original will that was not in their favor? Why else would they have murdered Stanley and tried to kill Lawrence? That is, if that's what the car accident had been about.

Alene was weary of the entire situation. Was everything connected or was it all just happenstance? Was Lawrence involved or not? Was it about Stanley's will? Hadn't Lydia said that the spouse gets a third of the estate no matter what's written in the will? Was anyone on Alene's list so desperately struggling with life that murdering Stanley seemed like the best option? No, they were all basically doing fine. Nobody had a good enough reason to take someone's life, even if that someone was an irritating, obnoxious man who always reeked of aftershave.

After at least a dozen more customers, Julian Evans pushed his stroller through the door. He was followed by three women with babies snuggled into forward-facing slings. Alene only knew one of their names but greeted them all with equal enthusiasm. She had a fleeting desire to ask the one with the most adorable baby for a quick cuddle, but the moment passed.

Julian parked the stroller at the table, annoyingly close to the counter, and approached Alene to order. Both boys were immediately out of the stroller and pressing their grubby hands and noses against the clean glass display case.

Alene could understand its allure – all those breads, cookies, brownies, cakes, and pastries. There were many scrumptious-looking things, all healthier than at just about every other bakery and café in the city. The two boys were getting in the way of customers standing in line. A cute young guy with snow-white hair and a skintight shirt stood behind the baby-carrying mothers. Then there were two women with similarly spiky hair, and large dangling earrings. It was funny how people tended to have friends or partners who resembled them, kind of like Julian and Phyllie with their frizzy hair and chocolate-colored eyes.

"Hey, Julian," Alene said finally, "could you please move your stroller and your children to a table farther from the counter? I'm afraid someone will trample on their little feet if they're not sitting down." She hoped she'd sounded friendly enough.

"Children should be sitting at all times in their seats," Edith called out from the smoothie section. She was like a Greek chorus, repeating what had already been said. "People are carrying hot drinks that could cause third-degree burns if they were spilled." Great thing to tell people in a café, thought Alene.

"Oh, I'm sorry, of course," said Julian, distractedly sweeping up his boys and placing them in their seats. But they didn't move to a different table. The older boy jumped up and ran back to the display case while Julian held onto the little one's shirt so he couldn't get down from his chair.

145

Then they settled down. The line at the counter moved quickly. Within moments they'd sold all four of their chocolate babkas, and Alene signaled to LaTonya, who promptly headed into the kitchen with the empty tray.

The little boys were making a big mess at the table when Heather and Miles arrived. They pulled two chairs from other tables and joined Julian, sitting close enough to the counter for Alene to hear their conversation. It wasn't even nine in the morning, but Alene started to think about leaving.

"I'll wait until the line lets up before I order," Miles said, dangling something he pulled from his pocket. "Want to look at my keychain, Ethan?" Alene watched Miles offer his keys, which, she noticed, were attached to a Swiss Army knife.

The two-year-old, with chocolate smeared around his mouth like a two-day shadow, grunted as he reached for the knife. Just as Alene was about to dive over the counter and lunge toward the table, Julian grabbed the keys and handed them back to Miles.

"What kind of idiot gives a knife to children?" Edith piped up in a loud enough voice for the whole café to hear. Alene shot her a disapproving look, but Edith had already turned her head. Miles apologized to Julian and said he didn't know much about children. As if he needed someone to tell him not to give a sharp instrument to anyone who didn't know how to sign their name.

Back in the kitchen, Kacey stopped Alene and asked if there was an update about Jocelyn. Alene picked up a hunk of dough and used a kitchen scale to divide it into thirty-six equal portions. As they worked, Alene said, "I can't stop thinking about Jocelyn. What if she found the original copy of her father's will, the version that included her as his child?"

Kacey said, "I can't imagine a father not including one of his own children."

"That's because your father was a good person," said Alene. "And even if your brothers have issues, I don't think they'd ever hurt you." She lowered her voice, "What if Jocelyn's brother tried to erase evidence of the original will so he could inherit everything?"

Kacey said, "I guess that's possible." She didn't look convinced.

"Or maybe Harrison tried to silence Lawrence, who probably knew all about who was supposed to inherit Stanley's estate," Alene continued.

Kacey said, "Maybe, but you're just guessing. There has to be proof."

"I know there has to be proof, but I'm just working through different scenarios. Here's another one," said Alene. "Maybe Miles and Heather were blackmailing Stanley. What if Heather enticed Stanley into sexually assaulting her again, and Miles filmed it?"

"That seems kind of farfetched, Alene," Kacey said. "We don't know what happened, and I don't understand why you think you need to solve it. Can't you let Frank figure it out? That's his job, right?"

Alene smashed one of the balls of dough onto the table. "You're right, but how do I shut myself up?"

Jack walked past them both, and said, "When I can't shut myself up, I try to imagine that I'm in the lake, letting the waves push me towards the shore. It's a trick I learned from one of my therapists." Alene wouldn't have expected advice from Jack to be successful, but she spent the next few minutes trying it, and it worked. She imagined being in the lake with Frank at her side, and her jumbled thoughts quieted down.

She covered the finished balls of dough to rest for a second rising and went back out to the café to pack a bag to take to the hospital. Customers still sat in groups of two and three, sipping, nibbling, talking. She'd be able to leave now. Heather and Miles were still sitting with Julian. The older child was busy with a box of crayons and the younger one had fallen asleep in his stroller, his face a mess of chocolate.

Alene scanned the room. Here was a woman with long eyelashes carrying her fluffy support dog and there was a

147

fine-boned man with wire-rimmed glasses and long, tapered fingers. The family who'd come in the previous week with two pink-clad little girls now had them dressed in matching canary yellow outfits. At least five people were glued to screens of one kind or another. What a pleasure, Alene noticed, that people weren't toting around Better Be Fit bags now that it was temporarily closed. Edith could barely keep up with smoothie sales, they'd sold out all their muffins, and she needed to make a new batch vegetable and bean spreads. Alene felt nothing but relief that Stanley was gone. Not guilt, not sadness, nothing.

Chapter 12

Just as Alene was about to leave, Kofi limped through the door, his leg covered in a professional-looking bandage. He shuffled over to Julian and Heather's table. Alene saw him scowl and heard him growl something that sounded harsh, but Julian didn't respond. She wondered how they knew each other. Last thing she needed on a lazy Saturday morning was to deal with personal disputes.

Alene made her way to the table, but Olly got there first. He began removing empty cups and shooting the breeze with Kofi, asking if he'd found anything worthwhile that morning, and wondering if the gash on his leg was healing all right. Jack had followed Olly out of the kitchen and hovered near the table with a broom.

"I found a rusted tricycle and locked it with my bike," Kofi said, flashing his dimples. "I can do a lot with a rusted tricycle." Julian kept his eyes on his plate, clearly relieved that Kofi's attention was distracted.

"Like what can you do with a rusted tricycle?" Jack asked."

"Truth is," said Olly, sounding a little too enthusiastic. "I'm standing here because there were some raised voices coming from this table, and I want to remind you that you shouldn't be bringing your little squabbles into Alene's café."

"Cut it out, Olly," said Julian, with a weary sigh. "And I didn't say a word."

"That's because you don't have a leg to stand on," Kofi said, "You were at the tournament, Olly, and you know why I don't want to see his face."

Jack whispered to Alene, "I'll just stand here in case things get out of hand." Alene gave him a thumbs up. It was another sign that Jack was becoming more of a team player.

Olly circled the table, talking non-stop. "It was very exciting to watch you in action, Julian," he said. "I admit it, I had no idea you could move that quickly. I gotta say, there's nothing I like better than watching two men in physical combat. Especially when one of them cheats."

Kofi hadn't moved. "Just leave," he said quietly to Julian. Kacey had reached Kofi by then and tried to pull him away from the table. Alene helped Julian buckle in his kids, and when they'd finished, he pushed the stroller out the door without speaking. Jack cleaned up their mess.

Alene grabbed Olly before he could return to the kitchen. "What just happened?" she asked. "Why did Kofi want Julian to leave?"

Olly pantomimed pulling a gun from a holster as he swaggered, saying, "Because that's how we handle things here at the O.K. Corral, little missy." Sometimes he refused to be serious.

Edith called out from the smoothie section, "I thought it was extremely rude of Kofi, and you shouldn't allow that sort of thing, Alene. We can't have people coming in off the street and being rude to our customers."

Alene didn't respond. She lifted an eyebrow and Olly laughed. "Well, if you must know, last Friday night, there was a bit of an incident, and those two gunslingers duked it out," he said.

Alene followed Olly into the kitchen wanting more details, and Edith tailed closely behind. "I hope you don't mean they were shooting guns at each other," Edith said.

150

"No, Edith, I was joking. They were actually at a Jiu-Jitsu competition," said Olly. He headed to the sink to wash his hands.

"Why didn't I know that?" Alene asked.

"You did know it, Alene," said Edith. "Julian told you that's where he was when his mother was rushed to the hospital. That was the day he had some acid reflux, and I suggested..."

"Fighting is what people are supposed to do at a competition," Olly said, interrupting Edith, "but Julian broke some rules. You know I've been trying to get you to take a Jiu-Jitsu class for the past three years. Seriously, Alene, it'll change your life."

"What do you mean when you say that Julian broke some rules?" asked Alene. Even though she needed to get to the hospital, she had to get to the bottom of this first.

Olly said, "It was kind of sad. Julian Evans, also known as the-Incredible-Hulk-just-before-he-turns-green, made a couple of illegal moves. It's a guaranteed way to get kicked out."

"What exactly did he do?" Alene asked. She couldn't believe Julian Evans was a competitive fighter. He always seemed so lethargic, and he'd been such a meek teacher, allowing obnoxious sixth graders to disrupt his classroom, according to Sierra, nearly every day.

"I don't know which thing got him kicked out," said Olly. Everyone at the baking table followed the conversation, turning their heads while they continued to knead or measure. "It was either the head butting or the kick to Kofi's groin. I'm not sure the ref noticed the illegal move Julian made with his elbows, but I think I can say, without exaggerating, that Julian Evans is a cheating cheater who cheats." Olly turned his back to Alene to put on oven mitts and lift a tray out of the oven for one of the bakers.

"That's awful," said Alene. Noah had begged her to enroll him in a Jiu-Jitsu class after she'd taken him to observe one of Olly's classes, but she thought it had been way too violent. Jocelyn had tried to convince her that Krav

151

Maga would be a better alternative for all three of the children because they'd learn to protect themselves in real life. Alene had planned to sign them up for after-school classes in the fall. The younger two would probably love it, and she'd let Sierra decide whether or not she wanted to take a class. Ruthie's kids were already doing something or other. Ruthie thought learning self-defense provided character building just like music lessons and team sports.

"Kofi and Julian both come in all the time," said LaTonya. "How'd they miss running into each other before today?"

Everyone in the kitchen had an opinion about it, and LaTonya suggested that Julian always came in the morning, well before Kofi ever showed up. "I don't know and don't care. I just don't want fighting in my café," Alene said, taking off her apron and grabbing her purse from the chair behind her desk.

Julian hadn't seemed like someone who cheated, but she'd already been wrong about him being competitive. And he didn't look like someone who would commit a murder, but it would be silly to assume that murderers were required to look the part. Maybe he'd gotten away with other crimes as well, all because he looked like a nerdy science teacher who wrote science fiction stories and spent a lot of time with his mother. "I'm sure Frank already looked into Julian's story about where he was the night of Stanley's murder," Alene added. She made sure everything was set and said her goodbyes.

Olly followed Alene out the back door. "Did Frank mention anything about the DNA?" Olly asked. "It's been over a week."

Alene turned in the alley and said, "I read that the state is backed up for at least half a year on getting DNA results. I wouldn't even bother asking Frank."

Olly whipped his head around so that his curls bounced. "Guess you'll have to keep Sherlocking it on your own, boss," he said.

She waved goodbye to Olly and started walking to the hospital. She was still thinking about Julian twenty minutes later as she passed Sylvie's room. Sylvie's door was open, and she was asleep. Even from the hallway, Alene could see that her face was puffy, and she didn't look any healthier than she had looked earlier in the week. Maybe her doctors had figured out that there was no cure for narcissism.

Alene rushed past. Cal slept through Alene opening his door, sitting down beside him, and answering emails for twenty minutes. He finally woke up and smiled to see her. "Hello, Sweetheart," he said. His eyes were more focused. "I'm going crazy here." He thumbed towards Sylvie's room.

"If she starts yelling while I'm here," Alene assured him, "I'll go over and say something."

"Can the thing you say be. 'Shut the hell up?" Cal wore his exasperated expression. "Actually, it'll give me. Great pleasure to do it myself." Alene thought his sentences seemed longer.

They heard Sylvie then, her voice like a saw cutting through steel. Alene didn't want her father to get up before he was ready. She said, "I'll take care of it, Dad." She hustled over to Sylvie's open door.

"Well finally," said Sylvie, patting her bed as if she thought Alene was going to come in and sit down next to her. "I've been trying to get your attention. You have no idea how hard it is to be stuck in the hospital."

Alene didn't want to argue. She said, "I'm sorry you're having a hard time Sylvie, but my father can't rest with all the noise coming from this room." As if other people were also shouting and barking out orders.

Sylvie looked confused. "I don't know what noise you're talking about," she said, "but since you're here, I wanted to chat with you. I wasn't going to say anything, but I'd really like to know why you keep using that Polish woman to clean your apartment."

That was a weird non-sequitur. "Are you asking me about Blanca?" she asked. "She's my father's caregiver. Did

153

she do something to upset you?" Alene knew that Blanca enjoyed rattling people who annoyed her.

"Yeah, I'd say so. She slept with my husband, and that's why I fired her." Sylvie pressed her hands together as if she spent most of her day praying, her voice hushed as if she were sharing a state secret that Alene didn't have clearance to hear. "And she never dusted the pictures or move a single chair to clean underneath the dining room table." Sylvie sucked in her cheeks and frowned at Alene over the top of her big red glasses.

Alene remembered Blanca complaining about the Huffs. There was no way she'd have slept with Stanley, and she always dusted the pictures. Also, Sylvie hadn't fired Blanca, she'd quit. Alene said, "You must be mistaken, Sylvie."

Sylvie snorted. "No, I'm not mistaken. That woman is a whore."

Alene shook her head. "That is ridiculous, Sylvie." Blanca was always meeting men through her church, and she would assess their husband potential, gossiping to Alene about how this one made a good living but never laughed, or that one was too stingy to take her out to dinner. Blanca had street smarts and longed for a real relationship. There was no way she'd have slept with a married man, especially not Stanley Huff. She'd thought he was old and pathetic.

The only question, Alene thought with disgust, was why she'd just let Sylvie get under her skin.

Sylvie pointed at Alene and said, "I have proof. Here's a lonely, undocumented Polish girl who can always use extra money, and there's Stanley, who can't stop chasing women."

"That's not proof, Sylvie," said Alene. "She's not a girl and she's lived in this country for over twenty years. She's also not the kind of person who would sleep with someone's husband."

Sylvie said, "Well, maybe she's not like you. Maybe she needs a man."

Alene felt her mouth go dry. What would Ruthie do in this situation? "Shame on you for speaking like that about

154

someone you don't even know," Alene said. At least she'd refrained from using the kind of expletives that Sylvie deserved.

"Oh, I know the kind of person she is," Sylvie said. "Have you seen her diamond stud earrings?" Alene stared out the window at the Chevron sculpture near the Diversey Harbor as Sylvie blathered about how the studs had a diamond on one side and a sapphire on the other. Stanley had given them to her for their fifteenth anniversary, and she kept them in the original velvet box in her jewelry drawer. Alene tuned in when Sylvie added, "Those earrings have disappeared, and Blanca was the one who took them."

Alene took a deep, cleansing breath. "I'm sure you'll find them when you get home, Sylvie," she said. "Blanca would not have stolen your earrings. She has plenty of her own jewelry."

Julian came in the room and Alene nodded at him, thinking that he slouched too much to be a practitioner of Jiu-Jitsu. Not that she knew what they were supposed to look like. She turned to leave without a word. That was the last conversation she intended to have with her no matter how long Sylvie Huff stayed in the hospital.

When Kacey showed up an hour later, Alene was scrolling through Instagram, and Cal was contentedly engrossed in a book about the history of human civilization. "How's everyone?" asked Kacey, kissing Cal on the cheek. He put down his book as Alene vented about Sylvie's accusation. She hadn't shared it yet with her dad.

"It's nonsense," Cal said. "Blanca has better taste than that."

Kacey said, "If I let everyone trigger me the way you do sometimes, Alene, I swear I'd be so twisted in knots I'd probably throw myself in the lake and let the rip tide carry me away."

Alene hated hearing Kacey speak so casually about suicide after everything she'd been through — the drugs, the overdoses, the rehab programs, and then her father's murder. "I don't let everyone trigger me," Alene replied,

155

trying to convince herself that it was true. "Well, most of the time, that is."

"Ruthie would yell at you for listening to Sylvie's gossip," Kacey said. Ruthie never yelled, but she would have been disappointed.

"Blanca is. An exceptional person," said Cal. "I can't wait to be able to take a walk with her. Play a couple of games of chess. Talk about news of the day." He looked wearily at Kacey and Alene, and added, "It's nice to have the two of you here. But I want to go home."

Kacey gave him a rare smile. She stayed in the room chatting with Cal, telling him all about Kofi, until Lydia and Theo came. Kacey got up to leave. Cal, looking disappointed, said, "Plenty of room for everyone. Kacey, honey."

"Plenty of room for everyone," Theo repeated as he pulled a chair closer to the bed. Alene sincerely hoped he made Lydia happy. "How are you doing, Cal?" Theo continued. "My mother sends her regards. Maybe I should get her on the phone." He pulled out his cell. "She'll probably tell you all about the incredible weather they're having in Naples this summer. Not too hot at all."

"Glad to hear she's doing well, Theo," said Alene. She reached for Kacey's hand. They were all used to hearing about Theo's mother. It was nice how much he cared about her, compared to Neal, who only called his mother when he needed her help with the kids. Even though Alene didn't have a lot of patience for Theo, he did all the grocery shopping, cooked dinner when they didn't go out to a restaurant, and had put up with her sister's selfishness for nearly four years. She should be more grateful to him for marrying Lydia. Alene couldn't' imagine how unhappy Lydia would be on her own. "Kacey and I are going to leave now so the two of you can have some time with Dad." She said it in as cheerful, friendly a tone as she could manage, and dragged Kacey out the door before Lydia or Theo had time to look up from their cellphones.

In the hospital lobby, Kacey said goodbye and headed outside, while Alene turned to the reception desk to get

156

Lawrence's room number. When she got there and peeked in, she saw that his face was swollen, pallid, and covered in tiny bandages. The accident must have shattered his car door window. He was asleep and alone in the room, so Alene didn't linger. She'd come back when Lillian was there. Lawrence looked old and fragile, no longer a murder suspect, but he could still be on the murderer's list of victims. Alene thought again about Stanley's legal wills, both the one that included Jocelyn and the one that left everything to Harrison. But wouldn't Harrison have a lawyer of his own, and wouldn't that lawyer have explained how inheritance works in Illinois?

Real life wasn't like in mystery novels, where the suspect soon makes another move that gives the detective enough information to zero in. Maybe she had to go back to the most logical explanation, that Stanley's death was an accident. Somebody came to his office the previous Friday night, started fighting for any number of reasons, Stanley had a heart attack and stopped breathing.

Lydia and Theo greeted Alene as she stepped off the elevator on the tenth floor. "Neal's mother is here now," Lydia said, "so we figured we might as well leave. I guess it's really good that they're friends." Lydia, who initially thought Alene's ex-mother-in-law had nefarious designs on their father, had come around to appreciating their relationship.

Theo repeated his wife's last words, "It's really good that they're friends.". His repeating was a tic of sorts, and Alene tried to be more accepting of it. "Because it isn't easy to be alone at that age," he added. "My mother never found anyone after my father died seventeen years ago. If she lived in Chicago, I know she and Cal would be close friends. She's happy with the weather in Florida, but she's lonely. I'd never give up family for the weather."

"I hear you," said Alene. That was the first time her brother-in-law had said anything even remotely negative about his mother. He hardly ever said anything negative about anything – maybe it made him feel vulnerable to admit that his world wasn't perfect. Or maybe he was just an

157

optimist, which had its pros and cons. What if he was incapable of commiserating with Lydia's suffering regarding her infertility, and she'd had to face all that disappointment on her own? That would explain some of her recent prickliness. Alene wondered how she could help her sister going forward. She wasn't disappointed that Theo and Lydia left so soon after they arrived. It meant more conversation with Mitzi Dunn.

Neal's mother was sitting next to Cal, holding his hand. He loved having his hand held while he dozed. Alene had to remember to do it more often. She and Mitzi started chatting about the children and the café, while Cal nodded and smiled, clearly happy to have them sitting by his side. Alene always thought of Mitzi as her consolation prize for divorcing Neal. She was loving and generous with Alene and the children and always demanded better behavior from her son. Alene was grateful every time Mitzi smoothed over a problem that Neal caused by forgetting to pick up the kids, neglecting to feed them, or disregarding their needs in some way.

When Frank came by a while later, Mitzi whispered to Alene that he seemed like a good guy and shooed the two of them out into the hallway. "You could at least give me some time alone with your father," she said with a wink.

In the hallway with Cal's door closed behind them, Frank kissed her forehead, which was comforting, and asked how both she and her dad were feeling. They spent a long moment gazing at each other until a noise behind her made her jump. It was just someone pushing a cart filled with drinks. Until the distraction, Alene had felt like they'd both been trying to see into each other's souls. Was that what real love felt like?

Frank swept a stray hair off her face. "You look beautiful, but tired," he said.

"I'm all right. Thanks for going to visit Lillian this morning," Alene said. It always embarrassed her when someone called her beautiful because she knew it wasn't true. "I know she was grateful."

He wrapped his arms around her. "We never got to say a proper goodbye," he said into her hair. "And you smell good."

"Thanks," said Alene. How could she smell good after a morning at the café and several hours in a stale hospital room? "Did you learn anything from Lillian or Lawrence?"

"Lillian reminds me of my mother," said Frank, ignoring her question. "She's so competent and calm about everything. Lawrence slept through the whole visit. Apparently, he volunteers at the hospital and people adore him, so there were several other visitors while I was there. I was sorry I couldn't do anything to help regarding the accident, but nobody called in a witness statement. We had nothing to go on."

It felt so delicious, she wanted to stand there for hours with her face resting against his shoulder. But they had to talk, so she pulled away. "I need you to be honest about what's going on, Frank," Alene said. "What if Jocelyn isn't the only one in danger?"

"I think you're pretty safe at the moment," he said as he ushered her away from Cal's room, "but the world can be a dangerous place." She'd hoped to hear that they'd figured out who murdered Stanley. It was too late to remember Sylvie's open door.

"Detective Shaw! You might be interested in this, Detective Shaw," Sylvie hollered from her bed. "Alene didn't let me finish telling her before, but this is important."

Alene hung her head. She should have warned him about Sylvie's latest outburst. Frank said, "Hello, Mrs. Huff, I hope you're feeling better."

"You have no idea," Sylvie retorted. She still boomed, as though they wouldn't hear her while they were standing in the hallway.

"Is there something you need to tell me?" Frank asked quietly, from just outside her door.

"Well," Sylvie narrowed her already half-closed eyes. "I tried to tell Alene, but she refuses to believe me. I have proof

159

that her cleaning lady was having an affair with my husband."

Frank just stood waiting for Sylvie to continue. Alene said, "It's not true. She's talking about Blanca, my dad's caregiver."

"It's about the earrings I saw her wearing," said Sylvie, as if that settled everything.

Alene said, "Blanca's earrings only prove that she's an excellent shopper."

"Oh, no," Sylvie said. She blathered on about her diamond studs. Alene thought she must have lost them while pulling a shirt over her head. And how could she have recognized earrings from ten feet away while Blanca was hurrying down the hallway? It was absurd, and not just because most diamond studs looked the same.

Frank nodded thoughtfully and said, "Thank you, Mrs. Huff." He took Alene's hand and pulled her away from Sylvie and towards the elevators. After walking a few yards down the hallway, he whispered into her ear, "I'm on it, Alene. No worries." He squeezed her hand, and they walked out together, not speaking until they were outside the hospital.

"First, don't let her get to you," said Frank, as they headed across the street towards the outdoor bar at Diversey Harbor. The line moved fast, and he bought two beers. "Sylvie Huff is what we call an unreliable witness," he added after they found a place to sit.

Alene said, "No kidding." She started to tell him about Julian cheating during the Jiu-Jitsu tournament. Frank said that several people had mentioned the tournament, including Julian, who hadn't said anything about cheating or being tossed out. Frank hadn't thought it was significant to the investigation.

Alene disagreed and would not let go of the subject until he told her that he'd check into it. "Now we get to relax, right?" Frank asked. They sat back in Adirondack chairs and sipped their beer. It was after five, but the sun was still high and the air still hot and still. Could Frank see the sweat stains under her arms?

"Can I ask you just a few more questions?" she asked.

"You can ask as many questions as you want," he said, his expression warm. "But I thought you'd been compiling evidence this whole time and I also thought you were going to let me rest for a while."

It was hard to concentrate when he looked at her in that way. She shook herself and counted off using her fingers, "You said there were signs of a struggle in Stanley's office. I want to know what they were, and did any foreign substances show up in his lungs? Also, did you find anything else of interest?"

Frank said, "Chair tipped over, papers strewed, clothing messed. Nothing in his lungs. Did I mention initials in the nine o'clock slot on his calendar? We haven't figured them out."

"So that's why you wanted my employee list," said Alene, now sitting forward in her chair. Why had he taken so long to tell her? "What were the initials?"

"Three letters, R.G.S." He'd closed his eyes and was basking in the still-bright sun. "It feels good out here, doesn't it?"

"It wasn't one of my employees," said Alene, her mind spinning. Was it anyone she knew? "And yes, it is really nice to be here with you. I promise I'll stop bothering you soon."

"It's no bother, Alene," Frank said. "We don't know if the initials are for a name or several names. The R could have been for retirement plan or register to vote."

Alene smiled, "But it was nine o'clock on a Friday night."

"True," said Frank, sinking deeper into the chair. She wanted to read his face with her fingers, especially to outline his mouth and rest her hand on his cheek. She'd never dated such a handsome man before.

Alene said, "I guess you've already checked Better Be Fit's client list." His answer was to squeeze her hand in his. A squirrel scampered across the path, causing a tiny tan-colored dog to bark uncontrollably. It was ridiculous to think that she'd come up with an answer, especially as he brought her hand to his mouth and kissed it.

They leaned back in their chairs as the soft breeze relieved a bit of the heavy heat. There was a clinking of glasses from a nearby table and another squirrel dashed up the trunk of an old oak tree. Leaves of all shades fluttered in the surrounding trees. Listening to the uninterrupted chattering of squirrels and other people in the park, they sat side by side, sipping their beer.

Then Frank's cellphone buzzed.

Chapter 13

Frank sat forward in his chair. Where?" and "When?" he
barked into his phone. Then he told Alene, probably before
he realized he'd said it out loud, that he was working
outrageous hours, and Lee, his partner, was inexperienced.
"The CPD just doesn't have enough resources right now,"
said Frank. "Sorry I have to get back to work."

"Me too," said Alene. She'd read about challenges the
Chicago Police Department had been facing. Just last week,
there was something in the Tribune about how the previous
mayor had closed two of the city's five detective bureaus.
"Too bad Lee can't handle whatever it is." Although, she
thought, it was obvious that Frank was better at talking to
witnesses than his partner.

"Really too bad," said Frank, "that he doesn't have
enough experience. We weren't so overworked last
summer."

Alene wasn't sure how to respond. He'd stated
everything matter-of-factly, so it wasn't that he was
complaining, but he obviously didn't expect her to jump in
with helpful ideas. She settled on saying, "It must be hard
on you."

Frank shook his head and sighed. She liked his composure, knowing she'd have grumbled nonstop to anyone who would listen if she had to deal with an inexperienced partner, budget cuts, and extra work. And she liked that he didn't even feel the need to remind her that everything he told her was just between them. He only said, "Thanks, A. I like having someone to talk to."

She liked that he had a special name for her, even if it was just her first initial. Her phone pinged with a text message that she quickly read. "It's Sierra," she said. "The kids are on their way home, so I've got to bounce too." It was hard to pull herself out of the comfortable chair.

Frank reached for her hand to help her out of the chair. "I can drop you off on my way," he said, giving her a look that made her want to sit back down. "Really sorry I have to cancel plans again."

"Me too," said Alene. Frank probably accepted being alone with as much equanimity as he accepted his potentially dangerous job. She guessed that he'd never, unlike her, spent a Saturday night scrolling through Instagram to see how many of her old friends were out having fun while she, probably the first one in her high school class to get married, have children, and get divorced, was trapped at home. They'd hardly talked about his marriage or children.

Now that they'd spent a night together, it was time for him to tell her more about his family. Maybe he had a healthier relationship with his ex than she did with Neal. She said, "I don't want to be the kind of person who constantly whines about my ex-husband, but I always ask Neal to give me advance notice and then nearly every time, I get a text saying they'll be home in fifteen minutes."

Frank held her face with both hands, kissed her mouth and said, "And I sure wish people who commit homicides would take weekends off." They hurried to his car holding hands. Getting a ride meant a few more minutes with him.

She was in time to see Sierra slam the passenger door of the bright yellow Camaro that Neal was driving that month. The kids loved riding in convertibles, but Alene always worried that Neal drove recklessly when he was trying to show off a fabulous car. Someone must have traded it in, probably a divorced husband whose ex-wife wouldn't let her children ride in it.

Quinn and Noah hopped out of the back seat and came running into the building. Just as she was feeling grateful that Neal had been picking them up nearly every week, giving them happy memories, the three children started complaining. Turned out they'd been locked in Neal's apartment all day while he was at work. Alene would have liked to confront him, but he'd already pulled away with a dramatic screech. Sierra was irate because she'd had to watch Quinn and Noah all day.

Alene asked, "Wasn't Dad going to take you to a street fair?" They stared back with blank faces. Even taking them to his car dealership would have been more fun than leaving them in his apartment. They'd have had people to talk to and lots of activity around them.

Sighing with immense drama, Sierra said, using finger quotes, "It was another emergency. Also, remember two weeks ago when Noah asked some kids if they wanted to play, and they hid in a backseat of a car on the lot and the customer couldn't find them when he was ready to leave? Dad said we were all punished because of Noah and that's why we had to stay in all day."

Nobody had mentioned that incident, and Alene was furious. What kind of father traps his children inside his apartment on such a perfect summer day? He could have called Zuleyka or one of the other four babysitters whose phone numbers she'd given him. Or, he could have called his mother, who would have left work early to make sure they had a wonderful day. Mitzi had told her dozens of times that she was ready to jump in and help every time Neal had the kids.

Luckily, it was one of those summer days that go on forever. Alene let the kids invite one friend each for dinner while she got Neal on the phone and chastised him. He kept telling her to calm down, which made her even angrier. He claimed, predictably, that he'd had to rush into work when one of his salesmen called in sick. He promised to take the kids for both days the following weekend, but Alene treasured her Sundays with the children. Sierra was fast approaching a time when she wouldn't be willing to hang out all day with her siblings and her mother.

Everyone found a friend who was happy to have something to do on a Saturday night. Within the hour, Alene was walking on the lake path with four bubbling children plus two pre-teenage girls who were trying, but failing, to look older. They all headed to play mini golf in the park at Diversey Harbor, near the Adirondack chairs where Alene and Frank had recently sat drinking beer. Alene rented golf balls and clubs and kept score for the forty-five minutes it took to play a round. Then she ordered pizza from the grill, and they ate sitting outside, swatting away mosquitos. Sierra and her friend spent much of the time whispering and giggling, while the younger children ran around until it was time to leave. By the time the friends had gone home, and her children were showered and in bed, they'd had enough fun to make up for the dismal day, and all three seemed content.

The next morning, after they'd finished their Sunday chores and Alene had checked in with Ruthie at the café, she helped the kids pack for a day at Montrose Beach. There'd probably be several thousand other Chicagoans with the same plan. When everyone was ready, wearing bathing suits under their shorts and T-shirts, with hats, drinks, lunch, towels and sunscreen in their backpacks, Alene called a Lyft. To begin the day with everyone in the best possible humor, Alene let Sierra sit in front while she squeezed between Quinn and Noah in the back.

By one o'clock in the afternoon, the children had built a sandcastle, searched for and found other friends, lounged on the towels, complained about the lack of waves, and finished their lunches. Later, when Alene was ready to leave, Sierra and Quinn grumbled because Noah got to stay at the beach with a friend's family. The girls wanted to go straight home, but Alene insisted that they stop first to visit their grandfather at the hospital.

Cal expressed delight in seeing Sierra and Quinn and opened his mouth in a huge grin. When they were little, Cal had taught both girls to reenact a scene from "Little Red Riding Hood" whenever he made his wolf face. Sierra had already outgrown it, but Quinn was happy to exclaim, "What huge teeth you have, Grandfather."

"The better to eat you, my child," Cal answered, reaching to tickle her the same way he'd tickled Alene when she was a child. "What brings you pretty girls inside, on such a beautiful day? And where's my grandson?"

"You sound absolutely normal, Dad," said Alene. What a relief. And his color looked good. She wished she could just pack up his things and take him home.

"When wasn't I normal?" Cal asked. "Maybe I was testing you all. To see if you missed me. And now I'm ready to come home. Wait just a minute," he squinted at them. "Did you go to the beach today without me? Is that where you lost Noah?"

"We didn't lose Noah, Grandpa," said Quinn as she skipped over to the window.

Sierra added, "Some people in the family always get to stay at the beach longer than other people."

"He's with a friend's family," Alene clarified. The girls gave Cal the play-by-play about their day while Alene settled into a chair. "We can go again tomorrow after camp if you want, Dad," she said. "You'll probably be sprung from here by then, and the sun is supposed to shine for the next day or so."

"Who knows if I can even walk on sand. After being imprisoned in the hospital. All week," said Cal. He still wasn't completely back to normal, but at least he wasn't stopping to breathe after every two words. Both girls had climbed onto the window ledge, and Quinn said, "This is a better view than we have at home, Grandpa."

"Just don't push on the window," Cal said with a sly grin. "Last week a couple of kids fell out, and it was apparently tragic." He shook his head, frowning.

The girls rolled their eyes, and Alene was about to respond, but she heard the usual commotion coming from the room next door. She had to stop her daughters from running to look. "I thought Sylvie went home yesterday," she said.

"Nobody tells me anything," Cal sighed.

"Grandpa's neighbor in the room next door screams at some of her visitors," Alene said quietly to Sierra and Quinn. "Sometimes being sick makes people do things they wouldn't normally do."

"Or you could just tell them that she's a nutcase," said Cal. Alene gave him a dismayed look she hoped he'd understand. He shouldn't speak like that in front of the girls. "I mean," he amended his comment, "I feel sorry for her because she wanted to go home. And they must have made her stay an extra day. Just to torture me."

After kissing him goodbye and promising to come back if he didn't get to go home soon, she hustled the girls out of Cal's room. They passed Sylvie's open door. Miles was pacing while Heather, looking fragile and pale, sat as far from her mother as she could manage in the small room. Sylvie called out to Alene, as she had before.

"We're just leaving," Alene said, continuing to walk, "so this isn't a good time."

"Hold on," said Miles, who'd come to the doorway. "I've got to clear things up with you. Please come in and give me a minute to explain what's going on."

Alene was torn between wanting to get out of there and wanting to hear what Miles had to clear up. She said, "Girls, would you please wait in that sitting area next to the elevators so I can talk to this man?" She didn't think they needed to know who Miles was. "The lake is beautiful today and I think you can see the driving range."

Quinn took off running. Before turning to follow her sister, Sierra said, "I hope you don't think we're going to sit

168

in a hospital lobby for an hour." She was impatient like her Aunt Lydia.

Alene smiled at Sierra and turned back to Miles, who repeated, "I want to explain something."

"You should really be talking to Officer Shaw," said Alene, "if it has something to do with Stanley's murder."

"No, it's just that I need to tell you why I came to work at Better Be Fit in the first place." Miles exchanged glances with Heather. He told Alene that three years before, he'd started taking one of the supplements Stanley sold at a previous Better Be Fit location. He'd nearly died. Miles paused to take a deep breath. "The supplement I took has a lot of different names. Stanley's was labelled as Ripped and Ready DNP. People have died from it."

Heather piped up, "It's also used in photography and to make dyes and explosives."

Miles gave her a grateful nod. "I started researching DNP and learned that in Chicago, they can either buy it online or directly from Better Be Fit."

Alene still stood in the doorway. A lot of her customers carried those Better Be Fit bags. Some had probably bought that exact product. "Is it for building muscles?"

"And weight loss," said Miles with a bitter edge to his voice. "I mean, I didn't always have this body." He was toned and didn't look like he could spare an ounce. "I used to weigh nearly three hundred pounds."

Heather shook her head and said, "After he recovered, he wanted to sue Stanley, but then he started researching the whole supplement industry and decided to do something bigger."

"I began serious weight training, built up my body, and became a personal fitness trainer. Six months ago, Stanley opened the Better Be Fit next door to your café," said Miles. "He was happy to let me bring my twenty-three clients."

"That's when we met," Heather interjected.

"We probably met before, but you wouldn't have given me a second look," said Miles.

From her bed, Sylvie said, "I was starting to worry that she'd never meet anyone," and got a vicious look from Heather.

Alene said, "So, you might have died because of something you bought from Stanley. Then you came to work for him. The police would probably consider you a pretty good suspect." It wasn't like he could strangle her or bash her in the head right then and there.

Miles said, in a steely voice, "I was going to expose him and everyone else who sells DNP. The supplement industry brings in over thirty-seven billion dollars a year, and I'm working with a group doing a nationwide project to educate the public about the dangers of vitamins and supplements. The project is underwritten by the House Center for Public Health. You can google how it's financed by a private family foundation and named after the TV show."

"I loved Hugh Laurie in that show," said Sylvie, triggering a scowl from Heather.

"So, you're working for Stanley in order to do this research," said Alene, wishing she'd sat down. Miles had seemed kind of bumbling when Kacey fainted in the alley, but maybe Alene had misjudged him.

Sylvie interrupted to say, "Stanley doesn't hire employees, so Miles wasn't actually working for him."

"We work for ourselves and pay Stanley for the use of his gym. It's an awful place," said Miles. "No sense of being on the same team, just everyone out for himself." Was it awful enough for him to want to get rid of Stanley?

Miles went on, "Before I moved my clients to Better Be Fit, I was volunteering for a different House Center project. We were looking into free-standing emergency clinics that lack equipment and resources. Some of those places cost as much as actual emergency rooms, so it turns out that if you have a serious problem, you should go straight to a real emergency room."

Alene nodded. "I think I read that somewhere." Or her father had read it out loud from one of his newspapers. He loved anything having to do with shenanigans in the medical

170

industry. But it had nothing to do with Stanley. Just then, Sierra came in and started tugging on her shirt. Alene whispered, "Please give me another five minutes, sweetie." Sierra stomped away with an exasperated expression on her face.

"Miles probably contributed to that article," said Heather. "But he wanted to research the supplement industry. Supplements are not considered drugs, so they don't have to be regulated."

Miles said, "Even though some of them are extremely dangerous."

"Just because something comes from nature doesn't make it safe," Heather added. "Even healthy-sounding herbs like comfrey or green tea can be toxic to the liver."

Quinn ran up behind Alene as Miles said, "Folks have been sickened or killed because some companies don't list all their ingredients."

"Thanks for filling me in about your research," said Alene, "but we have to go."

As she turned to steer her away, Quinn asked, "Why do people get killed when companies don't list all their ingredients?"

Sierra had returned, and both girls listened to Miles rant about the Dietary Supplement Health and Education Act of 1994. "It allowed the sale of unregulated products as long as they weren't advertised as a cure for anything. So it's legal for companies to advertise sugar cereals as being good for your heart, or candy that claims to be low-fat."

Sierra nodded. "You mean they're trying to trick people into thinking that they're eating something that's good for them even when it isn't."

"Exactly," said Heather, now standing next to Miles. "Alene, did you know it was Senator Orrin Hatch of Utah who pushed the act? His son was a lobbyist for the supplement industry. Some of the biggest quack product makers were based in Utah, and they gave boatloads of money to Hatch's campaign."

"No," said Alene, as Quinn started pulling on her arm. "I don't remember that. I was thirteen-years-old in 1994." Cal probably knew all about it – he paid close attention to stories of elected officials who traded away the rights or health of constituents, in exchange for hard cash. "Is any of this connected to Stanley's death?"

Heather said, "Why would you even ask that question? Absolutely not. Miles was trying to stop Stanley from selling potentially harmful supplements." She looked nervously at Miles as if she wasn't sure she'd said it correctly. "And that had nothing to do with my mother staying in a marriage with an abusive ..."

Sylvie interrupted. "I never said he was abusive. He was just mean."

"The way he treated you, Mother? That was psychologically abusive," said Heather. "He fat-shamed you. My therapist thinks he had a lot to do with how I am now."

"That's ridiculous," said Sylvie.

"I'm not going to argue with you," said Heather, "but someone might try to murder you next, maybe someone who wants to inherit Stanley's estate."

Alene couldn't believe they were having this exchange while her daughters were standing there. "Let's go, girls," she said, starting to back away. Sierra stood firm just inside the door, mesmerized.

Sylvie continued, "I'm not worried about inheriting Stanley's money. I already own half of everything." She gestured with her arms.

Miles said, "That doesn't change the fact that someone might want to kill you next."

"You're both being overly dramatic," said Sylvie, studying the veins on the back of her hand with an aggrieved expression. "I still think Stanley simply had a heart attack and died."

Heather and Miles exchanged looks. "Okay, Mom, let's go with that," said Heather.

Listening to Sylvie was destroying brain cells. "That's it," said Alene, a hand on each daughter's back. "We're going now." They hurried to the elevators. It would have been nice to stop by Lawrence's room, but Alene couldn't ask the girls to wait anymore while the sun was shining. A big canopy of trees shaded much of the way, so it was a pleasant walk home.

Finally in the apartment, as the girls sprawled on the couch staring at screens of one kind or another, Alene looked up some of what Miles had said about the supplement industry. She read a few paragraphs, and it was interesting, but she had too much on her mind. She closed her laptop and called Ruthie to discuss how the day went. Ruthie reported that Whipped and Sipped had sold five containers of Alene's cashew-onion dip, nearly all the bread, and the homemade fruit and vegetable popsicles they'd been experimenting with all summer. Customers had loved the unusual flavors, plus the fact that there was no added sugar. Ruthie also wanted to share that Edith had been unfailingly polite and hadn't said a single negative thing all day.

"Not sure what we're doing," said Alene, "but it seems to be working."

After signing off with Ruthie, Alene called Frank. He said he'd been hectic all afternoon, still working the same case he'd dealt with the previous night. She told him about her conversation with Heather and Miles. Frank said that after his talk with Miles, he'd vowed to be more careful about checking ingredients before buying things. "Excellent idea," Alene said enthusiastically. She'd been doing it since college.

And Frank told her that Jocelyn's bank card had been used to take a few hundred dollars out of an ATM just a few miles west. They were checking it out. He said it could be either good or bad news.

Chapter 14

None of Alene's employees were ready to takeover Jocelyn's job of opening most days, so Alene and Ruthie took turns. It was Alene's turn, and she had to skip her morning workout. Now Olly, her opening partner that day, charged up the alley on his bike, ready to show Alene that he knew the protocol. She watched him unlock the door, turn off the alarm, and start turning on ovens, his expression atypically glum. "Turns out I don't like living alone as much as I used to," he said.

That meant Jocelyn hadn't come home yet. "Stay positive, Olly," said Alene. She felt about as despondent as he looked.

It was a typical Monday with a steady stream of customers until half past nine. Kofi came in then and sat at a table near the crimson wall. Kacey hurried out of the kitchen to join him as Alene glanced around the café. At one table, two mothers sipped coffee while their toddlers made a mess, at another, two women were eating breakfast while thumbing their cellphones. At a third table, Toula and her husband were bickering, as usual, and in front of them, a woman Alene didn't recognize was filing a fingernail. She debated going over to recommend a nail salon up the street.

Royce, Toula's husband, abruptly pushed his chair back and stormed out of the café for the second time that week. Neal used to stomp around like that when he got upset, and Alene had often thought about telling him to go to his room back then. Now Toula burst into tears, and this time, Alene decided to go over and commiserate. Toula was pretty, even with blotchy skin and a red nose. The gap between her teeth made her look younger than forty-three. "You seem so unhappy," said Alene. "Ruthie's breakfast babka has been known to lift spirits if you're interested. My treat."

"Thanks, Alene, but I don't think I can swallow right now," Toula said, dabbing at her eyes with a tissue. "You know how when you're young, you think your life is going to turn out one way, and you try to make it happen, but suddenly you realize that you're a mess? And it's too late to undo the damage because some things are final and can't be changed, no matter what?"

She was preaching to the choir. "Yeah," Alene said. "I know exactly what you mean."

Toula's violet eyes glistened and she gave Alene a weak smile. "Anyway," she said, standing, "it's been nice coming here. I always like the food and the music, all the friendly people, and it's right next door to Better Be Fit. But it's been hard. I haven't worked out since Stanley died." She hesitated. "But I keep eating as if I did." She sat back down and told Alene about how she'd met Royce at a bar where she'd gone with a couple of girlfriends to celebrate someone's birthday. Alene wondered how she'd gotten those fresh bruises on her arms if she hadn't been working out all week, but maybe her skin was fragile.

Toula talked about falling in love with Royce, and how he'd always been a little gruff. They'd had several good years, and then, she didn't know why, he started suspecting her of all kinds of things. She'd begged him to go to couples' therapy, but he'd refused. And lately, they didn't have a lot to say to each other. "Anyway," she concluded, "I know it's my fault that the relationship is so terrible right now, but I don't know what to do."

Alene reminded her that everyone was just doing the best they could, and she shouldn't be so hard on herself. Toula looked at her watch, said she had to go, thanked Alene for listening, and ran out the door. Alene cleaned up the table, wishing she was the kind of person who could help solve other people's problems. She couldn't even solve her own.

Ruthie came out of the kitchen and made herself an oat milk latte. She sat down with Kacey and Kofi, who was leaning back looking pleased, one hand flung over Kacey's shoulder, the other holding a blueberry apple hand pie. Alene wished she could make everyone stay seated on all four legs of the café's chairs. Last thing she needed was for Kofi to fall back and crack his head. She made herself a cup of peppermint tea and joined Ruthie, Kacey, and Kofi. Olly hovered and chatted the way he always did. Kofi asked him if he'd noticed any homophobia in the Jiu-Jitsu world. "I saw those guys messing with you last week and I've been meaning to ask," Kofi said. "Just so you know, if you ever need backup, I'm there."

Hadn't they just been arguing about how Julian got thrown out of that Jiu-Jitsu tournament? They must have made up. Kacey said, "That was really sweet, Kofi." He looked away as if the compliment embarrassed him.

"What'd you do when they messed with you, Olly?" Alene asked. She was surprised he hadn't mentioned it before, since that tournament kept coming up in conversation.

"Just what anyone would have expected me to do," Olly said. He didn't usually have such dark circles under his eyes, and the paleness of his skin made his freckles look three-dimensional. But he struck the pose of a boxer and displayed a few air punches. "I beat the crap out of them."

"Olly!" Ruthie's tone indicated her disappointment, and Olly quickly lowered his arms. She abhorred violence, or any talk about violence.

"Yeah, right, that's exactly what you did," Kofi said, laughing. He turned to Alene and Ruthie. "They were younger kids, and he threatened to give them a lesson if they so much as thought that way again. Some of them probably wet their beds that night."

"Don't worry about me getting insulted, guys," Olly interrupted. "I've dealt with homophobia my whole life and I'm not ever going to let small-minded, ignorant people ruin my day."

He'd gotten everyone's attention with his drama, and most of the café's customers watched Olly sashay back to the counter, tossing his curls and jumping into a monologue that grew in volume with each sentence. "That's what I learned from my friend and roommate, Jocelyn DeVale, who is still missing in case any of you didn't know or have already forgotten." He stopped to stare accusingly at Kacey and Kofi. "I'm getting more and more worried about Jocelyn, so the bottom line is that I cannot pay attention to the little challenges of being who I am, when my best friend is missing." His arms flailed in the air, and his last movement was to place his right hand on his heart as though he was about to launch into the Star-Spangled Banner.

There was a moment of silence that Edith broke by announcing, "Jocelyn is my best friend, too." Edith pulled up a chair, so Alene glanced over to make sure someone was still serving customers at the counter. "And Jocelyn wouldn't hesitate to protect Olly if people were making fun of him," Edith continued. "She knows Krav Maga, and she says it's even better than your Jiu-Jitsu."

"My Jiu-Jitsu?" asked Kofi. He chewed slowly and said something to Kacey about Jocelyn being so fast that she could have crushed him if she'd been in that tournament. Alene wondered if Jocelyn knew that Edith viewed her as a best friend.

"Maybe she could have beat you, Kofi," said Kacey, "but Jocelyn does all that stuff to protect herself. She'd never start a fight or put herself in a dangerous situation."

Olly said, "I agree with Kacey, and for sure Jocelyn would never have hurt her father, if that's what any of you are thinking."

"Nobody's thinking that," said Edith, pulling her floral cardigan around her bony frame, her hair a flat cap. "No matter how badly he treated her," she continued, addressing them like they were students at an assembly. "She was sad, but not surprised that he was murdered. He wasn't a kind man, he made a lot of enemies, and he cheated people. Jocelyn thought someone just snapped and killed him on the spur of the moment."

Everyone looked at her. Edith enjoyed gossiping, but it was generally negative. Now here she was defending Jocelyn. "And she couldn't get past the fact that her father never accepted her the way she was," Edith continued in her lecturing tone. "It was terrible for her because she had always grappled with her identity."

Ruthie, who hadn't spoken much, said, "That's really perceptive, Edith."

Edith blushed, and said, "Well, she knew early in her life that she was supposed to be a girl. Oh, there's someone waiting for a smoothie." Edith jumped up and ran to the counter to serve a woman with straight black hair.

"That was unexpected," said Alene, exchanging looks with Ruthie and wondering when Edith had developed insight into Jocelyn. "I still want to understand the whole Jiu-Jitsu tournament situation." Maybe someone left there to go straight to Better Be Fit, either during or after.

Kofi said, "I'm kind of over arbitrary Jiu-Jitsu tournament regulations. Julian screwed up, but it's not like he went there planning to screw up. It happens. And I've been thinking about switching to Krav Maga. Jocelyn says they don't make such a fuss about rules."

"What do you mean they don't make a fuss about rules?" Alene asked. Jocelyn had been encouraging her to register her children for Krav Maga classes. "Do they let children hurt each other?"

Ruthie said, "I hope that's not what you meant, Kofi." Ruthie looked like she was ready to march over to the nearest Krav Maga studio to give them a talking-to. "There's a huge difference between protecting yourself and hurting other people." Alene loved Ruthie no matter how preachy she got.

Kofi, looking peeved, sat up straight. "Some people don't have a choice about learning how to fight, ladies. You think you'll always be there to protect your kids? Krav Maga comes from a part of the world where one group of people is trying to push the other group into the sea. You come up across that kind of hate, you better be prepared to do whatever it takes to protect yourself and your family."

"I want my kids to learn self-defense," Ruthie said, "but I don't want them to turn into bullies."

"I'm not a bully," said Kofi, looking a little offended. "I just want to be sure nobody kicks my skinny butt." He finished his pie and gave Kacey a half-smile that showed just one of his dimples.

Alene had never heard Kofi say so much in one sitting. Too bad none of the martial arts were going to protect him from getting banged up while searching for cast-off materials. His scratches and lacerations probably came from transporting bulky things and digging through building sites. She said, "I wonder if Krav Maga skills would allow someone like Jocelyn to overcome someone who was much bigger and stronger?"

"I've never seen her lose a fight," said Olly, who'd come back to the table and now flopped down onto a chair with an iced tea he'd made for himself.

Kofi pivoted to look at Olly and acknowledged LaTonya, behind the counter, by raising his chin. LaTonya kept glancing at their table, looking like she wanted to join the conversation.

"If Jocelyn had been at that tournament, it wouldn't have been so boring. It would have been majorly quiche." Olly was either Alene's source for the latest slang, or he made up new meanings for words. Calling something "quiche," he'd told her, meant that it was sexy.

Kacey said, "It probably got even more boring after Kofi and Julian left."

Alene sat up straight in her chair. "I thought only Julian got kicked out."

Kofi said, "I left too. Don't worry, I already told your boyfriend all about it." Frank hadn't said otherwise, so what if both Kofi and Julian were still suspects? Maybe she'd be careful about tossing around accusations this time.

"I have a question, Kofi," said Alene, glad to have thought of a perfect way to change the subject. "Any chance you know where Jocelyn is?"

"Nope," said Kofi, his eyes holding hers. "I haven't seen her." Of course, he'd say that.

"As soon as I get the moves under my belt," Kofi added, "I'll look forward to sparring with her, although I might not be ready to be humiliated by a girl." Alene frowned. He meant it as a compliment, but Jocelyn would be upset that he'd called her a girl instead of a woman. She'd be grateful that he didn't call her "trans." Alene imagined a big guy trying to force Jocelyn into a car with shaded windows. In her vision, Jocelyn fights back and the guy ends up writhing on the ground. It was a cheering image.

Ruthie had gone back to work and now poked her head out to beckon Kacey. Kacey hugged Kofi and headed to the kitchen. Alene said goodbye and also left the table. She hoped Jocelyn was hiding in a comfortable place with good Wi-Fi and had just spent the past week catching up on all her Netflix shows.

A few hours later, Edith, who'd been strangely silent all afternoon, must have thought it was time to weigh in again. As the lunch crowd thinned, she left the smoothie section and walked over to Alene. "You might be interested to know that I started taking beginning Krav Maga classes with Jocelyn," she said. "I'm trying to do whatever it takes to make sure that nobody ever manages to bash me in the head again. Jocelyn says that I have a lot of muscles and hardly any extra body fat. And she's grateful for my help with her cat."

It sounded like she was angling for a compliment. Alene rang up a triple espresso. She was about to call Jack over to restock the small under-counter fridge where they stored the different kinds of milk, but she stopped to stare at Edith. "Are you, did you just ...?" She had to consider exactly what she needed to ask. "Edith, are you taking care of Jocelyn's cat?"

"Well, she doesn't know how to deal with bacterial infections," said Edith, unable to keep a judgmental tone from creeping in. "When she was growing up, her mother was allergic. Then when she was about eight, her parents got divorced, and her father married Sylvie, who always had a cat. Jocelyn always says that was the one good thing about that marriage. She loves cats, but she never learned how to take care of them when they're sick."

Edith had been bizarrely cheerful, hardly dampening anyone's spirit, not at all depressed about Jocelyn being missing all week. She must have been dying to tell someone what she knew. Alene leaned over the counter and whispered, "You know where she is."

"I'm not saying a thing," said Edith with a self-congratulatory little nod. "We're very close, and Jocelyn trusts me."

Alene moved closer to Edith and whispered, "She's at your apartment, isn't she?" It would be a perfect place for Jocelyn to hide out, and Edith had kept the secret until she couldn't hold it in any longer. Alene shook her head slowly, feeling a bubble of anger rise to her throat. "You never said a thing, Edith, and I've been sick to my stomach worrying." She hoped the intensity of her voice didn't sound threatening the way she knew it sometimes did.

Edith looked away. "I'm pretty sure I told you, but you rarely listen to me."

"Really, Edith?" That was one thing Alene would have heard.

Edith leaned forward and murmured in a hushed voice, "She was afraid that whoever killed her father would come after her, so I did my best to keep her safe. And she knew she could count on me."

Alene closed her eyes, inhaled, and tried to control herself from saying something she'd later regret. Jocelyn had definitely not instructed Edith to keep her whereabouts a secret from Alene. That was Edith's doing. Alene walked back to her office and wrote a note on an old envelope, then returned to where Edith stood behind the counter and handed it over. "I know I can trust you to deliver this, Edith," she said, in a much calmer tone, although she still had to control her anger. Maybe it was useless to be angry. As Ruthie always said, everyone has limitations.

Edith took the note and stuck it in a pocket before looking around like a wannabe spy, nodding with a knowing look and proudly smirking. Alene would have liked to rush over to Edith's apartment and demand an explanation, but did Jocelyn owe her one? Alene thought they'd become friends over the past half-year, but maybe to Jocelyn, she was just another boss. An hour passed, Alene packed up, said goodbye, and headed to the hospital, glad to get far away from Edith.

Cal was still asleep, so she zipped over to visit Lawrence and Lillian. She hadn't thought it through though, because it was Monday, and Lillian was at work. Lawrence lay in the bed, still swathed in bandages. He clearly had a long recovery ahead of him. He greeted her with a weak smile and thanked her for stopping by. She asked how he was feeling.

"I'm uncomfortable, I'm bored, and I need help doing everything," he said, looking defeated, his voice weaker and raspier than when she'd heard him speak before.

"At least the staff here is wonderful," said Alene. "I know because my dad's been on the tenth floor for a week." She hoped the doctor would release Cal that afternoon now that he was well past his myasthenia crisis. "He can't wait to get out."

"It ain't easy," Lawrence nodded. "Your dad's lucky to have you."

"He's the only dad I have, so it's my pleasure. Also, my kids and I live with him. We're all looking forward to him coming home." Alene didn't know much about Lawrence except that he'd done legal work for Stanley. Was he widowed or divorced? Did he have children? Maybe he was one of those people who rarely share information about themselves.

Lawrence asked, "Have they figured out who murdered Stanley? Lillian told me that you're somewhat involved in the case."

"I'm not really involved," said Alene, "but I don't think they've figured it out yet."

"We had our professional differences," said Lawrence. "I didn't agree with all of his methods and we didn't always see eye to eye, but he was a disciplined man and a heck of a personal trainer. I know he also had a child who needed him. Lillian told me she'd gone missing."

Alene said, "That's true." Should she still consider him a suspect? He wouldn't be asking these kinds of questions, unless he had nefarious reasons for wanting to find Jocelyn. Still, it was unlikely that he'd planned to be nearly killed in a hit-and-run accident just to distract the police.

"She'll come home safe," he said, although his mouth formed a distinct frown.

Alene said, "Hope so." She started to inch backwards toward the door. Lawrence was a gentle, sweet old guy, and Lillian was too good a judge of character to keep company with a criminal, but what if the actual murderer had purposely tried to hurt him? Again, she went back to the work Lawrence did for Stanley and the possibility that the murder had something to do with money. She asked, "Do you think your accident was connected to Stanley in any way?"

Lawrence shook his head. "What a funny question. I can't imagine why anyone would want to hurt Lillian or me. And even if someone did, how could they have known where we were going to dinner that night? I think we're just going to have to accept that another distracted driver refused to take responsibility, and I'll just have to pay more for car insurance."

184

Alene wished Lawrence a speedy recovery and returned to her father's room. He was sitting in the chair next to the bed looking bored and irate. He held a plastic grocery bag in his hands and was looking intently out the window. There was something zippier about the way he was leaning forward as if he wanted to see what was happening outside. He turned when Alene came in, and said, "I think they want to keep me here forever."

"I won't let them do that, Dad," said Alene. "I promise." He was better. That was a long sentence, and he was sitting in a chair instead of lying in bed.

"I can't take another day," said Cal, waving the plastic bag at her. He seemed more like himself, stroking his nonexistent beard and tapping his foot impatiently. "This is my stuff. You carry the ceramic cup and my book so we can get out of here before they notice anything."

"Did the doctor release you, Dad?" she asked, sitting down next to him. She couldn't have guessed how much she'd miss her father calling out to her from his favorite chair, echolocating whenever she left the living room.

"Well, this isn't prison," Cal bristled. "I don't need permission to leave."

"We need release papers if you expect Medicare to foot the bill, Dad." Alene stood to kiss him on the cheek and pulled out the box of assorted cookies, scones, and muffins she'd brought from the café. She was grateful to see that his spirit was reviving. He'd been so vibrant before the disease. "I also brought you a thermos of good coffee," she said, pouring some into the ceramic mug that now had a few extra chips after nearly a week at St. Darius. "It's still sunny and hot outside. Let's relax for a bit."

Cal looked exactly like Noah did when he was disappointed. His mouth tilted down, he gave her an accusing look, and his shoulders sloped. "You're going to need to do an intervention then," said Cal. "If I hear what's-her-name screech one more time, I might go smother her with a pillow." Even his crabby voice was back to normal.

185

"Dad!" Alene said, exasperated. It was too soon to joke about murder.

"Just kidding," said Cal, leaning back in his chair. "What happened to your sense of humor?"

They heard a commotion coming from outside the room and Alene walked over to peek out the door. Sylvie was trying to push past Julian into the hallway. She reported back to Cal, "It looks like Sylvie is also trying to escape, but Julian's blocking her."

Cal shook his head. "She should definitely wait in the hallway and make a lot of noise. That way she can bother everyone on the tenth floor. It's not like anyone is suffering from pain or anything." He took a sip of his coffee and chose a tomato-basil scone from the box. "I'm going to start with savory before sweet," he added. He was even back to announcing his eating plans.

"Enjoy," said Alene. "I'll be right back." She walked out to the hallway, pondering what she should ask Julian about the night Stanley died.

Julian stood in front of Sylvie, who was leaning against the hallway wall, dressed in billowy pants and a long white tunic that looked a bit like a bathrobe. Sylvie said, "You've got to help me Alene. I want to go home but Julian is making me sit in that stifling room with no air."

Alene was not in the mood to engage with Sylvie in any way. She said, "Julian, I heard that a few of you were disqualified in a Jiu-Jitsu tournament last Friday."

Julian said, "Yeah, it was stupid of me to go in the first place."

"Did you go straight home afterwards?" Alene asked.

He gave her a puzzled look. "I should have stayed home, cleaned up after dinner and helped put our sons to bed. Maybe Phyllie and I could have talked. Maybe we'd have watched a sitcom and laughed together, but instead, I went to that asinine tournament and now my life is a nightmare of running back and forth between two women who can't stand each other."

186

He hadn't answered her question, but his face turned beet red, and he paused to clutch his chest as if he were having trouble breathing. He took big gulps of air. Alene put a hand on his arm and asked, "Should I get help for you?" Maybe she should take him off her list of suspects, or move him down to fourth, after Harrison, Sylvie and Phyllie.

Julian shook his head. Not to be outdone, Sylvie managed to muster some maternal feeling, or at least to act the part by looking at him with a loving expression and softening her tone. She said, "I'm sorry Julian, I forgot how upset you can get. I shouldn't have argued with you. Let's go back in the room so you can rest."

As she watched Julian accompany his mother into the room, lean back into the chair, and put his feet on Sylvie's bed, Alene detected a satisfied smile on his face. She'd just helped Julian out-manipulate his mother. Until that moment, Alene had thought that Sylvie was the master-manipulator.

Chapter 15

Cal called Alene at the café three times the next day to grouse about having to wait for the doctor to sign him out of the hospital. Alene worked all morning and headed over after lunch. A few hours later, after his official release, she followed her father as he shuffled out the door and into the sunshine.

Cal chatted with the Lyft driver and sang the first lines of the Sir Henry Bishop song he'd memorized as a kid: "Mid pleasures and palaces though we may roam, be it ever so humble, there's no place like home." And as the driver pulled up to the front door of their building, he added, "A charm from the skies seems to hallow us there, which, seek thro' the world, is ne'er met with elsewhere." He got out of the car and spent a few minutes chatting first with his favorite doorman, and then with the concierge.

Blanca opened the door to the apartment and pulled him into a warm hug, making a fuss about how she was going to trim his hair and give him a good shave. The kids were already home from camp. Sierra said, "Hi, Grandpa," from where she was lying on the couch, but Quinn and Noah jumped up and hugged him.

"This is more like what I expected from my grandchildren," Cal said. "Sierra, honey, are you sure you don't have time to give me a hug?" Sierra bounced over, briefly forgetting her pre-teen surliness.

Even though she hated to rush out the door so soon after her father's return, Alene gave dinner instructions to Blanca and kissed everyone goodbye. She ride-shared to Edith's and texted Frank on the way to tell him that Jocelyn had been staying with Edith. Maybe she should have let him know earlier that morning. Or she should have waited until she saw Jocelyn. At Edith's building on Damen near Belmont, she pushed the doorbell six times, until a disembodied voice whispered, "Who is it?"

Alene said, "You better let me in or I'm going to stand outside and yell your name for the next hour." Jocelyn buzzed her in, and Alene trudged up the stairs thinking about what she was going to say. Finally, there she was, wearing a fitted floral sundress and looking freshly made-up, with her hair teased into a flip like a 1950's housewife. "I had no idea if you were even alive," said Alene, harsher than she'd intended. "Why would you scare everyone like that?"

Jocelyn drew her into a hug, and said, "I'm sorry." She must have been under a lot of stress, but she looked surprisingly well-rested and calm.

"Frank said you used your debit card," Alene said. Edith's living room was jammed with carved, antique furniture on top of a floral Oriental rug that reminded Alene of one of Edith's cardigans. On one side of the room, a glass-fronted cabinet was filled with cat sculptures, and there was an intricate floral arrangement on the sideboard that looked like it was made of beads.

"It was a mistake to let Edith use my card, but I didn't want her to keep paying for everything," Jocelyn replied as she fidgeted with her pearl earrings.

Alene was pleasantly surprised to learn that Edith had been generous without bragging about it. "You might be a suspect in your father's murder, Jocelyn."

"Frank doesn't think so, does he?" Jocelyn asked. "I told him everything. Wow. I can't believe he'd think I was vile enough to hurt my own father. I mean, how could I? I wouldn't want to have to live with that for the rest of my life. I have enough regrets."

She probably did, thought Alene. She was sitting on a fussy, uncomfortable high-backed chair. Jocelyn sat on the chartreuse sofa across from her, and a large, fluffy cat jumped up and sat on her lap. Alene could see that cats had scratched up the carved legs and velvet cushions. Edith could have bought one of those towers for them to scratch and climb on instead of sacrificing her furniture. "Truthfully, Jocelyn," said Alene, "I don't even know what to say to you." It had been such a draining week.

"You know I didn't do it, right?" Jocelyn asked. "He wasn't the most supportive father, but he didn't deserve to be murdered. I ran away because I was afraid, you know?"

"No, Jocelyn," said Alene. "I don't know." Alene had known Jocelyn for less than a year, so any thoughts about her innocence were based on gut feelings, not solid evidence. Frank would probably suggest that amateur detectives stick to milder crimes. "Who would want to hurt you, Jocelyn?" Alene mentally ran down her remaining list of suspects; Julian and Harrison, although she still couldn't let go of Sylvie. Jocelyn didn't respond, so Alene added, "Frank is working on your father's murder, but he's not sharing much with me."

"It's the only thing I've been able to think about," said Jocelyn. "I'm just dragging myself through the days. Edith has a good soul, but she hasn't been helpful with passing along useful information. I keep asking if anyone is talking about Stanley. I want to know what's happening with the investigation, but Edith focuses more on things like who argued, who didn't clean the blenders, and who wasn't nice to her."

That sounded like Edith. If only Jocelyn hadn't hidden herself away, they could have been brainstorming together. At least now they were talking face to face. Maybe if Alene shared her thoughts, she'd be able to read something in Jocelyn's reaction. "I'll tell you what I'm thinking," said Alene. "I don't think it was Heather or her boyfriend. They were visiting Sylvie at the hospital and I got to hear all about how Miles is researching and writing an exposé on the supplement industry. Do you want to hear about it?"

"No, thanks," said Jocelyn as she buried her fingers in the cat's fur."

Alene went through her reasons for crossing off Lawrence and Kofi. "Also," she added, "I'd originally ruled out Julian, but then I heard about how he cheated at that tournament. Both Julian and Phyllie are still on my list. And Frank says it would have been impossible for Sylvie to do it, but I don't trust her for one second." She'd shared who was off her list, but she didn't need to share who else was on it until Jocelyn asked.

Jocelyn made a dismissive face. "I agree that it wasn't Lawrence or Kofi, but I don't know why cheating would put Julian back on your suspect list. He's still a mama's boy."

"I can't disagree," said Alene, "but do you remember seeing Kofi and Julian leave the building after Julian got kicked out?"

"Oh, I get it," said Jocelyn as she adjusted her blouse and fidgeted with her necklace. "You think Julian and Kofi might have gone straight from the tournament to Better Be Fit."

"No, I already ruled out Kofi," Alene said. "It's just that Julian could have gotten over there within the time frame.

"We don't need to figure out who did it," said Jocelyn, leaning back on the uncomfortable sofa and closing her eyes. "We just need to figure out how to avoid that person. I've spent all week thinking about how my father cheated everyone. He's probably got people going back decades who've wanted to wring his neck. At least that's what my mother always implied. We just don't know enough to be helpful."

Either Alene hadn't paid attention, or that was the first time Jocelyn had mentioned her mother. Maybe Edith was right, and Alene never listened. "Was your mother still angry about the divorce all these years later?" Alene asked.

"You've got to be kidding," Jocelyn said with a bitter laugh. "My mother always said that she was relieved when Stanley moved out. She's happily remarried and lives in a cute little house in Albany Park, not far from our first house. I thought about going there after I left the police station, but it didn't feel as safe as this place. Nobody knows where Edith lives."

"That's true," said Alene. "I'd forgotten that you and Olly grew up in Albany Park." Maybe Jocelyn had been lonely all week with nobody but Edith to talk to. "Do you know the names of any of those people your dad cheated? Do you know if he was fighting off lawsuits and getting threats all the time?"

"No idea," said Jocelyn. "He never shared anything with me, so I only know the stories from my mother."

Alene reported what Frank told her about Stanley's desk calendar. "Do the initials R.G.S. mean anything to you?"

"Wow. He always liked initials," Jocelyn said with a faraway look. "When we were really little, he called Harrison 'HH' and I was JH. Later, he just called me J. I remember he used to call my mother SP for Sweetie Pie, and our grandmother was the OWP. Those were her actual initials, but my father said it stood for Old Wrinkled Potato." She stifled a smile. "I'm trying to recall, but I don't recognize RGS. Did Frank have any leads?"

"Not that he told me about," said Alene. She wished Jocelyn could ask her mother about all those people who might have hated Stanley. "Jocelyn, was there someone specific who frightened you these last few weeks or months?"

Jocelyn shook her head and said, "I can't think of anyone." Her hand tremored though, and she seemed apprehensive. "Except maybe my brother, but I don't want to talk about that. I'm going to keep thinking about those initials. Maybe I'll come up with something."

Alene understood. She told Jocelyn about how Stanley had appropriated her trainer's clients as his own and then accused Michael of stealing them. "That's why it would be helpful if you could ask your mom for the names of some of the people who hated your father. Also, did Edith tell you about Lillian and Lawrence getting rear-ended? That was the night you disappeared. I thought whoever murdered your father might have also tried to hurt Lawrence, but I visited him in the hospital, and he said he was pretty sure that it had just been an accident."

"I thought the guy seemed solid, but old," said Jocelyn, who picked at stray cat hairs on the couch and couldn't seem to find a comfortable position. "I don't think Lillian's elderly boyfriend could have overpowered my father." She'd lost some of her regal bearing, her spark.

"No, I don't think he did it. I meant that he might be at risk because of having been Stanley's lawyer, which would also put Lillian at risk," said Alene.

Jocelyn rubbed her forehead. "I don't know who would have done either thing," she said, eyes tearing up, "I just pray it wasn't Harrison. Even though he doesn't seem to remember that we're related, he's my only brother."

Alene understood. "Why, though? Why would Harrison murder his own father?"

"Money, of course," said Jocelyn, exhaling slowly. "He was always competitive, but money influenced everything he did. As a child, he used to come up with all kinds of schemes, like a delivery service for neighbors, or mowing lawns. Our mother used to make him drag me along sometimes. And he worked all through high school and college. But he buys and sells multi-million-dollar homes these days, so why would he be worried about money now? I'm relieved that the initials don't match his."

Alene tried to recall why they were so sure RGS were the murderer's initials and not something Stanley wanted to remember to buy, like red grapes. She stretched her neck and asked, "Jocelyn, why are you hiding here at Edith's?"

Jocelyn sighed. "I didn't think Harrison and Rhea would find me here."

Edith walked in then and set two bags of groceries on her little round kitchen table. From the snippy set of her mouth, Alene could tell she was unhappy to be sharing Jocelyn with anyone. The cat slipped away from Jocelyn and disappeared into another room. "I know he's your brother, Jocelyn," Edith said, "but every time I've met them, Harrison and his wife have been nothing but rude to me. That kind of behavior says something about what to expect of them."

Alene would have contradicted Edith, but Jocelyn looked like she was about to cry. If rudeness indicated a propensity to commit murder, there'd be a lot more crime in Chicago and everywhere else. She hadn't seen enough of Harrison or his wife to form an opinion, but they hadn't struck her as obviously evil. Of course, malevolent people probably practiced hiding behind pleasant manners. Alene said, "According to the newspapers, and probably all research on such things, some of the most heinous crimes in this country have been committed by people described as perfectly polite."

Edith winced. "I guess anything I say is going to be wrong." She turned to Jocelyn and asked, "Do you want to know what I think?"

Jocelyn shrugged and raised her palms as if she didn't know what she wanted, but Alene wasn't in the mood to be swept into another Edith drama. "I'm going to call Frank now," she said, punching his number into her cellphone. They hadn't spoken since earlier that afternoon and he'd said he was going to be working late, but he'd probably come straight over the minute Alene told him that she'd found Jocelyn.

"He'll be pissed," Jocelyn said, still miserable, "and the last thing I need is to be arrested."

"I don't think 'being pissed' is an acceptable reason to arrest someone," said Alene. On the other hand, Frank would have a lot of questions. "You can tell him that you hid because you're afraid of Harrison. Say you were worried that he might be psychotic or something."

Jocelyn shook her head. "I never thought he was psychotic. I mean, how can you tell what someone is going through if you never have a real conversation?" Alene thought uneasily about her sister. When was the last time they'd had a real conversation? What if Lydia had been trying to communicate something important and Alene kept failing to hear her?

"I think you should just call him and talk to him, Jocelyn," Edith said. She rehashed everything she'd heard Alene say, and added, "What if Stanley was trying to remove you from his legal will, and Harrison fought with him on your behalf?"

Implausible, thought Alene. "Edith, are you saying you think Harrison murdered their father with Jocelyn's welfare in mind?"

"That's not what I said, Alene." Edith made a big production of putting away some cans of cat food. "I think siblings should take care of each other. I might not have been the best sister in the world, but my brother took care of me until the day he died, and you have no idea how hard my life has been since he passed away."

Alene blinked. Was calling Harrison a good idea? If he'd murdered his father, he might not have any qualms about taking down his sister, along with her friends and even her boss. Why should Jocelyn let him know what she suspected? "We all miss Gary," Alene told Edith. "He was an exceptional brother to you and a terrific neighbor and friend to us."

"Yes, he was," said Edith, nodding primly, "and I'm not sure anyone realized how generous he was."

Jocelyn stretched her neck with a pained look. "Harrison was never the kind of brother yours was, Edith. I was just a pest as far as he was concerned. Why do you think he'll even answer the phone?"

"Maybe after losing a father, he doesn't want to lose his only sibling," said Edith. "You could text first and ask him how he's doing. Even the most horrible people like to be asked about themselves."

Had Edith just dispensed some wisdom? "You're right," said Jocelyn, "but I'm not quite ready to talk to my brother. I am ready to stop being afraid of him though, and I don't want to hide anymore. Come on, ladies, it's a beautiful summer evening. Let's go outside."

Edith basked in the glow of being right, flushing with a small smile as she placed a package of cheese in the refrigerator and three deep red apples in a bowl on the counter. "Thanks, but not me," she answered, "I have things to do."

"You'll be glad when I finally move out, won't you?" Jocelyn asked.

"Oh no," Edith gushed. "I love having you here. I wish you'd move into my second bedroom, Jocelyn. Olly's apartment is probably tiny with just that one bathroom. Maybe it's closer to the café, but is that worth the lack of privacy?"

"Olly and I go way back, Edith, and I'm totally comfortable there," Jocelyn answered, tapping her nails on the table the way she sometimes did, "but I can never thank you enough for taking care of me all week."

Edith gave a satisfied smile and continued to bustle around the kitchen, emptying her grocery bags. Alene arranged for the two of them to open the next morning so that she could work out and be home to get her children ready for camp. Blanca was competent and wonderful, but they occasionally liked seeing Alene when they woke up. "If that's okay for you, Jocelyn," Alene said. "I mean, that is, if you're sure you're not afraid."

"What can happen? I highly doubt that the murderer, whoever it is, is going to shoot me in front of everyone at the café. No, I'm done cowering," Jocelyn said, tossing her hair.

Edith started to ask about getting the code to turn off the café's alarm. Alene said, "Let's talk about that another time." She felt a flood of relief. At least some things would go back to normal.

Jocelyn said, "Let's go for a walk and get some fresh air." She jumped up and was out the door before Alene had time to smooth down her shirt. She caught up at the building entrance and watched Jocelyn burst out into the night.

They slowed down and Jocelyn mused, "I don't hate Harrison, you know. He just wasn't very supportive."

"And there's a chance that he's a murderer," said Alene.

"I don't know," said Jocelyn. She sped up again, as if those past feelings were chasing her. "I can only imagine that it was an accident, you know, like they were arguing, and things got out of hand." Her voice trailed off. "I remember how upset Harrison was when our mom got remarried. He started staying at friends' houses on weekends and I hardly ever saw him. And he's eight years older, so I was in fifth grade when he went off to college."

"What about your mom?" Alene asked. She was getting winded from Jocelyn's brisk pace.

"She hated when she had to deal with my father," said Jocelyn. "He was always angry and yelling about something or other." They were walking next to a fence that surrounded a park. The other side of the street was lined with cottages, probably built for workers in the nineteen thirties. They passed one with gables that reminded Alene of a witch's house.

"Have you ever talked to Harrison about your childhood?" Alene asked.

Jocelyn replaced what began as a guffaw, with a more refined chuckle. "As if Harrison ever wanted to waste a minute of his time having a conversation with me," she said, turning to look sideways at Alene, her mouth trembling like she might cry any second. "My gender identity embarrassed him, and I always thought he hated me. He's the reason I started doing Krav Maga when I was fifteen. He was already out of college and working. One time when he was home, he punched me and made my nose bleed for three days. I had to have it cauterized." She touched her nose. "He said it was an accident, but my nose was never the same after that."

"Did he apologize?" Alene asked, looking sideways at Jocelyn's nose, which looked straight and perfectly lovely. Maybe Jocelyn meant that her breathing had never been the same. And how could her nose have accidently gotten in the way of Harrison's fist?

"Are you kidding? My father told me I'd better stop acting like a wimp or I'd never be able to stand up like a man," said Jocelyn. "He was horrible to me. I was just a kid, but I hardly ever saw him. And then he'd want to take me out for dinner, usually at a steakhouse, and it would be like he was auditioning for the role of best father in a sitcom. He'd get all sentimental and after dinner he'd make a big thing about wanting to hug me."

"Maybe he was trying to be a better dad," said Alene.

Jocelyn gave her a brief sideways glance accompanied by a frown. "He called them RBHs, which stood for Really Big Hugs. He used to say, 'Time for my RBH, JH.' It was all fake, because a minute later he'd have this disgusted look on his face, and he'd yell at me for wearing my hair in a ponytail, or because he thought my voice sounded too effeminate."

"And you just wanted him to accept you," said Alene.

Jocelyn said, "That was never going to happen."

"He could have called you 'JH' even after you changed your name to Jocelyn. It would have made it easier for him." Alene considered the initials in Stanley's calendar, but again, nothing sprang to mind.

"Yeah," Jocelyn responded. "He could have called me JH, but he hardly ever talked to me by then."

She sounded so wounded. Alene wished she could think of something comforting to say. They walked a bit without speaking. It felt good to be outside, but they both had to keep an eye on cracks in the pavement. Alene wondered if she was doing enough to make her own children feel loved and protected. "I bet your mom stood up for you and tried to make Stanley be a better father," said Alene.

"My mother was always halfway out the door," said Jocelyn. She sounded as low as she'd ever been, but at least her posture was still exemplary. "And my brother was away at college or busy living his own life. Even when he saw it with his own eyes, Harrison pretended he didn't realize how our father was treating me."

Alene had always thought Stanley projected an intimidating image, but it was hard to imagine why he'd acted that way with his own child. It was clear that Jocelyn could have used more understanding and acceptance. If one of her children chose a different path than the others, a path Neal didn't approve of, would Alene be able to force him to change his behavior? He could think whatever he wanted, as long as he treated all three children with equal respect.

The air was still hot but not as sweltering as it had been during the day. A slight breeze felt good against her face. Again, she wondered if Harrison had gone to Stanley's office and they'd fought that night? Maybe it had been an accident, like Jocelyn's broken nose.

"Hold on," said Jocelyn, interrupting Alene's thoughts. They'd just crossed the street onto a poorly lit block of small, brick houses. "Did you just hear something?"

"It's probably Frank pulling up," said Alene. She'd already been feeling jumpy even though nobody, except Edith, knew that she and Jocelyn were walking around the block. It was time to get back inside, and Alene had to get home to make dinner.

Chapter 16

Late that night, thunder rattled the windows. Quinn and Noah crawled into Alene's bed and were still cuddled on either side of her when she woke up early Tuesday morning. The storm had calmed to a drizzle. The children slept as she got ready to go running and were still asleep when she tiptoed in forty-five minutes later.

She showered, dressed, and whipped her hair into a braid. She opened her father's door and snuck a quick look. It was a relief to see him sprawled out, snoring lightly in his own bed. Then she made lunches, woke the kids, gave them breakfast, and got them off to camp. She even had time to skim through one of her father's newspapers and chat a bit with Blanca and Cal before heading to the café.

The kitchen was in full swing and the cafe was humming with customers. Ruthie, wearing an old-fashioned bib apron adorned with yellow snapdragons and a matching ribbon tied to her braid, rushed over to give Alene a hug. As they caught up on everything that had happened since the day before, Alene recalled finding the apron while scouring garage sales with Ruthie one long-ago Sunday morning.

Behind the counter, LaTonya was serving a man with snow-white hair and Jocelyn handed a box to the woman whose tattoo reminded Alene of wallpaper. Jocelyn wore a short black pencil skirt with a cute magenta top and her hair was pulled back in a low bun. How did she manage to look so chic, so early in the morning? Alene thanked Edith and Jocelyn for opening the café that morning, and turned to Jocelyn to say, "I'm glad you're back." She wondered how Jocelyn had explained her absence to everyone.

Jocelyn smiled brightly and turned to greet two well-dressed young women who looked like they had an important meeting to attend. Several regulars grabbing coffee and muffins hailed her and said they'd missed her for the past few days. During the next hour or so, Alene watched as people popped by to visit Jocelyn, especially Olly, who was like a puppy barking in excited bursts now that his best friend had returned. After his third visit to the counter, LaTonya asked how he'd survived the two years Jocelyn had spent in Afghanistan.

Alene assumed that Olly responded with a sarcastic quip even though she walked away and wasn't close enough to hear. The Tuesday knitting group had started trickling in. Alene looked forward to edging the striped comforter she was nearly ready to donate to a newly settled refugee family. Everyone in the group was using leftover yarns, and nobody was following a pattern, which sometimes led to lovely art, and sometimes not.

She'd just said goodbye to the knitting group and put her project back in the office, when Julian and Phyllie pushed their stroller through the door. Julian got in line at the counter while Phyllie got her boys busy with crayons and paper at the big table.

Alene savored the constant flow of customers and employees. Jack was busy cleaning spills, tossing trash, restocking paper goods, and taking empty muffin trays back to the kitchen. Zuleyka, Jocelyn, and LaTonya were behind the counter, creating or serving drinks and taking orders. Olly delivered plates of food to the tables, and Alene filled in wherever she noticed a gap, ringing up credit cards or helping unload platters coming out of the kitchen.

Kofi arrived and sat on the other side of the café from Julian, and Jack ran back to the kitchen to inform Kacey. Alene hoped Kofi and Julian would avoid each other. She kept an eye on customers coming and going and watched as Miles Taylor held the door open for Heather and her mother. So, Sylvie was home again. Alene was surprised to see her out and about so soon after getting released from the hospital.

Sylvie's lipstick-colored hair was freshly dyed and styled, and she wore the big red eyeglasses that made her look like a bug. She hobbled unsteadily in a bright floral dress that reminded Alene of an old cereal commercial she'd watched as a child. The three of them sat at Julian and Phyllie's table, and the little boys immediately climbed off their chairs. They tried to hug Sylvie's legs, but she squealed that being touched was painful. Phyllie pulled them away as Julian continued to wait at the counter.

Toula and Royce entered and got in line three or four people behind Julian. The two of them stood silently, reminding Alene of the joke about a young couple watching an older couple at the next table. The young wife mentions how sad it is that the old folks have nothing to say to each other, while the older wife points out how sad it is when young couples feel the need to jabber constantly. Alene, passing carry-out boxes across the counter, hoped she and Frank would reach that comfortable, nonverbal stage in their relationship, one day.

Ruthie hurried out of the kitchen, a splotch of flour on her cheek, cheerful as usual. She walked over to hug Sylvie, asked how she was feeling and made a fuss about how good she looked. Sylvie explained that she'd just come from the hair salon. Ruthie told her how sad her own mother would be to miss seeing the family, since it was a weekday, and she was at work. Sylvie announced that Lillian had called her the previous night to tell her that Lawrence was doing better. He was probably getting out of the hospital on Friday, and the big news was that he was going to move in with Lillian. They were still discussing the financial pros and cons of getting married at their age.

Sylvie added, "Obviously they should avoid getting married. Too many problems."

Alene walked away when Ruthie and Phyllie began to argue about marriage. Ruthie waxed rhapsodic about finding someone who loves you best of all, while Phyllie made cracks about some men never growing up. It was not a subject Alene wanted to weigh in on at the moment.

As planned, Olly and another employee started strolling through the café, handing out small samples of Ruthie's Chocolate Banana Nut-Butter frozen pie. Customers oohed and aahed, commented on the pie's creaminess, marveled that it was low in sugar, and asked for the recipe. Alene trained employees to answer that Ruthie was happy they enjoyed her creations, but her Whipped and Sipped contract didn't allow her to give away recipes. It wasn't true. Alene thought a Whipped and Sipped cookbook would be a wonderful idea, but Ruthie didn't want to share her recipes. She argued that people preferred sitting in a café to eating in their own kitchens.

The samples were in small muffin cups served on cute paper coasters that advertised Whipped and Sipped as a party venue. Olly had designed them in the crimson color of the café's art wall, juxtaposed with a graphic of the barn-style door that connected to Tipped, Brianne's bar. When those doors were open, they could comfortably host up to seventy-five people. They'd hosted occasional small parties over the years and had just scheduled a larger event for August. The server handing out samples with Olly was planning to take the new job of catering manager.

Olly brought out a tray of warm rosemary-onion turnovers and crouched behind the counter to fill the case. LaTonya accidentally bumped into him and absently spilled a little of the drink she was carrying. Jack swooped in with his mop. Now, several customers rushed into the café after being caught in a sudden downpour. Some were dripping water on the floor with their umbrellas, so Alene signaled to

Jack, who rushed over. The next two dripping people to enter set their umbrellas in the umbrella stand – thank goodness some customers understood its purpose.

When Jocelyn stiffened and slipped away from the counter, back into the kitchen, Alene realized they were Harrison and Rhea Huff, Jocelyn's brother and sister-in-law. They were coughing and sniffling. Alene quickly moved to take their orders, hoping they weren't spreading germs all over the café. If they started arguing with Sylvie, or anyone in that family, Alene was going to ask them to leave. A shouting match would drive all the other customers out the door.

"Of all the gin joints in all the towns in all the world," she whispered to LaTonya, who shrugged. Not everyone watched old movies like Alene did with her father.

Rising from behind the counter, Olly said, "That's from Casablanca. But Gin Joint? That reminds me of the two ingredients you should add to the café's offerings. I'm thinking we should do gin-inspired cookies and marijuana infused brownies. Everyone's doing it these days." LaTonya laughed, which had probably been Olly's objective.

Alene just shook her head and greeted the Huffs. Harrison ordered the spinach turnover salad plate with coffee. Rhea asked for a veggie lunch burrito and herbal tea. As he inserted his credit card, he said, "I've wanted to meet you, Alene. I'm Jocelyn's brother, Harrison Huff, and this is my wife, Rhea."

It seemed like a good start that he'd called Jocelyn by her chosen name, but Alene felt a little nervous talking to them both. Harrison and Rhea had more of a motive than anyone else Alene had thought about. She'd read that prosecutors in a criminal case don't have to mention motive, as long as they can show intent. Had it been Harrison's intent to murder his father, or had he only hoped to inherit his father's estate? She was getting ahead of herself. If Harrison was guilty of anything, Frank would figure it out.

"Thanks for coming in," Alene said guardedly, with a small smile. "Of course, I know who you are." He shared

Jocelyn's long face and beautifully arched eyebrows. Jocelyn was still hiding in the kitchen. If, as she'd told Alene, she wasn't going to live in fear anymore, this would be the perfect time for her to face Harrison. He probably wasn't going to create a scene in the middle of the café.

"I've been trying to reach my sister," Harrison said, looking for a moment at the crimson wall. Alene wished Jocelyn had heard him call her his sister. Maybe he'd softened over the years and there was some possibility of a relationship. Unless, of course, he'd murdered their father.

Rhea Huff said, "Sylvie is always gushing about this place, so we all decided to meet here today."

If they'd planned a family reunion, why hadn't anyone told Jocelyn? "It's because of Ruthie Rosin's stellar baking," said Alene.

Harrison and Rhea probably knew Ruthie because of her mother's friendship with Sylvie. They seemed younger than Alene, probably early thirties, and neither looked like they'd spent much time in the sun. Alene knew they'd moved back to Chicago recently. Maybe it hadn't been easy moving to the city just in time for the hot, sticky weather. And then they'd had to grapple with Stanley's death. Maybe that's why they seemed tense.

"I hope it's not a bad time," Harrison said, sounding congested and worn out. "As I mentioned, I've been trying to reach Jocelyn all week." Hadn't Jocelyn said that he wouldn't talk to her? Families could be so complicated.

Olly popped up from behind the counter, where he was unloading another tray. "Jocelyn wasn't reachable this week," he announced cheerfully. Alene remembered how he'd disappeared into the kitchen the last time Harrison came in.

Harrison blinked. "I thought I glimpsed her when we first came in. Look, we just need to set up a time to go over some details regarding our father. Maybe we can leave a message since she's not answering my texts."

Rhea added, "We've tried calling too, but she didn't return our calls. We just want a quick meeting." Alene

206

couldn't help taking another look at her broad shoulders while imagining female murderers she'd seen depicted in the movies. Why just a quick meeting? Was it because they'd slip her some poison and be on their way?

Olly said, "I can't believe you don't recognize me, Harrison. I used to hang out at your house all the time with J. I've never met your wife." He waved. "Pleased to meet you. I'm Olly Burns."

"I remember you, Olly," said Harrison, smiling in a friendly way. Alene couldn't help thinking about the good-looking serial killer who kept fooling women into trusting him before he abducted them. "You and J always took up both couches and spent hours watching abysmal music videos."

"Ah yes," Olly responded good-naturedly, "I'd forgotten that you were always an authority on high culture." He elbowed Alene and added, "You don't need anyone's permission to speak with Jocelyn. She's an adult."

They were either very sneaky or very professional criminals. Alene glanced at the umbrella stand, recalling the true story of a Bulgarian operative who used a poison-tipped umbrella to assassinate a Russian diplomat. "Why don't you choose a table and Jocelyn will bring your food when it's ready," she said. Olly would keep a close eye on them, just in case.

Jocelyn must have reconsidered, because now she returned to the counter, holding onto Jack's arm. She stood slightly behind him as if he were a bodyguard. Jack stood up straighter than usual, no longer slouching. His jaw jutted forward, and he acted like protecting a beautiful woman was one of the things he did all the time. Alene couldn't help feeling a little proud to have helped bring out this side of Jack.

Holding her chin high, Jocelyn put a manicured hand on the counter and said, "If you're trying to get me to sign my inheritance over to you, Harrison, I can give you some helpful advice about where to put important papers."

Harrison responded with a loud coughing fit. Alene waited on the next customer, hoping it was just reflux or asthma, and not contagious. Jocelyn tapped her fingernails and watched Harrison warily. Finally, he said, "Can we talk, Jocelyn?"

Her head fell forward, either to consider her response or to cry. Maybe that was the first time he'd ever addressed her by her chosen name. Alene's customer held her credit card in the air and watched the unfolding scene, until Alene pointed out where she should insert the card.

As Jocelyn wavered, Edith inched close enough to say, "You should be ashamed of the way you treated your sister all these years, Harrison."

Olly, LaTonya, and Jocelyn all stopped in their tracks to stare. It was the first time Alene had ever admired Edith, who now patted Jocelyn on the back like a coach about to give a pep talk.

Harrison looked at his wife, who'd linked her arm through his. "What am I supposed to do now?" he said with a defeated sigh. "I tried. Let's just go."

"No, we're not going," said Rhea, firmly gripping her husband's arm, "not before you talk to your sister. You can't expect her to welcome you with open arms after a lifetime of treating her like crap. You don't need me to tell you what you have to do next."

Alene liked the woman's style. Rhea added, "Please, Jocelyn, give him a chance to apologize. He knows how your father treated you, and he feels bad for going along with it all these years." Jocelyn, tears streaming, looked helplessly at Alene. "He should have stood up for you," Rhea added.

Alene was plagued with a tiny bit of doubt as she watched Harrison and Rhea head to a table. What if they were trying to get Jocelyn to let down her guard by pretending to have had a change of heart? As soon as she trusted them, they could arrange for her to have an "accident."

Jocelyn followed Harrison, who turned and touched her arm. The small gesture gave Alene a sense of hope. Maybe

Harrison really was trying to make amends for the way he'd behaved. Then Jocelyn swatted Harrison's hand away from her arm, and Alene delivered a veggie burger smothered with shredded, roasted carrots to another table. She needed to stop dreaming about everyone getting along with each other.

Moments later, Blanca arrived with Cal, who waved and blew kisses from across the café. Alene helped them to a table and took their order, hoping none of her other customers would assume they'd get that kind of personalized table service. The rest of the staff came out of the kitchen or from behind the counter, a few at a time, to welcome Cal back. Alene watched her father happily soak up the attention. She hoped he didn't notice Sylvie Huff, sitting on the other side of the café. He'd been so glad to get out of the hospital and away from her.

Blanca should bring him to the café more often. Maybe they'd set up a few tables with chess sets, since her father loved to play. He'd taught Alene and Lydia when they were younger, but only Lydia had enjoyed the strategizing. The café could offer games in the afternoon, after the lunch rush. They could even host chess tournaments. She'd have to investigate buying relatively inexpensive chess sets along with the necessary timers.

There was a low murmur of people ordering or chatting at their tables. Then, Julian's two-year-old, who'd been leaning against Phyllie's leg eating half a grilled cheese sandwich, suddenly propelled himself to the next table, where Toula sat with her husband, not speaking, as usual. The child averted a tumble to the ground by grabbing Royce's leg with his greasy hands. Royce shook his leg to loosen Richie's grasp, and spluttered, "Get this kid off me."

The little boy fell hard on the floor and started wailing as if someone had stabbed him. Julian jumped from his seat to swoop him up. "He's only two," Julian said to Royce. Alene wished he'd yelled louder at the large adult who'd come close to hurting his child.

Royce stood and said, "We're done here. Let's go." There was still food on their plates.

But Sylvie had risen from her chair and now stood directly in front of Toula, who put her fork down. "Just one minute," Sylvie demanded in her nasal voice, as she pointed at Toula's face. "Where did you get those earrings?"

Just a few feet away, Alene heard her father say, "no way, you've got to be kidding me."

She asked Sylvie to lower her voice. Sylvie grabbed Alene's arm, sending a cloud of sickly-sweet perfume into the air. Alene made a note to turn up the air-conditioning the second Sylvie let go. "Those are my earrings," Sylvie shouted, and then with less volume, added, "I already told you about how Stanley gave them to me for our anniversary."

"You accused Blanca of stealing them, Sylvie," said Alene. "And now you think one of my customers took your earrings. How many more people are you going to accuse?"

"I don't take your ugly jewelry, Sylvie Huff!" Blanca said loudly.

Cal said, equally loudly, "Some people might need a little more recovery time before they venture out in public after a hospital stay." Alene hoped that was all he was going to say about Sylvie.

Sylvie doubled down, paying no attention to Cal. "They're half-carat diamonds on one side and sapphire on the other. Nobody else has earrings like these." She slowly rose from her seat, leaning heavily on the table with her face scrunched in anger. Customers were staring as Alene tried to come up with a way to prevent more drama. It looked like Sylvie was working herself into a relatively quick frenzy, her pointer finger now much too close to Toula's face. "Those are my earrings," she shrieked. "Where did you get them?"

All conversation in the café stopped. A few customers took out their phones and began snapping photos or videotaping. Alene stepped in front of Sylvie to address Toula. "I'm so sorry," she said, "This is Sylvie Huff, who just lost her husband. She's been ill, and got out of the hospital

210

yesterday, so she might not be completely well." As if that would explain Sylvie's rudeness.

Toula, in a shaky voice, said, "I know who she is."

Ruthie had come out of the kitchen by then and headed straight to Sylvie. "I'd hate to see your blood pressure go up again." She reached for Sylvie's hand. "Come sit down with me," she said soothingly, "and we'll figure this out together."

Sylvie flicked Ruthie's hand away. "My husband gave her my earrings," she said, oozing with scorn, "because she was sleeping with him."

Edith called out, "You should never re-gift anything." Several people snickered, which caused Edith's eyes to well with tears, because she hadn't meant to be funny. Alene pointed at the blenders, hoping Edith would remember that she had a job to do. How many hurt feelings could a person deal with at the same time?

"Toula always wears lovely jewelry," said Alene, still hoping she could diffuse the unpleasant situation. Sylvie's earrings were probably hidden in a sock at the back of her freezer. Alene wore small hoops that she could sleep in, and envied women who had the wherewithal to change their jewelry every morning. "Those earrings are not yours, Sylvie, so please sit down and don't ruin lunch for everyone in my café."

Alene was shocked and angry when Sylvie pushed her out of the way. "Yes, they are mine," Sylvie screeched, again pointing just inches from Toula's head. It looked like she meant to grab the earrings out of Toula's ears.

"Please sit down, Sylvie," said Alene. "If you can't calm yourself, you're going to have to leave immediately." Only a few people continued to eat. Most were staring.

Toula reached her hands to her face and felt both of her earlobes. "I've had these earrings forever," she said with a slight tremor.

Sylvie continued sputtering about the earrings, now directing her ire at Toula's husband, who sat stiffly with his eyes darting to whoever was speaking. His face was the color of a beet, and he clenched and unclenched his hands, cracking the joints and reminding Alene of a teapot about to blow its top. Was he going to attack Sylvie for casting aspersions about his wife or would just he add a few more bruises to Toula's arms?

Jocelyn, Kofi, Kacey, and Jack quickly surrounded Royce while Alene pulled Toula toward the kitchen. Sylvie pushed Jack out of the way and got ahold of Royce's shirt. She thrust her finger into his face as she screamed about her earrings. Out of the corner of her eye, Alene could see Olly trying to lighten the mood by sending café coasters flying like frisbees. It wasn't calming anyone down, but as Alene closed her office door, she hoped it distracted a bit from the volatile yelling match that had erupted between Sylvie and Royce.

Chapter 17

Alene was surprised to see Toula break down in tears as soon as she crumbled onto the couch in Alene's office. How many more people were going to cry today? Alene offered Toula the tissue box and said, "I'm really sorry about all that. Sylvie is seriously not well. You should take everything she says with a grain of salt, and I should have made her leave the minute she started making a commotion. This is my fault."

"No, none of this is your fault," said Toula, dismal, but a little calmer. "It's all just been so impossible." Alene held her hands in a time-out sign and ran to pour water for the two of them.

Handing one glass to Toula, Alene asked, "What's been impossible?"

"Everything," Toula said. "My husband, for example."

"I got divorced about eight years ago," Alene said, "so I'm pretty familiar with going through rough patches in a marriage. You don't have to explain anything to me."

"Our marriage is a mess," said Toula, blowing her nose and taking another tissue. "I'm surprised it lasted this long."

Alene said, "You can't blame yourself if you tried and failed, believe me."

"I did try," Toula said in a small voice, "but some things can't be repaired." Alene felt like she knew exactly what Toula meant.

"He wanted to eat here," Toula gave her a look and started crying. "These past few weeks? He wanted to hear what people were saying."

"What do you mean? Saying about what?"

"About Stanley," said Toula, taking gulps of air as she sobbed.

"Why did he care about Stanley?" Alene asked, although she suddenly understood. Royce had smothered Stanley and caused his heart attack. Frank was going to be amazed that she'd figured it out. While Toula pulled herself together, Alene texted him, "Come to café asap. Hurry."

"Stanley was my trainer," said Toula, pounding a fist against her forehead. "And we." She stopped. "We didn't mean to, but we..."

Alene knew. "You had an affair?" Toula nodded. She was curvy and beautiful, and her husband wasn't kind to her. It wasn't such a surprise. "How can I help you, Toula? I just contacted the detective and he's probably on his way."

"You don't understand," Toula started crying again. "It was all my fault."

Alene said, "It wasn't your fault, Toula. Even if you and Stanley had an affair, Stanley's death was not your fault."

Royce had somehow managed to get into the kitchen and had started pounding on Alene's locked office door. He yelled at Toula to shut her mouth, which reminded Alene of her conversations with Frank about abusive husbands. She thought about watching Royce and Toula sitting at their table with nothing to say, remembered how he sometimes snapped at her, grabbed her arm, or pushed her out the door. Maybe Royce caught Toula and Stanley together, and was so enraged that he tried to kill them both, but only got Stanley. Frank was not, after all, a hammer who saw everything as a nail.

Toula stood. "He's going to testify against me if I say anything," she said, opening the door before Alene could stop her. Royce roughly shoved her back toward the café. He didn't see Jack Stone coming from around the pastry table until Jack's foot tripped him. Reaching out for support, Royce knocked over bowls of dough and batter as the bakers scurried to the other side of the counter. Toula got out of his way as he fell, but he managed to push Alene against one of the ovens. It was painfully hot, and it took the wind out of her.

"Thanks for slowing him down," Alene said, breathing heavily and wincing as Jack helped her to her feet. She'd never appreciated him as much as she did now.

Jack said, "But he's dragging Toula through the kitchen door and back into the café."

Alene limped out and immediately toppled against Phyllie, who knocked into Toula as Julian swooped the older boy up in his arms. Toula sat down hard on the floor, and stayed there, quietly hugging herself. In that fifteen second interlude, Jocelyn tackled Royce and Olly immobilized him with his arms behind his back. Alene worried that they were going to hurt him. Olly looked at Alene and said, "And that, in a nutshell, is why I love Jiu-Jitsu."

Jocelyn gave a snort of laughter and said, "All you did was help me while I tackled this guy like he was carrying the ball." Alene shook her head and glanced over to make sure that her father and Blanca were still sitting safely at their table. Some customers had gone, disturbed by the altercation, but Alene noticed some still taping with their phone cameras. She shuddered to think about the whole episode going viral.

Royce had threatened to testify against Toula? Now he was struggling against Jocelyn and Olly, so Kofi jumped up to help, and in a few swift moves had Royce stilled.

Everyone in the café froze, except for Julian and Phyllie's little boys, who bounced up and down in the stroller. The younger one thrust out a fist and shouted, "Again."

The kitchen staff had stumbled into the café to watch. Now Ruthie strode forward to put a gentle hand on Toula's shoulder. "Are you all right?" she asked. Alene's thigh already ached where she'd slammed it into the oven.

Toula was bent over and sobbing. "I just needed someone," she said. "Someone who cared about me."

Royce, thrashing but immobilized, growled at her to stop talking. His face was tight with rage and his eyes were angry slits. The veins in his thick neck throbbed. Alene wondered if he'd unleashed this part of himself on Toula regularly. Toula closed her eyes as if to build up courage and said, "I didn't want anyone to get hurt."

"I told you to shut up," Royce growled again.

Frank and his partner rushed in then, and Alene finally exhaled. She pointed out Royce to Frank and pantomimed a baseball player swinging a bat. Frank immediately understood and signaled to Lee, who pulled out his handcuffs and approached Royce. Alene pointed to Toula, and Frank helped her to her feet. "Are you hurt?" he asked.

Toula nodded, weeping.

"She murdered her boyfriend," Royce barked. "Cuff her if you're going to cuff me."

Everyone slowly turned to stare at Toula, who stiffened. Then her head fell forward and she said, "He wouldn't let me get up. Until Stanley. Stopped moving. I didn't want him to die."

Alene couldn't help butting in to ask, "What do you mean?"

"It was my fault," Toula said, now looking straight at Alene. "Stanley died because of me."

Frank got out his handcuffs and said, "You have the right to remain silent. Anything you say can, and will, be used against you in a court of law. You have the right to an attorney."

"It doesn't matter," said Toula, expressionless. "I can't live like this."

Royce said, "You're digging your own grave." He'd stopped fighting and his face had started to drain of all color. Now his face was hard and bitter.

"You wanted me to die too," Toula said, as calmly as if she were reading a grocery list. "You laid on top of me until he stopped moving. You wanted me to die too, but all you managed to do was break my heart."

Alene felt tears erupting. People were murmuring and more cameras came out. Her staff seemed petrified in stone, but what could she do? It didn't seem like the right time to issue directions. Toula added, "You're never going to touch me again."

Royce sneered. "I wouldn't be so sure, sweetheart. I'm still your husband."

"I'd rather rot in prison," Toula said miserably. Alene tried to put an arm around her, but she shook her head and moved closer to Frank. "You said I have the right to an attorney. I'll need one, because Royce said he'd make sure I'd get the death penalty."

"He can't do that, honey," Cal said from the other side of the hushed room. "There's no death penalty in the state of Illinois." He and Blanca were sitting far enough from the action to still be holding their cups. Cal looked positively energetic. Nothing like a good fight to make him feel alive.

Olly, now smoothing his mussed-up shirt, helpfully added, "It was repealed in 2011."

As Lee got Royce out the door, Frank helped Toula to a chair and called in the arrests. He told everyone to stay in the restaurant until they gave him their name and contact information. They all followed his directive – probably very few of them had ever witnessed the arrest of a murderer. Alene wanted to yell at her customers to stop gawking and get back to their laptops and coffees. Some were still holding up their phone cameras, and some outside the café were staring through the window. She gestured to her staff to get moving. What a devious thing, to hold Toula down until Stanley stopped breathing and then convince her that she was the one who'd smothered him. She was lucky Royce hadn't killed her too.

Frank pulled Alene close and whispered that she'd handled it well. Toula removed her earrings and reached over to give them to Sylvie. Sylvie held them up with a triumphant gesture and announced, "She obviously doesn't know how to take care of good jewelry."

Cal said loudly, "As Mark Twain wrote, 'Never argue with stupid people.'"

"You're right, Cal," said Blanca. "So many stupid people in the world."

After Frank got everyone's information, he left with Toula. Other customers gathered their belongings and headed out, and the café started to calm down. Jack Stone cleaned up the tables, everyone went back to eating and drinking, and after a while, it looked almost like nothing had happened.

Alene was upset that she hadn't figured out what was going on between Royce and Toula. She felt like she'd failed an important test. Ruthie said they'd all missed the signs that Toula was being abused. She thought they should invite someone from the nearby women's shelter to do awareness training with the whole staff.

The baking staff took turns speculating about why Toula and Royce had been coming to the café so often. Olly said he didn't buy that Royce wanted to hear if people were talking about Stanley and suggested that Royce's goal had been to humiliate Toula. Ruthie said, "Everyone in the neighborhood remembers that you helped solve a murder, Six. Maybe Toula wanted to be here because she hoped you'd figure out what was going on."

Alene didn't want to spend any more time thinking about Toula and Royce. She encouraged everyone to concentrate on their work, but just then, Jocelyn sidled closer and whispered, "Do you remember those initials in my father's appointment book?"

Alene nodded.

"Do you also remember that my father used to say, 'Time for my RBH, JH?' and RBH was a Really Big Hug? Harrison just reminded me that RGS was what he wanted from our mom."

"Oh?" Alene had forgotten all about Jocelyn's conversation with her brother. Nice that they'd spent the time reminiscing. Then she got what RGS must stand for. "Oh!"

"I think Royce scared Toula so much that she couldn't even give us a clue about what was happening," Jocelyn concluded.

Ruthie said, "That's what abusers do."

"They shouldn't be allowed to behave like that," said Edith, who'd come into the kitchen.

Alene was glad to have the opportunity to say, "Wise words, Edith. I couldn't agree more."

Chapter 18

Thirty minutes later, Alene breathed in the café's rhythms, the soft music, and the scent of freshly brewed coffee. The tables had turned over, but her dad still sat with Blanca, playing cribbage. Blanca always sat with her back straight as if she'd studied ballet as a child. She waved at Alene, who headed to their table. "I love being here," said Cal, "but are you sure you're all right, Leeni?" He'd been asking every ten minutes since Frank left. Alene worried that the outing had been too much for his first day out of the hospital, but he was smiling.

"I'm fine, Dad," Alene said for the fourth time, as she pulled up a chair. "But that was enough drama to last me for the rest of the summer."

"It was drama like television," Blanca said. "We enjoyed watching."

Cal shook his head, "I felt horrible for that woman."

Blanca snapped back, "She sleeps with a married man, bad things happen."

"I feel terrible for her too," said Alene, "even though I don't have a lot of pity for people who cheat on their partners." She couldn't help thinking back to when she learned that Neal was having an affair. Her phone vibrated, and it was Frank, asking if he could bring pizza and have dinner with her and the children.

"Yes, absolutely. It's about time, isn't it?" Alene said. "I don't know how we would have managed without you today, Frank."

"You'd have handled it," said Frank. "No doubt about it."

Alene still wanted to process everything that happened. "Were those really Sylvie's earrings?"

"Yes, but Toula didn't steal them," Frank said. "Stanley gave them to her." It was infuriating that Sylvie had been right. "Royce suspected the affair and followed her to Stanley's office that night."

Alene was grateful that Frank was willing to talk about it. "How did he force Toula to smother Stanley?" She asked. "I don't get that."

"He found Toula lying on top of Stanley, knocked the guy out and then physically held Toula down so that she was technically the one who blocked Stanley's air," Frank explained.

"That poor woman," Alene said. It was just as she'd speculated to Frank when she thought Sylvie might have murdered her husband. Toula had either already removed some clothes or she'd been wearing a microfiber material that wouldn't have been inhaled.

"She made some bad choices," Frank said. "People don't always consider consequences."

"Yeah," said Alene, remembering how Neal had suggested they have an open marriage. That was the moment when she realized that the marriage was over. Consequences.

Frank asked what kind of pizza the children liked, what time he should show up, and what was their favorite ice cream. After she hung up and put her phone back in her pocket, Cal said, "It was an unusually interesting afternoon, but will Sylvie show up everywhere I go from now on?"

Alene said, "Let's hope not." She kissed his cheek just before Blanca led Cal out the door.

221

Alene and Ruthie baked for the rest of the afternoon. People must have spread the word about what had happened, because they had more customers in the next hour than they had all week, and there were very few leftovers. Then they were alone, cleaning up and talking about how much they'd have to bake the next day. They joked about needing to stage some kind of drama now and then to spice up business.

Ruthie asked if Alene knew how Jocelyn's meeting with Harrison had gone. "I hope she got some closure," said Alene. "And I hope her life gets easier."

Ruthie said, "I think she's always going to have challenges."

"Aren't we all?" Alene responded.

As she walked home, Alene called her sister to tell her what had happened. Lydia calmly explained the legal possibilities. "It's horrible that the woman might also be prosecuted for Stanley's murder," Lydia said, adding that she'd text Alene the phone number of an organization that fought for the rights of abused or battered women.

"But this is a completely different situation," said Alene.

"Every situation is different, but she was still abused, and this organization might be able to help her," said Lydia. "In fact, I'm planning to do some pro bono work for them."

Alene said, "That'd be awesome, because word on the street is that you're a superb lawyer."

"Thanks, Alene," Lydia said. "I don't think you've ever said that to me." Alene felt a little awkward about that, but at least she'd said it now. She invited Lydia and Theo to join them for pizza, and texted Frank to tell him that there would be two more at dinner.

Frank arrived just after Lydia and Theo. He set three boxes of Lou Malnati's on the counter, saying that he hadn't wanted to disappoint the children, so he got each of their favorites; plain cheese for Noah, olives for Quinn, and the spinach stuffed "Lou" for Sierra. Alene had brought two sauces from the café: the first a Roasted Red Pepper Tahini and the second a Pumpkin Seed Pesto. They'd be delicious with the pizzas.

Cal was delighted to be home with both of his daughters and all three of his grandchildren. He sat at the dining room table eating, smiling and repeating variations of "I'm so lucky," or "You can't imagine how wonderful it is to look around this table and see your beautiful faces." Alene felt the same way. Frank had moved his chair so that their legs touched. She wasn't ready for the kids to see any serious displays of affection, but touching legs seemed harmless.

As they were finishing the pizza, Alene told the kids that Frank worked as a detective for the Chicago Police, and they all stared at him. "Do you have a gun?" Noah asked. "Like, are you wearing one right now?"

"Yes," said Frank." Noah's mouth fell open.

Sierra asked, "Why aren't you wearing a uniform?"

"Because I don't have to," Frank answered. Cal laughed at that.

Quinn asked, "Do you give tickets to children who don't follow bicycle safety rules?"

"Stupid question as usual," Sierra muttered. Alene gave her a look.

"No, I don't give tickets to children," said Frank, "but I like to explain what the rules are to them, because the rules keep them safe, don't you think?"

Quinn and Noah nodded, and Sierra shrugged. While Alene wrapped up and refrigerated the leftovers, Cal asked Frank about corruption in the department. Then, Lydia asked about recent Tribune articles criticizing the police.

Alene said, "Let's give Frank a little break from talking about his work." She was passing out the ice cream bowls when Quinn said, "I have a relevant story. My friend Sadie's mother was having lunch today and the police came because some people eating there did something bad, but Sadie didn't know exactly what, so they were probably bank robbers or something. And then, ..."

Predictably, Sierra, who didn't have patience for Quinn's winding stories, interrupted to say, "I heard about

223

that too, and I don't think they were bank robbers. Mom, you know my friend Camilla?" Alene nodded. This was a girl at camp whom Sierra had been talking about a lot. "So, she just texted me because their upstairs neighbor said the police raided the Whipped and Sipped Café."

Alene nodded, "Nobody raided the café, but...

Quinn interrupted to finish her story. "And then my friend Sadie said that her mom was having coffee with a real estate lady because her mom is pregnant and they're trying to move into a bigger place." Here she stopped to look sadly at Alene, who'd told her unequivocally that there would not be another baby in the family.

"Yeah," said Sierra, "Sadie's mom was having coffee at Mom's café."

Now Noah piped up, "Mom, did something bad happen? Were there robbers?"

Alene, Frank, and Cal exchanged glances. Alene said, "Robbers? I don't think they'd dare to come into the Whipped and Sipped Café. What do you think, Frank?"

"I think bad people shouldn't be allowed in cafés," said Frank.

Cal said, "but if there were no bad people, there would be no good lawyers."

"That's one of your best sayings, Dad," said Lydia.

Alene said, "I thought you wrote it, Lydia."

"No," said Cal. "That was by Charles Dickens, an old friend of mine."

Alene's children all looked confused. "I think your friend is wrong, Grandpa," Quinn said, "There could still be good lawyers for other things, but if there were no bad people, then we wouldn't need policemen." She smiled shyly at Frank.

"I'd be okay with that," Frank said.

List of Recipes:

GF = Gluten Free
V = Vegan

Apple Cinnamon Protein Bars (GF, V)
Almond-Berry Breakfast Cake (GF, V)
Banana Loaf or Muffins (GF, V)
Cashew Chocolate Chip Blondies (GF, V)
Challah Bread
Chilled Minty Cucumber-Melon Soup (V)
Chocolate Banana Nut Frozen Pie (GF, V)
Creamy Chocolate Sauce (V)
Dover Sole with Butternut Squash
Ginger Molasses Cookies (GF, V)
Guacamole Salad (V)
Lemon-Blueberry Cake or Muffins (GF, V)
Oatmeal Chocolate Chip Cookies (GF, V)
Orange Hummus (V)
Orange-Tahini Cookies (GF, V)
Pumpkin Apple Cake (V)
Roasted Red Pepper Sauce or Dip (V)
Skillet Chicken with Mushrooms
Sunflower Chocolate Chip Cookies (GF, V)
Sweet Potato and Black Bean Soup (V)
Vegetarian Cholent (Overnight Stew) (V)
Zucchini-Orange Loaf of Muffins (GF, V)

Apple Cinnamon Protein Bars

1 TBSP each (min. 2 of these) flax meal, chia seeds, hemp seeds
½ cup unsweetened coconut, almond, or oat milk
1 ½ cup unsalted, roasted almonds (can subsitute walnuts or pepitas)
½ cup plus 1 ½ cup old fashioned or quick oats
1 cup pitted prunes or dates (about 20 - can be mixed)
1 small or medium tart apple (like Gala), seeded, cut into 12 segments
1 TBSP unfiltered apple cider vinegar
1 tsp pure vanilla extract
1 tsp baking soda
1 ½ tsp ground cinnamon
½ tsp fine-grained sea salt*

In a small bowl, stir flax meal, chia seeds, and hemp seeds with the plant milk. Let it rest 10 minutes. In a food processor, grind almonds with ½ cup of oats into a course flour, about 60 seconds. Add prunes/dates, apple segments, vinegar, and vanilla. Blend until uniform, about 90 seconds. Stop to scrape down the sides, add the thickened seed mixture, and pulse 3 or 4 times. In a medium or large bowl, stir together 1 ½ cup of oats, baking soda, cinnamon, and salt. Spoon the apple mixture from the processor into the dry ingredients and stir together until blended. Refrigerate the bowl while you preheat the oven (350°F/180°C) and clean up (10-15 minutes). Line 1 standard, rimmed cookie sheet with silicone or baking paper, and lightly spray. Remove bowl from fridge and spread the dough to the edges of the silicone mat or the baking paper. Smooth the top and sides so that your bars will be even. Bake for about 15-17 minutes until toasty brown. Cool before cutting the slab into rectangular bars.

These bars will be soft. I freeze them and take out one or two for breakfast or a snack. These have no added sugar and are better than prepackaged bars. If you want crispier bars, add about ¼ cup regular sugar to the recipe. It's a small amount but it'll make a difference.

* *Sea salt is less processed than table salt and contains more trace minerals (in case you wondered)!*

Almond-Berry Breakfast Cake

1 cup almond or oat milk
1 small seeded sweet apple (like Gala, with peel), cut into 6 or 8
    segments
1 medium, THIN skinned orange, seeded (with peel*), ends cut, cut into
    8 segments
¼ cup coconut, canola, or extra virgin olive oil
½ cup real maple syrup
2 TBSP unfiltered apple cider vinegar
1 tsp pure vanilla extract
1 tsp pure almond extract
2 cups almond flour
1 cup quick oats
1 tsp baking soda
1 tsp baking powder
1 tsp ground cinnamon
¼ tsp fine-grained sea salt
1 to 1 ½ cup (10 oz) washed strawberries (about 12 large) or other
    berries
2 TBSP almond or other gluten-free flour (for coating the berries)

Preheat oven to 350°F/180°C and spray a 9" round or spring-form pan.
In a high-speed blender or food processor, blend plant milk, oil, apple,
orange, maple syrup, apple cider vinegar, and extracts until it all looks
uniform, about 90 seconds. In a large bowl, stir almond flour, oats, baking
soda, baking powder, cinnamon, and salt. In a separate bowl, toss berries
with flour and be ready to move quickly. Pour wet ingredients from the
blender into the dry ingredients and use a spatula to stir. Fold the berries
gently into the batter. Pour the batter into the prepared round or
springform pan. Bake for about 60-65 minutes until the cake is golden
and a toothpick comes out clean. Cool in the pan before plating or serving,
For a shiny top, microwave 1 TBSP maple syrup with 1 tsp coconut oil for
30 sec. Shmear. I like refrigerating this cake and eating it chilled, but it
can be left out on the counter for a couple of days.

* Even though oranges are usually zested, I started using the entire
peel many years ago. The peel contains vitamin A, C, B6, B5, calcium,
riboflavin, thiamine, niacin, folate and dietary fiber!

227

Banana Muffins or Loaf

2 TBSP flax meal* (ground flax seeds)
½ cup unsweetened almond or oat milk
1 ¼ cup mashed banana (about 3 very ripe bananas)
½ cup packed coconut or dark brown sugar
½ cup unsweetened coconut flakes
¼ cup coconut, canola, or extra virgin olive oil
1 TBSP unfiltered apple cider vinegar
1 tsp pure vanilla extract
2 cups any kind of oats (You could also use oat flour or any
     gluten-free flour)
1 tsp baking soda
1 tsp ground cinnamon
1 tsp ground coriander
½ tsp ground or fresh ginger
½ tsp fine-grained sea salt
Optional: ½ cup semi-sweet chocolate chips

In a small bowl, stir flax meal with plant milk and let rest in fridge while
you start the recipe. Preheat oven to 350°F/180°C. Spray or line a
standard loaf pan (I like using baking paper) or 12-muffin pan (I
use reusable silicone muffin cups). In a large bowl, mash bananas.
Stir in sweetener, coconut flakes, oil, apple cider vinegar, and
vanilla. If using flour, stir with baking soda, cinnamon, coriander,
ginger, and salt in a small bowl. If using oats, pulse with other dry
ingredients in a high-speed blender until uniform and flour-like,
about 60 seconds. Stir flax mixture from the refrigerator into the
banana mixture. Pour dry ingredients into the wet ingredients and
stir just until blended. If you are planning to add chocolate chips,
gently stir them in now. Pour the batter into the prepared muffin
or loaf pan. Bake about 45-50 minutes for a loaf and 20-25 minutes
for muffins (until a toothpick comes out clean). Cool in the pan and
then remove it to a serving platter.

*Flax meal is loaded with nutrients and health benefits. They sell it
everywhere. You can sprinkle it on anything and immediately add
protein (1.9 g per TBSP) and minerals!*

Cashew Chocolate Chip Blondies

1 TBSP flax meal
1 cup canned coconut milk
2 cups old-fashioned or quick oats
1 cup unsalted toasted or raw cashews (or almonds)
1 tsp baking soda
½ tsp fine-grained sea salt
1 tsp ground cinnamon
½ cup packed brown sugar
¼ cup canola or extra virgin olive oil
1 TBSP unsulphured molasses
2 TBSP unfiltered apple cider vinegar
2 tsp pure vanilla extract
½ cup semisweet chocolate chips + 2 TBSP extra for top

In a small bowl, mix flax meal with coconut milk and rest it in the fridge for 5-10 minutes while you line up your ingredients and prepare your pan. Preheat oven to 350°F/180°C. Line an 8 x 8" baking pan with baking paper. In a food processor, blend oats, cashews, baking soda, salt, and cinnamon until uniform, about 60–70 seconds. Add the flax mixture to the processor and pulse until blended, about 4–6 times. Add sugar, oil, molasses, apple cider vinegar, and vanilla. Blend for about 30–40 seconds until it is blended and creamy. Add ½ cup chocolate chips and briefly pulse just 2 or 3 times. Use a spatula to transfer the batter to the pan and smooth the top. Lightly press the extra chocolate chips (if desired) into the batter. Bake for 30–35 minutes until a toothpick comes out clean. Cool for about 20 minutes before serving (or tasting). Don't be surprised if you end up slicing off tiny pieces of this cake all afternoon — it's yummy with a cup of tea.

Challah Bread

6 cups (720 g) bread flour (If you can't get it, use all-purpose
    flour and start the night before)
2 room temp eggs, lightly mixed (plus one egg white if you wish
    to do an egg wash before baking)
1 ½ tsp (9 g) kosher or sea salt
¼ cup (50g) canola or any olive oil
1 packet or 1 TBSP (9g) active dry yeast
¼ cup sugar (50g) or honey (85g)
1 ½ to 2 cups of room temperature or lukewarm water (More as
    needed)

In a large mixing bowl, stir the yeast, sweetener, and 1 cup of flour
into 1 ½ cups of lukewarm water. It should start to bubble in a
moment or two. Add the rest of the flour, eggs, salt, and oil to the
bowl. Use your hands or a scraper to pull the dough into a ball,
adding water as needed into the bowl. When it forms a ball,
remove and knead until the dough feels like an earlobe (even
though it sounds gross) I count up to at least fifty turns, each turn
including the right and left side. Place in a large, lightly sprayed
bowl, cover with plastic wrap and let it rest at room temperature
(not in front of the window!) until it is double in bulk (about an
hour), or in the fridge overnight, or overnight on the counter (a
good method if it's a pandemic and you can't get bread flour).
Once the dough is doubled (or the next morning), punch it down,
cover the bowl loosely with a tea cloth or plastic wrap, let it double
in size again for about an hour. If you are making authentic
'Challah,' this is where you take an olive-sized piece of the dough
and bake it in the toaster after saying the traditional blessing.

This dough is enough for 2 good-sized loaves, 4 small loaves, or 8
personal loaves if you want to give each guest a separate loaf. For
2 loaves, divide the dough in half, and divide one half into the
number of pieces you want to braid.

There are plenty how-to braid videos, and you can get creative! I
do 4, 5 and 6 braid challahs, but 3-braided challahs taste just as
delicious. For beginners who haven't raised long-haired children,

divide each half into 3 pieces of dough and roll them into foot-long ropes. Set the three ropes of dough in front of you on the counter and pinch them together at the top. Now take the rope on the right and place it over the rope in the middle. Take the rope on the left and place it over the NEW middle rope (the one you already moved). Again, lift the rope on the right and place it over the middle rope. Keep going. Before you know it, you'll have a braid! Tuck the ends of each loaf under and set them in place with a little water. Place your braided loaves on a silicone mat-covered or sprayed baking pan with space in between. The loaves will poof up more. Cover the loaves loosely with a tea towel for the last rise, for about an hour, or until you are ready to bake. Then, preheat the oven to 350°F/180°C.

OPTIONAL: Just before you set them in the oven, in a small bowl, stir the white of one egg with a teaspoon of honey and brush the loaves. You can also sprinkle the loaves with poppy seeds, sesame seeds, or chopped dehydrated onion. Baking time will depend on the size of the loaves and on your oven. If you bake 2 loaves, check at 25 minutes — if they aren't golden brown and hollow when you tap, bake for an additional 5 minutes. If you are baking 4 loaves, check after 20 minutes. If you are baking 8 loaves, check after 15 minutes. And in each case, add an additional 5 minutes if needed. Final internal temperature should be about 200° — but the golden brown and hollow sound will tell you that the loaves are done.

Chilled Minty Cucumber-Melon Soup

1 honeydew melon, peeled, seeded, cut into chunks
1 large, peeled cucumber
Lime zest and juice from one lime
Handful of fresh mint
1/2 tsp kosher or sea salt
1 or 2 TBSPs tahini

In a food processor or blender, cream everything until smooth and frothy, about 60–90 seconds. Refrigerate until ready to serve. Add a small mint leaf to each bowl or glass. Serve in a small glass as an appetizer or first course.

Optional: serve with a sprinkling of sunflower seeds, chopped hazelnuts, or finely chopped cucumber (set aside a piece after you peel the cucumber)

Chocolate Banana Nut-Butter Frozen Pie

Crust:
1½ cup unsalted raw or roasted pecans*
¾ cup (8 to 10) dried pitted dates or prunes
2 TBSP organic filtered coconut oil
*Also, delicious when I replace the pecans with 10-12 of my own
      baked and frozen cookies

Filling:
2 cups unsalted cashews or peanuts
1 cup canned whole coconut milk
½ cup unsweetened coconut flakes
¼ cup unsweetened cocoa powder
½ cup packed coconut or brown sugar
1 ¼ cup mashed ripe bananas (3 medium or 2 large bananas)
1 tsp pure vanilla extract
½ tsp pure almond extract
½ tsp fine-grained sea salt
1 tsp ground cinnamon
1 TBSP instant coffee or decaf powder

Optional: Sprinkle ½ cup mini-chocolate chips on top, or for a more
dazzling presentation, add the chocolate chips and then finish with
powdered sugar or whipped topping

Crust:
In a food processor, blend pecans (or cookies) until completely uniform,
about 60 seconds. Add dates/prunes and oil, pulse just until blended,
about 5-6 times. Add oil and pulse 4 or 5 times. Press mixture into a
greased tart pan, pie pan or lined muffin cups (with silicone or paper).
Bake at 350°F/180°C for 8 minutes (in a muffin pan) or 10 minutes (in a
pie or tart pan). Cool on the counter (not on top of the oven) while
preparing the filling.

Filling:
Don't bother to rinse out the processor, just add all the ingredients except
chocolate chips. Blend until completely mixed and shiny (about 2–3
minutes). Smooth into the completely cooled crust (in either the pie pan
or the muffin cups). Toss mini chocolate chips on top. Freeze for at least
4 hours. Remove from the freezer about 20 minutes before serving. Add
the optional topping — although it's delicious without the final flourish.
Leftovers can be either frozen or refrigerated (for nibbling whenever you
want something sweet but nourishing). When refrigerated, it gets a
pudding-like texture.

Creamy Chocolate Sauce (or Icing)

1 ¼ cup water or any kind of plant milk (or half water and half plant milk)

1 small <u>baked</u> sweet potato (with skin). Wrap in foil and bake for about 45 minutes at 350°F/180°C. Bake several at a time and use them for snacking or adding to salads!

½ cup unsweetened cocoa powder

1 TBSP decaf or regular instant coffee powder or crystals

1 tsp ground cinnamon

½ cup real maple syrup

1 tsp pure vanilla extract

¼ tsp sea salt

Place ingredients in a high-powered blender and turn on the 'soup' setting. The heat will temper the chocolate, which will turn shiny. It should be smooth enough to pour or spread. If your blender does not have a soup setting, mix everything until completely smooth, pour into a microwave-safe container and zap for 30 seconds. Stir, zap another 30 seconds, and stir again until the sauce is silky and smooth. After a night in the refrigerator, the sauce will be thicker, like a ganache. Zap it in the microwave for 20–30 seconds if you need it to be easily spreadable. Use it to frost a cake, or dip strawberries, or enjoy teaspoonfuls of it all week (if it lasts that long. It's good in the fridge for up to two weeks).

Options for if you'd like the sauce to be sweeter or more interesting:

- Replace ¼ cup of water with a liquor
- Add a whole peeled orange
- Add a little brown sugar

Dover Sole with Butternut Squash

1 small butternut squash (or buy fresh cubes of it at Trader Joe)
1 medium onion, sliced
1 medium seeded apple, with skin, sliced
2 TBSP extra virgin olive oil
1 ½ cup water
½ tsp kosher or sea salt
¼ tsp pepper
1 lb. fresh or frozen Dover Sole (or any flat white fillet)
½ medium lemon (juice and zest)
½ tsp garlic powder
1 tsp dried basil
1 tsp dried dill
1 TBSP capers

Preheat oven to 350°F/180°C and spray a sheet pan. Bake whole butternut squash (or cubes) for about 45 minutes until soft and lightly browned. Remove squash from oven and let it cool. Slice up onion and apple and sauté in 1 Tbsp olive oil (5–7 minutes) until soft (don't clean pan yet). Add cooled onion and apples to a food processor and blend with water and salt until smooth. Add second tablespoon of olive oil and lemon zest to the same pan and turn heat to medium. Place fish skin side up and sprinkle garlic powder, basil, and dill all over. Cook for about a minute and carefully turn fish over (these are fragile fillets). Shake garlic, basil, and dill on the second side and sauté for an additional 3–5 minutes. Turn off the heat, squeeze the lemon juice and toss the capers on the fish. Serve with a crunchy green vegetable or bread (or both!)

Ginger-Molasses Cookies

2 ½ cups old fashioned or steel cut oats
1 tsp baking soda
½ tsp baking powder
¼ tsp fine-grained sea salt
1 tsp ground ginger (or fresh ginger if you can get it)
½ tsp ground cinnamon
¼ tsp ground nutmeg
½ cup packed coconut or dark brown sugar
¼ cup canola or coconut oil
¼ cup unsulphured molasses
1 TBSP unfiltered apple cider vinegar
1 tsp pure vanilla extract

Preheat oven to 350°F/180°C and spray or line 2 cookie sheets. In a processor or high-speed blender, blend oats into a fine flour, about 60 to 90 seconds. Add baking soda, baking powder, salt, spices, and sugar—30 seconds or until blended. In a medium to large bowl, combine oil, molasses, vinegar, and vanilla. Add dry ingredients to wet ingredients and stir together with a spatula. Moisten with 1–2 TBSP water if needed to form balls. Use a small scooper or wet hands to form 24–26 (1 inch/25mm) loose balls, placing 12 or 13 balls on each cookie sheet (these cookies will spread just a little). Bake for about 10 minutes until golden brown (if you over bake, they'll be yummy but dry). Remove from the oven and let them cool before eating. They can be frozen and eaten directly from the freezer (or zapped in the microwave).
OPTIONAL:1½ cup unsalted roasted almonds can be used in place of one cup of oats

I keep these chewy cookies in the freezer. Sometimes I make a little sandwich with a piece of banana in the middle, but mostly I just grab them for little bursts of gingery deliciousness.

Guacamole Salad

1 ripe avocado
2 TBSP salsa (our favorite is Trader Joe's Chunky Salsa)
1/2 cup chopped shallot or sweet onion
1 cup cherry tomatoes, quartered or halved
1 cup sliced red and yellow sweet mini peppers
1/4 cup (about a handful) chopped parsley or cilantro Juice of 1
      lime or about 1 TBSP Nelly & Joe Key Lime juice (keeps a
      long time in the fridge)
1/4 tsp each: kosher or sea salt and pepper (add more if desired)
Sprinkle of red pepper flakes or 1 tsp of Sriracha (also always in
      the fridge)

In a medium bowl, lightly mash up the avocado with the salsa —
leave chunks — don't make it super smooth. Add all the chopped
vegetables, lime juice, salt, and pepper. Gently stir it into a chunky
guacamole — it's not the usual kind, but when avocados are hard
to find or crazy expensive, it's still delicious! Serve as a side or with
a bowl of tortilla chips

Prepare it 20+ minutes before serving, and let it sit covered in the
fridge so the flavors blend.

Lemon-Blueberry Cake or Muffins

2 ½ cups old-fashioned or quick oats
1 tsp baking soda
½ tsp baking powder
½ cup unsweetened coconut flakes
½ tsp fine-grained sea salt
1 small seeded unpeeled sweet/tart apple (like Gala), cut into 8
    segments
½ cup packed coconut or light brown sugar
½ cup unsweetened plant milk (I use oat milk or coconut milk)
1 tsp pure vanilla extract
2 medium or 1 large, zested lemon (get every last bit of the zest!)
½ cup lemon juice (or as much as you can get from the zested
    lemons)
1 cup fresh or frozen blueberries plus more to sprinkle on top if
    desired

Preheat oven to 400°F/200°C and spray or line 1 standard loaf or
12-muffin pan. In a high-speed blender add oats, baking powder,
coconut flakes, and salt. Blend until flour-like, 60 – 90 seconds,
and pour into a large mixing bowl. In same blender, mix apples,
sugar, plant milk, vanilla, lemon zest and lemon juice, 90 seconds.
In a small bowl, toss berries in 1 TBSP of flour so they don't sink
to the bottom. At this point, plan to move efficiently to get the
batter into the preheated oven. Pour the wet ingredients into the
dry ingredients and fold just until all the flour is blended in. Very
gently fold in the blueberries (or leave a few to decorate the top of
the loaf) Fill the prepared muffin cups about 2/3 each, or pour all
the batter into the prepared loaf pan. Lightly press the extra
blueberries on top (unless you've already eaten them or mixed
them in). Bake muffins 20–22 minutes until light golden brown
and springy. Bake loaf 40–45 minutes until the cake springs back
when you press the top. Allow to cool for at least 10 minutes.

Oatmeal Chocolate Chip Cookies

2 cups old-fashioned, steel cut or quick oats
1 15 oz can of chickpeas — drain and save ¼ cup of the liquid
½ cup unsweetened flaked coconut
1 tsp baking soda
½ tsp baking powder
½ tsp sea salt
1 tbsp potato or corn starch
½ cup packed coconut or brown sugar
½ cup coconut, canola, or extra virgin olive oil
2 TBSP unfiltered apple cider vinegar
2 tsp pure vanilla extract
1 cup mini semi-sweet chocolate chips

In a food processor, blend oats into a powder. Add chickpeas, chickpea liquid, coconut, baking soda, baking powder, salt, and starch. Blend for about 60 seconds until the batter is smooth and uniform. In a large bowl, stir together oil, sugar, apple cider vinegar, and vanilla extract. Use a large spatula to fold the dry ingredients into the wet ingredients until just blended. Gently fold in the chocolate chips. Refrigerate until the oven heats up (or until you are ready to bake!). Preheat oven to 350°F/180°C and spray or line 3 cookie sheets. Use a scooper or a spoon to form 1"/25g (small) or 3"/76g (large) balls of cookie dough. Leave about 2"/50mm between the balls so they have room to spread. Makes about 30 small cookies and 18 larger cookies. Bake 10–12 minutes or until golden brown. Let the cookies cool completely. These freeze well and are good to nibble on right out of the freezer.

Note: There is only ½ cup of added sugar in these cookies, but the coconut flakes and the chocolate chips give them all the sweetness they need. After you blend the dry ingredients, you probably won't see or taste the coconut.

Orange Hummus

1 15 ounce/425 g. can of chickpeas (including the liquid)
1 medium orange (peeled and seeded, cut into 4 segments)
2 TBSP extra virgin olive oil (and an additional tsp for serving)
2 or 3 TBSP tahini (any plain kind) or 1 TBSP sesame seeds + ¼
    cup water
1 TBSP unfiltered apple cider vinegar
½ tsp each: garlic powder, cumin, coriander, turmeric, kosher or
    sea salt, pepper Paprika or ½ cup chopped parsley (to
    sprinkle over the top before serving)
Extra water as needed

Options to try so that your hummus does not always taste the
same. Try adding a couple of different ingredients now and then:
    1 Tsp Dijon mustard or ground mustard seed
    1 TBSP soy sauce or coconut aminos
    ½ cup of roasted red peppers
    1 tsp dried basil

Blend all ingredients in a food processor (not a high-speed blender)
about 60 seconds. If needed, add a little water to get a smooth,
creamy texture. Taste and add salt if it's not tasty enough (but I'm
rolling my eyes). If it thickens in the fridge, stir in 1 or 2 TBSP of
water or olive oil. To serve: dribble a little olive oil on top and
sprinkle with paprika for color.

Orange- Tahini Cookies

2 cups old fashioned, steel cut or quick oats
1 tsp baking soda
1 tsp ground cinnamon
1/2 tsp allspice or pumpkin pie spice
1/2 tsp fine-grained sea salt
1 medium, thin-skinned orange, seeded (with peel), ends cut, cut
into 8 pieces
1/2 cup plain tahini
1/2 cup real maple syrup
1 TBSP unfiltered apple cider vinegar
2 tsp pure vanilla extract

Options:
1/4 cup sesame seeds to sprinkle on top before baking
1/2 cup chocolate chips to make them into Tahini-Chocolate Chip
Cookies

In a high-speed blender, blend oats, baking soda, cinnamon, and
salt into a uniform texture, about 60 seconds. Pour into a large
bowl and set aside. To the same blender (don't bother rinsing it),
add orange segments, tahini, maple syrup, vinegar, and vanilla.
Blend until creamy, about 90 seconds (stop to scrape down sides).
Use a spatula to add the tahini-orange mixture to the dry
ingredients, and fold together. Set the bowl in the refrigerator for
about ten minutes. As soon as the dough is in the fridge, preheat
oven to 350°F/180°C. Spray or line 2 cookie sheets. As soon as the
oven is ready, use a small scoop to drop 1 1/2 inch balls of dough,
about 15 on each sheet (they won't expand much). Add a sprinkle
of sesame seeds to each cookie if desired. Bake for about 18–20
minutes until they look crispy golden. Lightly mash each cookie
with your palm, the bottom of a glass, or a fork to flatten so they
look a bit like peanut butter cookies. Cool 15–20 minutes. Gently
transfer to serving platter.

Pumpkin Apple Cake

2 cups all-purpose flour
½ cup old-fashioned or quick oats
1 tsp baking soda
1 tsp baking powder
2 tsp flax meal (ground flax seeds)
2 tsp pumpkin pie spice
1 tsp ground cinnamon
½ tsp fine-grained sea salt
1 small/medium apple, seeded and cut into 8 segments (with peel)
1 medium orange, seeded and peeled, cut into 4 segments
½ cup any kind of plant milk
2 TBSP unfiltered apple cider vinegar
1 15 oz canned pumpkin (or about half a fresh small baked pumpkin)
½ cup coconut or dark brown sugar
1 tsp (5ml) pure vanilla extract
1 cup (or up to the whole 9 oz bag) semi-sweet chocolate chips

Preheat oven to 350°F/180°C and prepare a Bundt, 2 x 9" round, or a 9 x 13 pan. In a large bowl, stir all dry ingredients (flour, oats, baking soda, flax meal, spices). In a large food processor or high-speed blender, blend apple and orange segments, milk, and brown sugar until smooth, about 90 seconds. Add pumpkin and vanilla, blend until uniform, about 30 seconds. Move wet ingredients from the blender (you'll need a spatula) into the dry ingredients. Stir gently to combine everything well. Fold in the chocolate chips. Transfer to a greased and floured Bundt, two 9" rounds, or a 9 x 13 pan. Bake in a preheated oven for 55–65 minutes until the top of the cake springs back. Remove from the oven and cool before removing from pan. If you used 9" pans: cinnamon buttercream or cream cheese icing goes well with this cake. Sprinkle with confectioner's sugar or cinnamon-sugar, if desired.

Roasted Red Pepper Tahini

5 or 6 large red peppers, seeded and cut into quarters
1 small or medium onion, any kind, quartered
Olive Oil spray
1 medium orange (peeled and seeded, cut into 4 segments)
2 TBSP Tahini
½ tsp garlic powder
½ tsp basil
½ tsp kosher or sea salt
½ tsp pepper

Preheat oven to 400°degrees Fahrenheit. Spray baking pan (or line with foil and spray with the olive oil). Place onion and red peppers skin side down and spray lightly. Bake for 20–30 minutes until peppers are soft and edges slightly browned. Remove from oven and toss into food processor with other ingredients, blend about 60–90 seconds. Taste before serving — might need a little extra salt

Skillet Chicken with Mushrooms, Scallions and Red Peppers

1 lb. (3 or 4) boneless chicken breasts or thighs, cubed
2 TBSP good olive oil
1 cup mushrooms (I use white or Baby Bella), cut in 4 slices
1 medium red pepper, sliced into sticks
2 or 3 scallions, chopped (or more if you love scallions)
8 oz can of tomato sauce
2 tsp dried tarragon
1 tsp dried basil (or a handful of fresh basil, if you have it)
1 tsp dried oregano
1 tsp garlic powder
1 tsp kosher or sea salt
½ tsp pepper
Optional: add 1 TBSP chopped jalapeno or ½ red chili flakes if
     you want the dish to have a kick

On medium heat, stir the chicken in olive oil until cooked through and white, about 5–7 minutes. Stir in the cut-up mushrooms, red peppers and scallions, simmer 2–3 minutes. Turn the heat to low and add in the tomato sauce, herbs, and spices. If you use flavored tomato sauce, less salt and pepper might be needed. Let the sauce simmer for an additional 10 or so minutes while you set the table, prepare a salad, cut up bread, or boil pasta. Or maybe someone else will do that, and you can enjoy a glass of wine.

I make this dish a lot because I usually have the ingredients in the house. I often use cooked, leftover boneless breasts (which I freeze in anticipation of making this easy, quick dinner), in which case, microwave the chicken, cut into pieces, and sauté along with the vegetables. Fresh cut-up chicken pieces require about five minutes of sautéing before adding the vegetables. Once everything is simmering in the pan, the flavors will blend. Taste before serving and add more salt and pepper if desired.

Sunflower Seed Chocolate Chip Cookies

1 TBSP flaxseed meal + ¼ cup cold water
1 ½ cup shelled, raw or roasted, unsalted sunflower seeds
1 cup (about 12) large, pitted dates or prunes (or mixed)
1 medium, thin-skinned orange, seeded (with peel), ends cut, cut into 6-8 pieces
¼ cup unsweetened coconut flakes
1 tsp baking soda
½ tsp fine-grained sea salt
1 tsp pure vanilla extract
¼ cup coconut, canola, or extra virgin olive oil
½ cup mini semi-sweet chocolate chips

Preheat oven to 350°F/180°C and spray or line 2 cookie sheets. In a small bowl, mix flax meal with water and set aside. In a food processor, mix sunflower seeds until flour-like, about 30–40 seconds. Add pitted dates/prunes and cut orange (with peel!) and blend until uniform, 50–60 seconds. Add flax and water mixture, coconut flakes, baking soda, salt, vanilla, oil, and vanilla, blend until uniform, 50–60 seconds. Add chocolate chips and do 2 or 3 quick pulses, just to blend. Use a small scooper to form about 30–32 cookie balls. Place 15–16 balls on each cookie sheet. Bake about 15 minutes until edges are slightly browned. Remove from oven and cool.

These cookies are soft, not super sweet, delicious, and healthful (no added sugar!). My husband loves them, but that is because he does not know they're sweetened with prunes and/or dates. They can be frozen and enjoyed directly from the freezer (or microwaved for a warm treat)!

Sweet Potato and Black Bean Soup

1 TBSP any olive oil
1 large onion, chopped
2 cloves garlic, minced (or 2 tsp ground garlic)
2 stalks celery, chopped
2 carrots, chopped or sliced
32 oz of water or vegetable stock (plus extra if needed)
1 large or two medium sweet potatoes, cut into ½ inch
   pieces
15 or 15.5 ounce can of black beans, drained (some brands
   have different amounts)
14.5 oz can chopped or diced tomato
2 tsp cumin
2 tsp dried basil
1/2 tsp smoked or regular paprika
1/2 tsp kosher or sea salt
1/4 tsp black pepper

Heat a soup pot (medium heat) on the stove. Stir chopped onion in olive oil until translucent. Add garlic, celery, and carrots. Stir about 4–5 minutes. Add everything else. Bring to a boil and then let soup simmer for about 45 minutes. Chop an avocado for garnish, or sprinkle with chopped parsley/cilantro — everything works, including just serving the soup as is. Even better the next day. Can be frozen and reheated

Vegetarian Cholent

(Overnight Veggie/Bean Stew)

1 cup uncooked pinto or kidney beans, rinsed
1 cup dry, uncooked garbanzo beans, rinsed
1 TBSP olive oil
1 large yellow onion, chopped
1 regular or sweet potato, peeled and cut into ½ inch pieces
1 small eggplant, cut into ½ inch pieces
½ cup chopped celery (1 or 2 stalks)
½ cup chopped carrot (1 or 2 carrots)
3 or 4 cloves garlic, chopped, or 2 tsp garlic powder
1 or 2 TBSP Dijon mustard
1 tsp each: kosher or sea salt, basil, cumin, dill, paprika, and
    turmeric
1 can (28 oz. diced tomatoes)
4 cups (32 oz) red wine and/or water (more liquid as needed
    during the long cooking time)
2 TBSP unfiltered apple cider vinegar
½ cup hulled or pearled barley (1 cup if you love barley, but then
    add 1 ½ cups liquid)
½ tsp black pepper (only if it isn't peppery enough from the
    turmeric and paprika!)
Optional: top with chopped fresh parsley, dill, or avocado. For
    extra heat add 1 tsp chili powder

The night before serving, cover the beans with water. Zap in the
microwave for 3 minutes and then let the beans soak while you cut
up the vegetables. Rinse after soaking. Place rinsed beans,
vegetables, and everything except vinegar and barley into a slow
cooker. Stir, and cook on low setting all night. Stir again in the
morning, and every few hours through the day. Add a cup or two of
water if needed. About an hour before dinner, add apple cider
vinegar and barley, and continue cooking. About ten minutes before
dinner, transfer to a serving dish (if you're planning to use one).
Taste before serving (add more salt if needed). If you prefer a
soupier stew, add a few cups of water or vegetable broth. Yummy to
add a handful of fresh chopped parsley to each bowl (if you have it).

Zucchini-Orange-Chocolate Loaf or Muffins

2 cup any gluten-free flour (it can also be made with all-purpose flour)

¼ cup unsweetened cocoa powder

1½ tsp baking soda

½ tsp baking powder

½ tsp fine-grained sea salt

1 small-medium zucchini (about 250 g) with skin, cut into 6-8 pieces

1 small, thin-skinned seeded orange (with peel), cut off ends and cut into 8 segments

1 small-medium seeded tart apple (like Gala) with peel, cut into 12 segments

½ cup packed coconut, brown, or monk fruit sugar

½ cup oat, almond, or coconut milk

2 TBSP unfiltered apple cider vinegar

1 tsp pure vanilla extract

½ to ¾ cups semi-sweet chocolate chips + ¼ cup extra for sprinkling on top, if desired

Preheat oven to 350°F/180°C. Line or spray a standard muffin pan, a standard loaf pan, or a 9" round pan. In a large bowl, sift flour, cocoa powder, baking soda, baking powder, and salt. In a food processor, blend zucchini, orange, and apple with sugar until uniform, about 60–90 seconds. Add plant milk, vanilla, and vinegar — blend until smooth about 30–40 seconds. Be ready to get pans into the oven asap after combining wet and dry ingredients. Use a spatula to transfer wet mixture into dry mixture, fold together. Gently fold in chocolate chips. Spoon into the prepared muffin pan, loaf pan, or round pan. Sprinkle a few chocolate chips over the top and gently press into the batter. Gently tap pan on the counter to get rid of air bubbles. Bake muffins 18–20 minutes, loaf or cake pan 25–28 minutes, until top springs back. Cool about 20 minutes before removing from pan

OPTIONAL: For a ZUCCHINI-ALMOND CAKE use almond flour instead, and replace cocoa powder and chocolate chips with 1 tsp pure almond extract

248

Acknowledgements

Many thanks to indispensable writer friends, S.L. (Sandi) Wisenberg, Natania Rosenfeld, and Thalia Bruehl for valuable criticism and encouragement, and especially to Sandi for her wise and patient editing. Unending gratitude to Annie Gottlieb, Raymond Zwerin, and my mother, Helen Pinsky, for their valuable feedback on early versions of the book, and to my niece, Sarah Pinsky, for all her patient help with social media. Thanks to my supportive children: Danielle, Rebecca and Gabriel, and my siblings: Milton, Martin, and Janet, all of whom suspect me of borrowing aspects of themselves to create my characters. And most of all I thank my loving husband David, whose writing is serious and profound (with nary a murder to be found).

Gratitude to readers, friends, and relatives who tested recipes and/or helped make my recipes easier to follow: Linda Ring Ash, Adele Brinkman, Ilana Craven, Marla Craven, Diane Halivni, Betsy Forester, Susan Greenbaum, Nancy Hitchcock, Sara Hoffman, Karen Kaplan, Susan Keisler, Linda Kupfer, Cathy Neistat, Mary Ellen Petrisko, Emily Pinsky, Frank Reid, Haley Reiner, Rachel Sapinsley, Jan Schwartz, Rachel Blum Siegelman, Sheila Small, Eli Sussman, Eric Vollrath, and Adina Weissman.

About the Author

G.P. Gottlieb holds undergraduate and graduate degrees in piano and voice. During her career as a cantor, a high school music teacher, and the administrator of the law center at DePaul University College of Law, she has also written stories, songs, and several unwieldy manuscripts. She is a graduate of the French Pastry School's Bread Boot Camp. Furthermore, she is the host of New Books in Literature, a podcast of the New Books Network and partner of LitHub. After recovering from breast cancer, she turned to writing in earnest, melding her two loves, nourishment for mind and body in recipe-laced murder mysteries.

CPSIA information can be obtained
at www.ICGtesting.com
Printed in the USA
FSHW010026290121
78021FS